I0747857

A LOST SHIP IN THE DARK GRAVE

THE LYRA CYCLE: EPISODE 2

RENE ASTLE

ARMCHAIR ALIEN

A Lost Ship in a Dark Grave

ISBN: 978-1-7773315-6-6

1st Edition

Contents

WHEN WE LAST LEFT OUR FEARFUL HEROES...

I F YOU'RE COMING STRAIGHT from book 1 — *A Dead Ship in the Deep Black* — jump right into chapter 1. If you're like me and can't remember what you read this morning, let alone yesterday, keep reading.

It was supposed to be a simple salvage job...but nothing is ever simple on board the *Lyra*. As soon as they arrived at the designated location, they knew they were looking at trouble. Which might have had something to do with the wrecked *Leviathan* floating dead in space.

Still, against the odds and a handful of nefarious forces, the crew managed to rescue the boy Ben and save him from the clutches of the shadowy factions who wanted to get their hands on him for reasons unknown. Though it might have had something to do with his unusual telekinetic abilities.

Along with their babbling saboteur, they delivered the boy into the care of the Sisters of Elazir — a shadowy faction in their own right. Besides their oath to care for the sick and orphaned, they're also the one organization powerful enough to protect him. Which might have something to do with their penchant for procuring arcane tech.

Using said tech, the Sisters opened a jump gate out of empty space — a feat even the emperor can't lay claim to — and sent the *Lyra* through it. On the other side, the klaxons start blaring. Which might have something to do with being dumped in the Green Zone — the not-quite-neutral zone between full Dominion control and the systems governed by the gang cartels.

The adventure never stops on the cargo ship *Lyra*. Even if Tink wished it did, if only for long enough to fix the black water back-flow flange.

Into the Green

1: ALEK

"ARGH!" ALEK WA YANKED on the control stick, struggling to pull the *Lyra* in a tight loop away from whatever danger had caused the ship to buck and the sirens to blare. The ship moaned its displeasure at his flying, and the stick shook in his grip. His shoulder muscles strained, and an old injury threatened to surface. Alek clenched his jaw, fighting the ship to keep control.

Despite having the power to conjure a gate out of empty space, the Sisters of Elazir apparently couldn't scan the space it dropped them into to see if it was clear. Or didn't care enough to check. His lips pressed together, and his nostrils flared.

"What the hell is that sound?" Captain Rebeka Mino loomed beside him, peering at the viewscreen, which only showed the empty black in front of them. "Cass, a 360 sweep please."

"Rear cameras offline." The AI's calm voice drifted down from over their heads.

"Can you turn the bloody sirens off?" Kandi shouted as she punched a finger into her console. In an instant, an unnatural quiet fell on the bridge. "Here's the last image from the rear...," she started, her voice too loud in the sudden silence.

A slice of space appeared on the viewscreen. In the distance, Alek made out an object, like a doughnut around a post. A flutter rippled through his gut.

"Magnify." Rebeka stepped towards the screen, blocking his view. But he'd already seen all he needed to.

"Bleeding Hades." Tink's tone indicated she'd seen it too.

A hand fell on his shoulder, and he turned his head to see her staring at the viewscreen. Her sentiment echoed his exactly, and tension wrinkled the space between her whiskey brown eyes. Alek pulled his gaze away before she caught him looking at her, which would result in her usual standoffishness returning.

"What is it?" Ish said, squinting at the screen.

"A Dominion station." Kandi tapped at her console. "We've been noticed. They're sending ships."

"Can you get us out of here, flyboy?" Rebeka turned to peg him with a hard stare.

"Strap in." He arched an eyebrow at her. "It's going to get hairy."

"Not kinetic?" Rebeka said, though she focused on following his directions.

"That too." He turned back to the controls. "Kandi, is there somewhere nearby we can hide?"

"Working on it." Her voice was tense, her words clipped.

"Looking for slip points." Ish's fingers moved over the holographic ripples in front of him.

"Can someone tell me where we are?" Rebeka's voice, edged with anger, filled the bridge. "Besides just the Green

Zone. You'd think with the tech to create a jump gate out of empty space, the Sisters could have dropped us somewhere other than the backyard of a Dominion station."

Alek frowned to hear her echo his thoughts. Even after minimal interaction with the Sisters in their Tower of Solitude, he recognized that they had their own agenda. The Sisters at the Tower were the most powerful in an already dominant organization. The Tower Sisters were different from those who served at the local hospices, like the one near where he'd grown up. For one thing, the Sisters at that old hospice hadn't known him as Alek Wa. A flicker coursed through his gut: maybe the Tower Sisters knew his real name.

"We're inside a solar system...." Tink's voice came from behind him.

"Not a lot of help, Tink," Rebeka said.

"I'm looking." Although he couldn't see her, he heard her fingers clicking furiously over her console.

"We're next to a gas giant," Kandi said. "There's a series of moons around it. Seeing if I can find it in the star maps."

Alek didn't say anything as he pushed and pulled the stick, forcing the *Lyra* onto the course Kandi plotted. Something whined as the ship expressed its irritation.

"Don't break my ship." Tink's voice was quiet but her tone serious. The whine petered out as a giant blue-green marble appeared on-screen.

"Ships incoming," Cass said just before sirens started sounding again. "They're sending a message: stand down and prepare to be boarded."

"Not too happy at having a ship pop into existence out of empty space, I imagine." Ish sounded way too pleased given their current predicament.

Alek shoved the stick forward, maxing out the ship's impulse engines, pointing its nose towards a rocky moon that looked like a promising hiding spot. "Hold onto your lunches." He twisted the ship into a roll around the icy moon to their left, hoping the plumes shooting from it would scramble the signal from their pursuers' marks. Without damaging the *Lyra* or her crew.

"Rear cameras back up," Kandi said as a new slice of space appeared on the viewscreen. "They're *Hogfish*." Her smile infused her words. "Slow. Not very maneuverable. The dregs of the Dominion fleet."

"So easy for a hot shot pilot to outrun," Tink said.

When Alek turned to scowl at her, he saw she was smiling. The captain, however, frowned at him. He turned back around to focus on flying.

"There's a slip point outside the orbit of this gas giant. At phi -35°, rho 12, zeta 7."

Alek made a quick calculation. He waited until they were past the rocky moon and into the shadow of the gas giant, then he tacked, changing course to head towards Ish's slip point.

The silent seconds ticked by, and they watched the *Hogfish* recede into the distance.

"I think I know where we are." Ish's tone was subdued as he reached for the holographic map in front of him. With a flick of his fingers, the wavy lines of his slip chart morphed into a star grid. As he rotated it, lines appeared, bisecting the three-dimensional image. "The Corican system."

The flutter in Alek's stomach turned to icy rock. "The edge of Dominion-controlled space."

"Beyond the edge." The anger in Rebeka's voice turned cold.

A blue blip showed their location near Corican V, still nominally part of the region patrolled by the Dominion, but the nearby station was staffed by the dregs of the army or those being punished for some infraction.

"Worse, out there sits the Selva system," she continued. At the far reaches of the Green Zone. Beyond that, the law of the cartels ruled. But in between the two there was no law at all.

And that's where Ten Selva sat.

"Why the Green Zone?" Alek stared at the coffee machine. At a sound overhead, he glanced up. Grim peered down at him, his jaws moving as the cat consumed something crunchy. Other than Grim, just him, Tink and Rebeka were in the common room. Kandi had taken food and drink to Ish, who was on the bridge navigating them through the slipstream.

"Maybe they're punishing us for saddling them with a strange kid," Tink said from the fridge before closing the door with a huff and heading to the table empty-handed.

Glass full, he turned to face the room. Rebeka stood opposite, leaning back against the glass that overlooked the cargo bay. Tink plopped down at the table and started fiddling with something he couldn't see. Both women frowned.

Alek walked over to the captain and handed her the coffee. "I doubt they consider Ben a burden. And certainly not enough of a reason to drop us right next to the last Dominion station."

"Right next to Corican V, the mouldy remains of the early Empire." Rebeka wrapped her fingers around her mug.

"But it's the old capital?" Tink bit her lip as she examined her widget. "Still Dominion."

"There's no work coming out of that city anymore." Rebeka wrinkled her nose.

"What are we going to do?" Tink asked. "In the Green Zone?"

He understood the engineer's misgivings. A quadrant of space between Dominion hegemony and cartel control, the Green Zone was a quagmire where anything was permissible...as long as you had the power to back it up. It certainly wasn't a place where honest people found honest work. In fact, honest people tended to live short lives out here.

Rebeka took a big gulp of coffee. Her eyes squinted at him over the rim of the mug, though he couldn't tell if it was the tension or that she still didn't trust him, even though he hadn't been their saboteur, and had, in fact, helped save the *Lyra*.

She shifted her gaze to Tink. "What we always do," she said as Alek returned to the kitchenette to make another drink. "Find enough work to keep the ship running and ourselves fed. And maybe a little bit more."

Tink shook her head. "You think they could have dropped us somewhere safer." She slapped a metal tool down on the table. "Do you think the Sisters knew where we'd end up when they sent us through their gate?"

Alek recalled the shimmer of blue and lavender the Sisters of Elazir had conjured up out of empty space. Jump gates required a solar system's worth of energy to build and maintain, and theirs had popped into being in front of them. He opened his mouth, but it was the captain who answered.

"What do *you* think? They made a gate appear out of nothing." She took another swig of coffee.

"They knew exactly where they were dropping us." He leaned against the counter and wrapped his fingers around his warm mug as he took a sip.

Rebeka straightened and downed the rest of her coffee. "At least they could have dumped us somewhere closer to a job." She strode over to him and placed her mug in the sink. She didn't look up when she spoke, but her hands went to her hips and her frown deepened. "But I know someone nearby who might need some odd jobs done."

Alek glanced between her and Tink. His stomach went cold despite the warm coffee. He was sure he wouldn't like this odd job, since the last one nearly got him killed.

2: Rebeka

THE HEAT AND HUMIDITY pressed down on Rebeka from all directions. The pinpoint light of the distant sun made her wonder how it could be so oppressively hot. With each breath, the heavy air squeezed her chest like a giant snake. Sweat sheened her face and crept along her stubbly scalp, making it itch. She reached a hand up before snatching it back down and curling her fingers into a fist.

A chittering noise brought her attention back to the cargo in front of her. She frowned then shifted her glare from the rattling crates to Sera Fox. Her old comrade-in-arms looked as cool and crisp as if she'd just stepped out of a chiller, which only made Rebeka even crankier. "It's illegal."

"It's not illegal." The statuesque blonde tore her predatory gaze from Alek, who peered out over the rippling swamp grass, resolutely ignoring Sera. Her pilot went up a notch in her esteem. Sera sighed theatrically in Rebeka's direction, tossing her hair over her shoulder. "They're just bugs."

"Smuggled bugs." Rebeka brought her hands to her hips, and a breeze caressed her armpits. She sighed at the slight cooling sensation, then the breeze died. Her shoulders slumped.

"Bugs that can make you hallucinate," Tink mumbled as she checked the seal on one of the crates, before jumping a step back when it rocked towards her. "Alive bugs."

"The gourmands want them alive. It's just good business. Besides, what harm can bugs do? As long as you don't eat them. Or lick them." Her mouth opened then snapped shut before she spoke again. "Maybe avoid touching them." Sera's gaze shifted over Rebeka's shoulder, squinting as she homed in on something. "You really do travel well these days, Mino."

Rebeka turned to see what had caught Sera's attention. Kandi strode down the gangplank, weapons strapped to hips, arms and thighs. "Sera, we could get in trouble if we're stopped."

"I have a permit."

"A clearly forged permit." Rebeka could see the pixelation in the seal.

"I have an official in my pocket." Sera shrugged a shoulder. "In my pants actually." Her voice dropped to a purr. "He quite likes it there. Call him if you run into any trouble." She flicked her attention from Kandi back to Rebeka, arching an eyebrow as she held out a tablet. "Do you want the job or not?"

Rebeka's jaw clenched, and she stared hard at her former troopmate. A skimmer flew overhead, causing them both to look up. She squinted but couldn't tell if the sleek, unmanned craft bore Dominion markings or none. And she couldn't decide which was worse.

Sera's lips quirked into an almost smile. "Some habits never die." She jerked her chin and the hand holding the waybill towards Rebeka.

Rebeka grimaced but swiped the tablet from her. "You swear we don't have to open the crates?"

"As long as you deliver them within the allotted time, they'll be fine. The tablet contains care instructions, though they don't need much. They're alive but dormant."

A crate almost jumped at Alek as he reached down to load it onto the hover cart. "You call that dormant?" He straightened up and stepped back.

Sera's predatory gaze came back, joined by a wolfish grin. "You should see them when they're wide awake. If there's a swarm of them, *you* become dinner." Her eyebrows twitched.

Alek's eyes slid from her to Rebeka, clearly unimpressed. Rebeka couldn't disagree with his assessment, but they didn't have much choice. They needed food and fuel to get them the hell out of the Green Zone and back into the oppressive but orderly Dominion sphere of control.

She gave Alek a sharp nod. He stepped back up to the crate, giving Tink a lopsided smile as she joined him.

"Let's get 'er done." Tink took hold of her side. "Sooner we load them, sooner we're rid of them."

"You're sure you can trust her?" Alek asked, nodding towards the closing cargo bay doors. A clank sounded, shutting out the sweltering haze of the hellish moon. Though now the cargo bay felt like a swamp, stuffy and damp and smelling slightly of rotten vegetable matter.

Rebeka slid her gaze from the door to the pilot. "No." She turned around to the piles of crates. "But she loves profit more than plotting. And there's no profit in turning us over to Dominion customs officers."

"You're sure about that?" Tink came to stand on her other side. A crate rattled and chirped. Something dropped from above them, landing with a thud. The grey shape resolved into a cat, and Grim's weight bore down on the crate, his eyes fixed on it as he made a chirring sound.

"She'd lose her cargo and gain notice of the authorities." Rebeka tried to make her voice sound more certain than she felt. "Shoo, not for you." She waved her hand at the cat. "There's already plenty of bugs living on the *Lyra* to keep you busy." Grim's green eyes peered at her as he waggled his rump before settling onto the pile of boxes.

3: TINK

BEHIND TINK, THE SLIPDRIVE hummed. That was the only sound in the otherwise quiet engine room. Abnormally quiet, even for being in the slipstream. The nape of her neck itched at the silence.

She glanced around. It had always been her solitary domain, at least after her uncle Emmon died, leaving the *Lyra* to her. And she'd always been happy to have it to herself. But something felt off. She cocked her head to the side, listening for some unwanted ping. She scanned the space, checking for a widget or a sprocket out of place. With a sharp inhale, she realized she missed Ben.

Even though he'd only been on the ship a short while before they'd delivered him into the care of the Sisters of Elazir, he'd spent a fair chunk of that time in the engine room. And the boy had an uncanny affinity for the workings of a starship. Tink's lips quirked into a smile.

"You'd almost think he had some Tinker in him." The smile slipped from her lips as an ache clenched at her chest. She couldn't pinpoint whether that was because of the scattering of her people and the slaughter of an extended family she barely knew or the loss of Ben.

The hum shifted up an octave, and she tipped her head left, then turned it right. The slipdrive was a black box, well, a black sphere actually. But either way, the inner workings of it and its fuel were a mystery to her. Despite trying, and enduring hours of painful tutelage by her uncle, she'd never fully grasped the astrodynamics of the slipstream.

She squinted and turned around. There was a chirp in the hum, she was sure of it. "Cass, run diagnostics on the slipdrive."

"That would be unwise while the ship is in the slipstream." The AI's disembodied voice warbled at the end, making her sound almost concerned.

Tink picked up her wrench and stepped towards the drive casing. Looking at the wrench, her shoulders dropped. "I suppose whacking it would also be unwise."

"Yes, it would," an entirely human voice said.

Tink spun around to see Kandi in the doorway. "Hey."

"Hey." The muscles on Kandi's bare arms twitched as she held her hands behind her back and glanced around the space. She was a rare visitor to the engine room, unless it factored into the circuit of a workout.

Heading back to the workbench, Tink sat down and put the wrench beside the hydrostatic pressure regulator she'd been tuning. "You've changed your hair." She jerked her chin towards the locks of electric blue that snaked into a braid along the top of Kandi's head. Her skin showed at the sides where the hair had been shaved short.

"Pink is so last week." Kandi remained standing in the doorway, feet apart, hands clasped behind her back. Almost like she was standing at attention.

"What's up?" Tink quirked an eyebrow as she picked up a brush to clean metal shavings off a piston. After a half minute of silence, she turned back to Kandi. Her jaw dropped open when she saw what the other woman held: the stave she'd retrieved from the Sisters of Elazir.

"Can you...." Kandi's lips twisted into a grimace. Tink frowned — the Antaran was the most self-assured, forward person she knew. "I...." Her blue eyebrows pulled together. She huffed out through her nose, before the words finally came in a rush. "It's temperamental, can you fix it?" She held the staff out to Tink.

Tink pulled away, unsure about touching the mythical weapon. The technology in the staves was a highly guarded secret. Her long fingers tensed as her mind raced. She hated technical secrets. But reverse engineering it could get her killed, either by the stave itself or the Antaran Martial Sciences Division. In the end, her curiosity got the better of her. She didn't take it, but she leaned forward and picked up her goggles. "Why?"

"I felt incomplete when I had to trade it for my brother's care." Kandi shrugged. "Naked."

"Couldn't you get another one?"

"Not another one like this." She went quiet for a few seconds, her fingers clenching around it. "And if it ever died, I'd have to ask the Matriarchs to fix it. I'm not asking them for anything ever again." Tink knew little of the Antaran culture or the world Kandi came from, only that it was ruled by a warrior class of women who had a strained relationship with their Dominion overseers. Questions burned in her head, but she bit her tongue as Kandi continued. "If the

Sisters have had it this long, the stave's secret is out. Might as well even the playing field."

Tink wracked her brain — she wasn't Antaran but there had to be a loophole that would let her tamper with the fabled tech, one where it wasn't illegal and wouldn't have her killed by an Antaran assassin. Then she blinked, realizing that here on the *Lyra* there was no regulation to stop her.

"If you don't want to...." Kandi's voice tapered off.

"No, I'll do it." Tink reached towards the weapon before Kandi changed her mind but hesitated at the grimace on Kandi's face. It took her a second to realize Kandi's eyes tracked something over her shoulder.

Pulling her empty hand back, Tink glanced behind her to where Grim amble out of the shadows. He'd finally left the crates in the cargo bay, at least long enough to hunt for a snack, perhaps realizing he couldn't reach those insects. Iridescent wings poked out the side of his mouth.

"Ewww." Kandi's nose wrinkled.

"You eat bugs too." Tink reached down to scritch Grim's head as he rubbed his chin against her ankle before turning to Kandi. A chirruping purr came from the cat's belly. Tink realized that was probably what she'd heard from near the slipdrive.

"Yeah, but ... processed."

"This ship would have a lot more of them if he didn't snack on them." Tink smiled to see the tall, muscular woman shiver and commiserated with her. She'd come across a nest of bugs more than once while working in one of the *Lyra's* many tight spots, unable to pull away. The way they moved and clicked and clacked and hissed. She rubbed the spot between Grim's ears. "He's doing us a service."

"The thought of a cargo bay full of them...." Kandi shuddered again.

"Oh, those bugs aren't the same. Culinary bugs are much bigger." Tink suppressed a grin as Kandi shivered.

She spun her head to gaze at Tink. "But they're in stasis, right?"

Tink nodded. "Pretty much. Torpor. Waking only enough to feed once in a while. The captain's contact said they'll stay that way until we drop them off." She held her hand out. "Give it here. I won't kill myself, right?" A ping sounded through the room, like a pebble hitting an empty barrel. Tipping her head, she listened for any follow-up sound as she gingerly took Kandi's staff.

She nearly dropped it when an alarm sounded and red lights flashed. She slammed her palm on the comms panel beside the bench. "What have you done to my ship, Ish?"

"Ish is a bit busy right now." Alek's voice sounded tinny. "We need to leave the slipstream asap."

Tink's stomach heaved, and she peered at Kandi with wide eyes. It felt like they were dropping through atmo too fast, which was impossible, being in the stream. Another ping, followed by a thud echoed through the ship, and a low growl emanated from Grim. Then Tink threw her hands out to catch herself on her workbench and stop herself falling to the floor. As she fought to stand straight, the ship rocked, and tools slid off the bench and clattered to the floor.

"What was that?" Tink asked, though even she wasn't sure who the question was directed at — Cass, or Ish, or Alek, or even herself.

Cass answered first. "Warning. Hull integrity breach."

"But why?"

"Something hit us," Alek's voice said. "Or broke off us." In the background, she could hear Rebeka and Ish but couldn't make out what they were saying.

Kandi went to the panel on the wall and started swiping through screens and tapping buttons.

"How? We were in the stream." Tink pulled over her tablet and flicked through the camera feeds. "Is this another one of Ish's monsters of the deep?"

"No." Kandi stood back from the panel and just stared at it. "Someone tagged us with a tracker. Poorly."

"The Dominion *Hogfish*?" When Kandi didn't answer, Tink went to stand beside her. Lips pressing together, she squinted at the image of the outside of the ship, seeing what Kandi was looking at: a hoary white halo surrounded a tiny hole and the partially torn off tag. "Who would track *us*? And what idiot would affix it to the slip sail?"

4: TINK

ARE YOU SURE ABOUT this?" Tink glanced sidelong at Alek, who stared at his breather as he flicked his finger at the status display. Again. His normally tanned skin had taken on an undertone of green. The tense muscles of his neck and the thin line of his lips screamed his nervousness. Apparently, his discomfort the last time they'd spacewalked wasn't a one-off thing. Tink smirked at the idea that a man so tall and muscular that he could barely fit into his own atmo suit was scared of a little spacewalk. Despite that, now that the ship had emerged from the slipstream, he was the one heading out with her to remove the tag and inspect the damage.

Looking up, he nodded sharply. "Yes," he croaked. Clearing his throat, he stopped futzing with his breather. Instead, he picked up the atmo suit.

It got warm in the suits so, like her, he was clad in underwear and a tank top. Tink tried hard not to peek as he pulled the suit legs over his chiseled thighs. Still, she caught herself staring at the scars criss-crossing his body like threads in a story. They were scattered across his torso and arms but converged at his knees. Clearing her own throat, she focused on putting her own suit on.

"It's either me or Kandi. And I lost the dice roll." He lifted his gaze to smile at her, but the smile fell away.

"There was no dice roll." Kandi's voice carried over the hum of crates filled with semi-catatonic insects. "We arm wrestled. He cheated, and now I'm stuck with the bugs."

"You really do hate them?" Tink asked, yanking her suit over her arms as Alek shrugged his broad shoulders into his. She didn't like it when the critters snuck up on her with their ticklish feelers as she worked in some tight cranny, but the Antaran warrior seemed to have a much deeper aversion. "You dislike spacewalking almost as much as he does."

Alek graced her with a grimace before picking up her breather and checking it over. He held it out so she could thread her arms through the straps.

"I don't hate spacewalking." He snugged into his own breather then lifted his helmet over his head. "I hate being surrounded by nothingness." Pulling the helmet on, the faceplate masked the sickly hue of his skin. "Completely different." His voice sounded hollow through the helmet.

Tink snorted as she put on her helmet. "If you say so." She tipped her head side to side as she made sure the seals were secure. When she lifted her gaze, Alek held out his arm, elbow crooked.

"Shall we dance?"

Despite herself, she smiled and threaded her arm through his. Together they walked into the airlock.

Tink huffed and her visor momentarily fogged up. She rapped the wrench on the sheared barb of metal on the slip sail mast. Her jaw clenched and her molars ground together. "If you're going to tag a ship with a big-ass tracking device, at least have the courtesy to do a decent job." Her voice rose. "And to not attach it to a delicate piece of equipment."

In her helmet, Alek's steady breathing stopped in that fraction of a second before she heard his voice.

"So, it's bad?" he asked when she shoved said big-ass device — now deactivated — into his free hand.

"The slip sail helps keep us steady in the stream."

"Doesn't look like a sail."

"More of a rudder actually." She held up her hand as Alek started to speak. "Don't ask," she said as he grasped at the fingers she waved in his direction before pulling his hand back to grab the jackline. "Something to do with currents and waves of light."

"Can you please hold on?"

"Safety line, remember?" She jerked the line with her other hand.

"Please."

She studied his expression — his lips thin and the skin around his eyes tight — and remembered their previous spacewalk. The one where a saboteur had cut the line and she'd almost floated into space. She smiled but grabbed the line.

"This isn't a Dominion tag." Alek turned back to the ship and waggled the hand containing the tag.

"Who does it belong to then?" she asked as she tucked the wrench in her belt and turned herself around to face the Black.

"I — I don't know."

In that moment, as she took in the view in front of her, Tink didn't care who'd tagged them; she was just glad it wasn't attached to her ship anymore. Keeping hold of the jackline, she pulled on it so her back was against the hull of the ship and her feet floating free, pointing at the planet they orbited. They were back at the fifth planet in the Corican system. Aconitia hung like a marbled pearl on black velvet. She sensed Alek move beside her and sighed, resigned to heading back into the ship sooner than she would have liked. But when she turned towards him, he was staring out at space, his jaw slack.

She smiled and turned back to the view. A moon was rising on one side of the orb and a small satellite glinted on the other. "Not so bad after all, eh?"

"No." Alek glanced at her and blinked. Quickly, he turned himself back to the ship. "Not bad I guess, if you spend your days with your nose in engine grease."

Tink blinked, her lips pulling down as something fluttered in her stomach. Her shoulders dropped, imperceptible inside her suit. "I have what I need. Let's get inside."

Alek peered at her, his expression flat beneath his faceplate, then turned his eyes to the slip sail. "You're not going to fix it?" He shifted his body so he could look back at the planet, then returned his gaze to her. "I don't mind hanging out with you a bit longer."

Tink clenched her teeth together before answering. "Can't be fixed. The jolt popped one of the directional wave sensing coils. We need a new one. Well, a refurbished one." She shoved at Alek. "Go on. Get out of my way."

Tink stepped out of the airlock to three faces staring at them from amongst the crates of bugs. Well, four if she counted Grim. The whole crew gathered around to hear their fate.

"So, we don't know who tagged us?" Rebeka asked before Tink even got her helmet off. The captain leaned against one of the crates, fingers pressed into the metal. "And we can't slip?"

Tink took a deep breath and placed her helmet down on the nearest box. "I didn't say that." She ran a hand through her hair, plastered to her head, and tucked a sweaty strand behind her ear. "We just *shouldn't* until we replace that coil. At least not deep. Not in any uncharted streams."

"All streams are uncharted." Ish arched an eyebrow. "Have you listened to nothing I've said?" he added, but his tone was flat, without the usually playful ribbing at Tink's inability to grasp something so fundamental to the ship. And so innate to him.

"Okay, not in any dangerous streams." As soon as she said it, Tink held up her hand. "All streams are dangerous. But we might not have to go deep...." She scuffed her toe along the grating.

"But you said you couldn't repair the part." Alek came up beside her. Glancing at him, she saw he'd stripped off his suit and stood in his underwear again.

Her own suit felt hot, and her cheeks flushed. She turned back to the captain. "You know where we are, right?"

"Corican."

Tink looked back at the floor. "And the next nearest system is—"

"No." Alek shifted beside her. "You can't mean...."

"Ten Selva." Rebeka exhaled sharply as she said the name.

"But why would you want to go there?" Ish stepped away from the crate beside him as something inside hissed. "It's a pit. A dusty, lawless pit of a planet."

"There's a Tinker living on that pit. At least there was as of 500 days ago, when the listings were last done." Tink unzipped the front of her suit, shrugging out of the sleeves. "She's more a trader than a tinker. If anyone nearby can get us a refurbed directional wave sensing coil, she can."

"But we're as likely to be stabbed in the port and the ship stolen as we are to get a part," Alek said.

"You have experience with Ten Selva?" Kandi ran a stone down the length of the blade in her hand.

"It's famous." Alek squinted at the floor.

"I think 'infamous' is the word you're looking for." Kandi held the dagger up, a smile quirking at her lips. Something squealed underneath her, and she jumped up from the crate. "I thought they were supposed to be in stasis." She glared at the box. "Maybe we can offload this lot there."

"Torpor. And no, not if we want to get paid." Rebeka stood up straight. "Better get dressed, Alek."

Tink glanced back at Alek, tucking a wayward curl behind her ear, which dislodged another strand.

"Race you to the showers?" His eyebrow quirked up.

"No point. I'm just going to get covered in engine grease again." Tink picked up the rest of her clothes and stomped off towards the engine room, still in her atmo suit.

5: ALEK

ALEK SAT ON HIS bed and glared at the tag sitting across the room as he stroked Grim, who twisted belly up in his lap. He'd told Tink the truth — he didn't know who'd attached the device to the *Lyra*. But he recognized the model. Old school. Favoured by a rebel operative who felt the new ones weren't made as well as they used to be. The operative who'd arranged for him to finagle his way on the *Lyra*. If he'd know then, what he knew now...he didn't know what he'd do.

He exhaled, his shoulders slumping, and grabbed his tablet. It was time to call his keeper.

Luckily, the ship was in normal space at the moment, with Ish keeping them shallow and coming out of the stream at the slightest ripple per Tink's recommendation that they shouldn't really slip but a little might be okay. Which meant his access to the Connect wouldn't be fed through the nav station. Or through Cass. He flicked the tablet on and scanned his eye to enable the encryption algorithm before punching in the destination number.

Alek lifted the tablet as Grim rubbed his chin against the corner, resting it on the cat's side instead. He brought his hand to his chin as he waited for an answer on the other end. The reason they'd given for putting him on the *Lyra* was to stop some nefarious plot by imperial agents. They'd done that — rescuing the unusual boy Ben from the cartels, the imperial army, and a rival rebel faction.

So why would they tag the Lyra now?

The black on his screen started to pixelate, and Alek pulled his hand away from his face when he realized he was biting his thumbnail. Drawing his shoulders back, he forced a cocky smirk onto his lips just as the picture resolved.

"Why didn't you call sooner?" The woman's dark eyes bore into him over the vastness of space.

No niceties then. He put on what he called his Arena face, equal parts fierce and haughty...or so he hoped. "Why did you tag the *Lyra?*"

There was a pause that could almost be excused as a Connect delay. Almost.

"Why do you think I did?" She tipped her head sideways, highlighting the still-red scar along her neck. The one she'd gotten trying to recruit him.

He crossed his arms over his chest, switching to the smirk again. "Really, Ze...." Noting the tensing of her lips, he recalled her code name. "Really, *Zinnia?* You don't think I'd recognize your work when I see it?"

"Not *my* work." She glanced over her shoulder, stretching the scar, then turned back to the screen. "Why didn't you bring us the package?"

"The boy, you mean?"

A lifted eyebrow was her only reply.

"That wasn't in the orders. Orders you gave me."

Her lips twisted into a smile, bringing to the surface a ghost of the person she'd been when he'd served alongside her, back when they'd both been soldiers. "Since when did you follow orders?"

"Since when did you kidnap little boys?" Alek dropped his smirk. "I might not follow orders, but I need more instruction if you're going to keep me in the dark about what my parameters of the contract actually are."

"You make it sound so transactional."

"Because I'm hired help."

"We both know you don't have an actual contract. Just a debt." One corner of her lips twitched. "Our mission was to keep that package away from the imperial scientists wanting to dissect it."

"*Your* mission." Alek breathed deeply and leaned back, acting casual. "And mission accomplished." He paused, unsure he wanted to say what was waiting on his tongue. "You can pick me up on Ten Selva. I'll slip away and—"

"No."

Alek's stomach churned at the word. He swallowed but stayed silent.

"Your debt isn't paid out. Stay on the *Lyra*."

"Why?"

"Because I say so."

"What are my orders, then?"

"To wait."

"And if I refuse?"

Zinnia's shoulder lifted. She tipped her head the other way, her halo of hair following a nanosecond later. "You can find your own way off Ten Selva." Her lips lifted into a lazy smile. "Isn't that where we picked you up? Running from that cartel, just because you were afraid of a little surgery." Alek's jaw clenched as she leaned forward, her face filling the screen as she reached black lacquered fingernails towards him. "I'll be in touch."

The screen went blank.

He stared at it for a second, then felt a gentle nip on his hand — Grim letting him know he was shirking his duty. He tossed the tablet aside.

Stay on the Lyra. Alek smiled at the thought of staying where he was, flying the cozy cargo ship and its crew from job to job. Then the smile fell. He sighed and leaned against the wall, pulling Grim closer to press his chin against the cat's head. Grim squawked but soon his stomach rumbled in a purr.

What do they still want with the ship? And its crew?

His was not to question why ... but he did.

6: TINK

TINK STEPPED OFF THE ramp onto the rust-coloured ground. Even the air had an orange hue. As she stepped forward to join Rebeka, dust eddies swirled up around her calves. Breathing in, her lungs burned and the hairs in her nostrils stung. The air tasted like she sucked on a nail. After pulling her goggles over her eyes, she tugged her scarf up to cover her mouth and nose. Even still, the sulphurous, metallic tang filled her sinuses. Tiny midges swarmed her, though she didn't know whether they were looking for moisture or a blood meal.

She shifted as Alek stepped up beside her.

He coughed and waved his hand in front of his face as he squinted at the monochromatic port. "Why would anyone settle here?"

"Because no one is going to bother you in a dust pit like this," the captain said. "Neither the Dominion nor the cartels."

"So, they want this hellhole to themselves." He slapped the side of his neck, then scowled at his hand. "At least the dark side is cooler. Well, frozen. Swarming with the rich and bored though."

"You don't have to come." Tink tapped at the panel on her wrist, trying to pull up directions to the Tinker's shop. She'd heard of Ten Selva but never been planetside herself, and certainly didn't know the layout of Excelsior, the only port town.

"Yeah, I do." His voice was so quiet she almost didn't hear him over the drone of the midges and the rumble of the port, which was surprisingly busy for such a backwater planet.

"Yeah, he does." Rebeka spoke more loudly, and Tink rolled her eyes as she glanced between the two of them. They both scanned the red-stained buildings that sprawled along the far side of the landing area. Alek strapped a second blaster to his hip and hoisted a pulse rifle up, tucking the butt in his armpit. Muscles flexed under his shirt as he hugged the weapon closer.

From behind her scarf, Tink grimaced at the amount of firepower on display. She bit her tongue and turned to the captain. "Kandi could come."

"Kandi's going with Ish to see if they can restock the food stores."

"What are you going to do?"

Rebeka slowly turned from staring at a person swathed in layers of rust-coloured clothes. "Get the lay of the land."

A headache pulsed across Tink's forehead as she and Alek walked down the main street of Excelsior, the sprawling ramshackle town that had sprung up around the dusty, so-called spaceport. When she squinted at her wrist tab, it took her a few moments to realize her goggles were coated with dust. After wiping them off, the map became marginally more readable.

"This way." She jerked her chin left, towards a small alley. Turning to head down it, she found herself stopped by Alek's hand on her chest. She turned to glare at it then at him.

"I don't think we want to go that way." His hand dropped to the inside of her elbow.

She shifted her attention from his hand to her map, frowning. Her mouth opened to protest — it was the most direct way. Then, at a sound, she glanced down the alley. Up ahead, 10 metres along, a brawl between a knot of people threatened to turn into a melee. She couldn't tell who was on which side — if there were sides — but knives were out and bloody. She took a half-step forward. "Shouldn't we do something?"

"An engineer and broken pilot ... what do you suggest we do?"

She peered at Alek, not seeing anything in his broad shoulders or chiseled torso that appeared broken. His grim expression swayed her. Swallowing, she turned back to the main road. "Right. Recalculating." She peered at the map, trying to find a route that took them along more peopled roads, though as someone bumped into her, she realized that more people wasn't always better.

Alek's hand shot out and grabbed a wrist of the person who'd jostled her. "Drop it."

Tink lunged forward and reached her hand out when she saw what the pickpocket had gotten hold of. She didn't have anything of real value on her, but the stink grenade would have left them all doused.

"Do you even know what this is?" She glared at the thief, then realized that it didn't matter. As long as the gaunt young man could trade it for a piece of bread, he'd have gotten what he needed. She dug around in her back and pulled out a bug bar, holding out her empty hand, she offered a trade. The pickpocket dropped the grenade into her palm, snatched the bar and ran off. She tucked the bomb back in her bag, her frown pulling her face further down. "Okay, turn left at this square then left again at the next."

Trudging along the next street, all the buildings were variations on a theme. Squat with small windows, red dust coated their original bright colours. Every few buildings, someone had gotten ambitious and added another floor. This street was wider, but Tink realized that just left room for the dust to drift into piles against doors and ledges. All the windows were shuttered, though she didn't know whether it was to keep out the dust and heat, or if they were abandoned. Or so their inhabitants could deny knowledge of what happened outside.

Finally, she broke the oppressive silence. "I can't reconcile this place with the stories I've heard. This isn't extravagant."

Alek made a sound like a cough. "You're only seeing the port, the dayside. A dusty, drab centre of illegal but still mundane commerce." He was silent for a moment before going on. "Take a trip to the nightside if you want to see the rich and the lawless."

Tink opened her mouth to ask how he knew, but the set of his jaw told her it wasn't something he wanted to talk about. And although she loved tales of outlandish piracy, debauchery and hedonism, at the moment she didn't care to hear. She certainly wasn't as interested in seeing it for herself as she thought she'd be. She was bone-tired and just wanted to get back to the *Lyra*.

"So, there's really no law here?" she asked instead, as they turned the final corner. She almost stopped at the silence from Alek.

"Oh no, there's a law," he finally said. Her wrist beeped and he continued. "Looks like we're here."

Looking up, Tink saw a sand-blasted sign that still held the impression of three interlocking gears. A twitter fluttered through her belly — it had been a long time since she'd dealt with another Tinker face-to-face. She took a deep breath and pushed open the door.

7: ΔLΘK

MACHINES, ENGINE COMPONENTS, AND unidentified contraptions — half-assembled or half-disassembled, Alek couldn't tell which — crammed the shop Tink led them to. The teetering piles reached up to the rafters in places. A patina of rusty dust coated everything, making it hard to pick out the actual rust.

He picked up a blob of interconnecting gears, using it as cover to examine the woman and her shop. Squinting, he scrutinized the woman, searching for whatever caused the itch at the back of his brain. He found few similarities between Tink and the shopkeeper. Elsbeth Aron, she'd called herself. Elsbeth was a couple of decades older than Tink. Grey peppered her frizzy hair despite an attempt to dye it, any colour nanos long since worn out and not recharged. The wrinkles that creased around her eyes as she smiled crept down towards her cheeks. The broad smile she gave them exposed a few missing teeth.

But it wasn't the teeth which caused a worm of doubt to creep through Alek's intestines. The smile seemed brittle, lacking in real warmth. Her eyes narrowed when her gaze flicked his way. The woman talked with her hands much more than Tink did. In that movement, Alek noted the only similarity between the two: her long, slender fingers were reminiscent of Tink's ... except for the beetle-dust stains between them. Thankfully, she wasn't smoking one of the noxious cigars at the moment. Though they likely accounted for her missing teeth. They would also cause the rhueminess in her eyes, though her gaze was too sharp for a full-on addict.

Even though Tink wasn't using her hands to barter with the woman, he noticed her fingers twitched, and she rocked ever so slightly back and forth on her feet. His free hand shifted, wanting to reach out, to help calm whatever made her nervous. Instead, he squeezed the blob he held.

The woman behind the counter glanced at him, her eyes squinting again, as she continued her monologue in her particular patois. He guessed it had a fair sprinkling of Ten Selva jargon, since Tink also seemed to struggle to understand her — she leaned progressively closer to Elsbeth as the woman orated.

Tink blushed, though he couldn't understand enough of what they were saying to know if it was something Elsbeth had said. She breathed in sharply, causing the woman to pause. "Let's speak Standard for his sake," Tink said into the gap, and jerked her head towards him.

Elsbeth's eyes slid his way again. "Standard. Fine. So, you want a directional wave sensing coil?" She shook her head. "I don't have one of those myself at the moment."

"But you have sources."

"Ha! Of course I have sources. A reputable trader always does, let alone a Tinker trader."

Alek turned to the shelf as his eyebrow quirked at the word *reputable*.

"Iyan!" Elsbeth shouted over her shoulder, towards the bead-covered doorway. Though as he looked at it, Alek realized the strands weren't made of beads; they were bolts and washers and capacitors.

A long-limbed young man emerged from the back, and Alek finally saw a resemblance to Tink. His brown eyes matched hers. He even had the freckles. "Ya'ma?" He glanced between Alek and Tink, his cheeks turning pink under their covering of spots.

"This lovely young lady is after a directional wave sensing coil." Elsbeth smiled at Tink, laying her fingers over the engineer's hand before Tink could pull away. Though it didn't look to Alek like Tink tried to break free. Instead, she graced the boy, Iyan, with a lop-sided smile and a shrug. Elsbeth patted the man's shoulder with her free hand, as if he really were a child, and pushed him forward.

His eyes rolled as the pink on his cheeks crept down his neck. "Na'ma!"

Alek took pity on the boy, forestalling Elsbeth's matchmaking. "The directional wave sensing coil ... can you get one?"

"Aish." Elsbeth scowled at him, and he scowled back. She didn't release Tink's hand as she looked at Iyan. "Who has one?"

"I'd have to check the lists. Haven't seen one come through for a bit." Iyan focused his gaze on his mother's hand, or Tink's fingers trapped beneath. His eyes flicked up to Tink's face every few words. "They don't break often so not a common stock part."

"Yes," Elsbeth said. "Very hard to come by. Very expensive."

"Yeah, ours didn't exactly break," Tink muttered as her shoulders sank.

Again, Alek fought the urge to reach out and squeeze her shoulder. "So, you can't get one?" he asked instead.

"She didn't say that." Iyan looked up at Tink, not Alek, with a small smile on his face. "I can get one." His mother grabbed his hand, drawing it towards Tink's. "And you get the Tinker's discount."

Elsbeth dropped his hand, and Alek almost laughed as her hand lifted in preparation to smack her son on the head. Halfway through, she shifted and stroked his hair instead, though her words were clipped when she spoke. "My boy. So generous."

"When do you think you'll know?" Alek stepped closer to the counter, closer to Tink. Iyan blinked at him, his smile faltering as his head tipped sideways.

"I'll have it for you tomorrow."

"Tomorrow." Tink nodded and smiled, a dimple forming on her cheek. She finally extricated her hand from beneath Elsbeth's, only to lay it on top of Iyan's, causing the young man to blush again. "Thank you." Then she turned towards the door.

"You can manage to not be thrown in jail for one cycle, ya?" Elsbeth's smile turned a little feral, and the worm of worry in Alek's gut twitched.

Tink paused, glancing at him before she turned back to the woman. "I thought there was no law here."

Elsbeth cackled. "Oh, there's a law. And her name is Echo Eris."

"Na'ma!" Iyan said while Alek paled at the name. The law had changed since he'd been here last, and not for the better.

8: ALEK

ALEK FLIPPED THE CHIT towards the table, looking for the sweet spot where it would bounce into the cup at the centre. Once again, it hopped over the glass. Despite the roar of the drinkers crammed into the saloon, he still heard the clink as it hit the pile in front of Ish.

"Urg!" Alek groaned while Ish beamed. He gave Ish a half-hearted grimace then took another swig of the vile grog the bar tried to pass off as suitable for human consumption. He peered into it with eyes too bleary for so early in the day. The liquid was tinted a reddish brown, like the world around them, even though it was straight from the bottle. He gave it a swirl, which disturbed the unidentified flecks floating in it. He put the glass down with a thunk and pushed it away, swearing not to look too closely at anything he was served here again.

The captain had kept them safely ensconced in the *Lyra* last night, which he'd been glad to comply with knowing Echo Eris was on the loose. But when they'd been freed this morning, with nothing to do until supplies and parts were ready for pickup, the others were restless. Someone had suggested a bar, which led to drinking games as a way to pass the time. It might have been him. He moaned.

"Nice reflexes, fly boy." Any sting was taken out of Ish's words by the smile on his face as he dragged the chits towards him.

"I deal with asteroids and moons, not tokens." Alek leaned back in his chair, taking a swig from the water he'd brought from the ship. "How about a game of Jacks instead? I'm aces at Jacks."

Kandi leaned forward at hearing that, her gaze sharp. "Deal me in."

"I wouldn't do that." Tink looked up from the automaton she was fiddling with. "She's a shark."

"I—" Kandi's hand came to her chest.

"A cheating shark," Ish added, smiling at Kandi, who arched an eyebrow at the navigator, though her lips quirked into a smile which told Alek that Ish probably spoke the truth. But there weren't really any rules against cheating as long as you didn't get caught.

"I'll deal." Rebeka pulled a pack of cards from her jacket, making Alek instantly wary.

"You're a cheating shark too?"

"Oh no." She peered at him, her expression flat, while she shuffled the deck, the cards moving in a blur. "I don't cheat."

"But she'll still eviscerate you." Tink didn't look up from her project.

"Tink, you're in." Rebeka lay a card down in front of her. Tink pulled her head up to protest. "Captain's orders. Your Tinker is the reason we're killing time in this bar."

"She's not *my* Tinker." Nonetheless, Tink huffed and put her automaton away.

"No, though she might be angling to be your mother-in-law." Alek smiled when Tink stuck her tongue out at him.

Nudging her tool kit aside, she picked up her cards. "Ugh. If it's going to be like this, I need another drink." She raised her hand to hail the rusty server-bot, which creaked and whined as it rolled over.

"Have you thought that not commenting on how bad your cards are might be the better strategy?" Alek picked up his own cards, holding them close as the captain finished dealing. He examined his hand and the cards Rebeka dealt face up.

"Braken," Tink told the bot.

Looking at his hand, he turned to Tink. "Ugh, get me one too," he said, even though he'd just sworn to avoid the stuff.

"That bad?" She quirked an eyebrow at him, but nonetheless passed his order to the bot.

"Ditto." Ish smiled as he sorted his cards.

"Ish, lesson one in being a shark: don't wear your hand on your face." Rebeka placed the rest of the deck in the centre of the table. "Braken all around?"

"Gods no! How can you drink that swill?" Kandi shook her head and turned to the bot. "Antaran firestorm. Neat."

"So, engine degreaser is better?" Rebeka arched an eyebrow, peering at her own hand.

"Antaran firestorm is the nectar of Aphrodite herself." Kandi sighed as she picked up her cards. "It reminds me of home, and the carefree days of my youth."

"I didn't think Antaran warriors had carefree days." Alek took a swig of the warm swill he'd pushed away earlier and grimaced. "Weren't all your waking hours spent training to be Amazons?"

Kandi frowned at him. "I am not an Amazon."

"Tell that to the Denovian at the bar who's been gawking at you all morning." Tink turned over the card on top of the draw pile.

Kandi tossed her blue hair over her shoulder to check out said person, giving them a wolfish smile. "Not my type."

"You have a type?" Ish commented, trying to suppress a smile.

"You're one to talk." Kandi bumped her shoulder against Ish's. Even though it was playful, Ish almost tipped out of his chair, and Alek joined Tink and the captain in laughing. Ish giggled as he righted himself.

"What about you hotshot?" He jerked his chin at Alek.

Alek's mouth dropped open, and he turned his attention to the card Rebeka laid down. "I'm definitely not an Amazon." He played a card on top of the captain's. "And I'll never drink Antaran firestorm again."

"You know what I mean." Ish picked up the card Alek had played. "What's your type?"

Alek watched the cards play around the table and debated his next move. "My type—" His gaze drifted towards the automaton Tink had been working on, but then a silence fell over the bar. He looked up along with everyone else at the table.

Echo Eris stood in the doorway.

"My type tries to kill me," he muttered as he scrunched down in his chair. His hair was different, and he had a new scar...maybe Echo wouldn't recognize him. Even as he thought that, her gaze travelled over where they were sitting, and her scan paused when it came to him. Alek shifted over behind Tink while trying not to actually move — movement draws a predator's attention. and Echo's gaze moved on, and he breathed out a heavy sigh.

Ish arched an eyebrow. "Who is that?" he whispered as he leaned forward.

"The Law," Kandi said before Alek could answer, as she stared daggers at Echo Eris. Her fist clutched her actual dagger. It looked like she might get up and confront the woman. Then his attention was drawn to a shout by the door.

"I didn't do it!" A man glanced around wildly, trying to enjoin the other patrons to his cause, as the men with Echo grabbed him and started dragging him away. Everyone in the bar either just stared at him or looked away.

"Igor Ashan, by the power vested in me by the Dominion—" Echo paused as a snicker passed through the regulars; she'd always loved drama. "—and the good citizens of Excelsior, and my skills with a blaster, I do hereby charge you with one count of theft."

"It was on the refuse heap."

"I thought you said you didn't do it," one of the men with Echo said, the scar on his face moving like a worm as he spoke.

"Shush, both of you, or I'll add contempt." Echo cleared her throat. "Witness, come forward." A man in the once-white robes of a mendicant order stepped from the shadows, limbs shaking. "Speak truth and prosper. Lie and share his punishment."

The man shrivelled, pulling his red-stained robes around him. "I ... I saw this man take the boxes." He glanced at the accused. "I didn't know what was in it."

"I thought it was garbage."

"Did you ascertain ownership and obtain transmittal?" Echo clearly struggled to maintain her seriousness as a smile played at her lips. Or, at least, it was clear to Alek.

The man shook his head, and Echo continued. "You have been deemed guilty—"

"Without a trial?" Tink glared at Echo's back, her arms crossing over her chest. "Without corroboration?" There was a hiccough in Echo's speech, and the captain shook her head at Tink.

Echo continued. "Because I am merciful, you will serve out your sentence in the iron fields of our own Ten Selva." The man's face blanched at that, and he renewed his struggles as Echo's men dragged him from the bar. Acid ate at Alek's stomach as his fists clenched his chair so hard his knuckles cracked.

"We should do something." Tink gestured towards the door.

"Their planet, their laws." Rebeka scowled at the open door. "We'd probably end up in the fields ourselves. We are still nominally in the Dominion after all." She turned back to the table. "Ha! Jacks!" She grabbed the card Alek had put down then slammed her hand down with more force than called for.

"Rebeka?"

Alek watched the captain's face go from angry victory to plain anger as she sat up, back as straight as a rod, and swivelled in her chair to face the rumpled man who'd spoken her name.

9: Rebeka

DUSTAN KEY." REBEKA'S HEART thudded and her stomach churned as adrenalin spiked through her system. She stared at her ex-husband. *Estranged husband*, she corrected herself — they'd never actually made it legal. His clothes were rumpled and looked like they hadn't been washed in weeks. His salt-and-pepper hair stuck out at odd angles, and his face hadn't seen a razor in days. Blue eyes sparkled above his ruddy cheeks, a clear sign he'd had more to drink than he should, which was nothing new. But the bags under his eyes were. And the wrinkles on his forehead were deeper. "You look like shit."

"And you look exactly the same, minus the hair. I liked the locks, but the shave suits you."

"A shave would suit you too." Rebeka tipped her head sideways. As she crossed her arms over her chest, she slid her gaze to the lanky young man who hovered by Dustan's shoulder before returning her focus to her ex. "What are you doing here?"

"Passing by." He glanced towards the door. "I go where the research takes me. Imagine my surprise when I saw you across a crowded room. Just like when we first met."

Rebeka's eyes narrowed. Her heart might still twitter when she thought of those early days, but she'd lived with Dustan long enough to know him. "Bollocks. No research would bring you to Ten Selva."

The young man's green eyes blinked when she swore, and his pale fish-belly cheeks flushed. It was like he'd never been outside of ... wherever Dustan had picked him up from.

She turned back to her ex, jerking her chin towards the man. "You conned a new fledgling into assisting you, now that Juniper's taken off to live her own life?"

"Our daughter helped me of her own free will, and Fennick is the same. Right, Fennick?" The black-haired young man swallowed and nodded but didn't speak as he fidgeted with the pendant that hung from a cord around his neck.

Rebeka ignored the intake of breath from the crew and the twist in her stomach — she'd never mentioned either her husband or daughter to them. Refusing to look at them, she rocked her chair forward and stood.

Dustan patted his assistant on the shoulder. "Fennick loves a mystery as much as I do." When her ex smiled, she caught a glimpse of the man she'd fallen in lust with...and unexpectedly found herself in love with when the heat turned to a rolling boil. Until he went on one crazy snipe hunt too many at the same time she'd defied the military, refusing to get modded. They couldn't order her to, but it resulted in dishonourable discharge, shunning and being forced to seek out employment in the few places she could find it. Acid still ate at her stomach when she thought about having to leave Juniper and Dustan, even if it was for their own good — she was supposed to be the reliable one.

Rebeka pulled out her chair and spun it around so the back formed a barrier between them before sitting down again. He gave her a look like he knew what she was doing, but he still pulled a chair up for himself. His assistant, Fennick, sank into a crouch beside him, but still came up to Dustan's shoulder.

"What are you really doing here, and what do you want from me?"

Dustan slapped a hand to his chest. "You wound me. When was I ever so mercenary?"

"Always." Rebeka arched an eyebrow.

"With you?" He dropped the hand to his lap, but she still noticed the tremble...when had they gotten so old?

She shrugged, conceding the point. He'd always been a loving husband and doting father, whatever she might think of his career choices. Or lack of career. He was smart and creative; he could have been a leading Professor with the Dominion Archaeological Institute. Instead, he chased after myths and phantoms.

He coughed, looking at the floor between them. "But now that you mention it, I could use your help."

Rebeka groaned. "I knew it." She heard chits changing hands behind her and turned to scowl at the crew. Kandi and Ish paused whatever they were doing, while Alek watched Dustan with intense interest. And Tink glared at her. Rebeka turned back to Dustan.

"You have a ship. I need a ride."

"Nuhuh. No more free rides. You'll have to find your own way off this blasted rock."

"Not a free ride." The words squeaked from the raven-haired assistant as he finally found his voice. "We can pay."

With both eyebrows raised, Rebeka looked from him to her ex. "Really?"

"Really. So hard to believe?" His blue eyes sparkled at her. "Okay, I know it's unusual for me to have money to pay for a ride, but this time...." He leaned forward, hands grasping his knees as his voice dropped. "This time I have an investor. An angel interested in my little hunt for a piece of history. For a legend."

Rebeka's lips pressed together. She didn't want to drag him or Juniper back into her ongoing game of hide-and-go-seek with her former Covert Ops commanders, but she especially didn't want to get herself or the rest of the crew involved in whatever escapade he'd cooked up.

"No." She started to stand but Dustan grasped her wrist.

"I...." He glanced around, mimicked by his assistant. "Will you sit down, hear me out?" Rebeka didn't move. "Just a minute. For old times' sake?" He stroked his thumb on the inside of her palm.

Breathing deeply, her stomach fluttered and her scowl softened to a frown. "One minute."

Dustan opened his mouth to speak, then looked at the crew.

Rebeka glanced back as she sat down. "Whatever you have to say you can say in front of them."

"No way I'm leaving anyway." Ish shoveled crispy bar worms into his mouth without taking his eyes off the two of them.

"And you'd better hurry." Rebeka leaned on the chair back. "Your minute is running out."

"I've found it."

"Found what?" she asked but then saw the answer in the glimmer of his eyes. She groaned. "Not this nonsense again. It's bad enough you almost got Juniper cast out from the Royal Academy of Archaeology over it."

"Found what?" Ish asked. When she glanced over at him, she saw him leaning halfway across the table.

Dustan's voice dropped lower. "I found the...." He cast his gaze all around then leaned even closer, looking at Ish. "The *Celeste*." He mouthed the word, barely a whisper.

For a minute, the silence was so heavy you could have heard a bar worm drop if it weren't for the rumble of the saloon.

10: ALEK

THE CAPTAIN SAID NO." Alek glanced sidelong at Dustan Key. He couldn't picture sharp, precise Captain Mino married to this rumpled man. "You're not getting a ride. And she scares me so don't even try to convince me to go against her."

"Smart man." Dustan picked up a pair of socks from a stall then put them down to follow along as Alek kept up his brisk pace. "But I wouldn't dream of it. I'm just going in the same direction." He waved his hand vaguely in front of them.

"You're going to the commissary?" Alek arched an eyebrow but didn't look at the man, instead keeping a wary eye on Ish, who spent too much time looking at wares on the scattered stalls. "Without a ship to provision?"

"Ha!" The rumpled man slapped his thigh. "Oh, you're not going to the commissary either." He waved his hand around at the ramshackle market stalls. "You're in it."

Alek glanced around – he'd never had to deal with provisioning the ship that had taken him to the night side. He tipped his head and peered at Ish, whose shrug confirmed Dustan's comment.

"It's a small port. No call for a fancy provisioners' market. Besides, it's cheaper this way."

The gnawing in Alek's stomach, a constant companion since landing on Ten Selva, sank as his shoulders dropped. It was going to be a long afternoon, going stall to stall, store to store, to find the provisions Ish and Kandi couldn't procure the day before.

"So, you really found the *Celeste*?" Ish said, looking around Alek at Dustan.

Dustan glanced all around as he hissed. "Chzzt! Do you want to announce it to the whole of the Green Zone?"

Turning to walk backwards in front of them, Dustan's assistant — Fennick, he'd called him — peered at Ish, a shy smile on his face. "This is huge." The words were a whisper. "The last of the legendary treasure ships from the old empire. From the Desolation. Still lost." His voice was hushed, and his eyes shone. "Long after the others were recovered, the fate of the Ce ... this one remains unfound. Until now."

Alek tried to dredge up long-forgotten history lessons. His grandmother would be unimpressed by what little he recalled of the old empire. She'd spent hours drilling him on facts and figures, luminaries and legends of the days before the Exodus. But he'd forgotten most of it; it was all lost to the Desolation anyway. Except the treasure ships, which every young adventurer had heard of.

"I grew up on tales of the twelve ships," Ish said. "Why they were lost and how they were found. The puzzles people had to solve to find each one. The still-undeciphered writing in the books the *Sunshin* carried. Bound paper books."

"I know." Fennick stepped in beside Ish. "I would love to be the one to solve that mystery. I've read everything about it. I have copies of all the books." He tapped the bag slung over his chest.

"You need to walk before you can crawl, Fennick." Dustin didn't sound entirely impressed by the young man's enthusiasm.

Fennick flushed and looked away. Alek frowned at Dustin, but the man's gaze trawled the stalls. Alek followed his example, though he was searching for Echo Eris as much as for something to buy. The sooner they got off this planet the better. Hopefully Tink succeeded in getting the part they needed from Elsbeth Aron. *And her son isn't succeeding in flirting with Tink.*

His frown deepened at the random thought, and he was almost caught by a vendor. His knee twinged but he managed to side-step the woman trying to sell him a snack with tentacles still moving. Ish wasn't so lucky, and they all had to stop while he paid. While Alek waited, he scanned the market looking for an excuse to ditch Dustan and his protege.

Ish finally escaped the woman, chomping into the creature, which thankfully no longer moved. Oil dripped down his chin as he bit into it again with a crunch. "Moffuyal." Whatever he intended to say was garbled by the bug bits.

Alek gave him a skeptical look. "There." He grabbed Ish's arm and pointed to a large stand at the end of the street piled high with staples, ready-made meal packets, boxes of freeze-dried bugs, and algae amendments. "Looks like they might have everything we need." *And nothing Dustan needs.* He set off towards the stall, assuming the others would follow.

"Halt."

Alek froze, and his intestines churned. Echo had found him. Slowly, he turned to face her. Only to see her attention focused on Ish, who had his hands up beside his shoulders, one holding the stick with half a body and one whole tentacle still on it. Her voice sent chills down Alek's spine, but he nonetheless stepped up beside Ish.

"Consuming sepidilus is a crime on Ten Selva." Her gaze slid his way. "You should know that Alek—"

"I'm not a street meat aficionado. How about harassing the woman who sold it instead of the tourists?" He scowled over her shoulder where he saw Dustan focused on his wrist patch — no doubt already looking for another ride off the planet.

"Selling it is *not* a crime."

"What?" Ish's arms started to drop, and she grabbed the skewer from him.

"Evidence."

Ish jerked back as she reached out and plucked a piece of tentacle from his chin.

"Surely we can come to some agreement." Alek hated himself as he said it, his stomach queasy at the thought of what she'd demand in payment.

She held up a black-gloved hand, the other going to the stunner at her hip. "Your next words better not be trying to bribe me. I take the law very seriously." Her eyes glinted as she stared at him.

"Excuse me, Sarge...um, Eris." Dustan tapped her on her shoulder just as her comm unit pinged. "I think you'll find that call is asking you to let this young man go."

Echo turned her fierce gaze on him, red creeping up her neck. "I am the law here. I don't take orders from anyone."

"Of course not." Dustan pressed his palms together in front of his chest and dipped his chin to his fingertips. "But you seem like a smart woman so I'm sure you do take wise council."

Alek almost gasped out loud and waited for her hand to shift from the stunner to the blaster. Instead, she tapped the bud in her ear, her head tipping just a bit sideways as she listened. Alek held his breath.

Lips pursed, she pulled herself up tall and straight. "This *is* a first-time infraction, and I'm feeling merciful. You're free to go." Her gaze flicked from Ish to Dustan to Alek. "But get off my planet asap and don't come back." She turned on her heels and strode away through the crowd.

After a heartbeat, Alek did the same, pulling Ish along with him towards the stall he'd seen earlier.

"How did you do that?" Ish asked Dustan, awe plain in his tone, as the man followed them.

Dustan shrugged, a conspiratorial smile creeping onto his face. "I told you I had an angel interested in the *Celeste*? Well, he's a powerful angel, and I called in a favour."

Alek's eyes narrowed, and his scowl returned. Powerful angels were bad news.

11: HARBIN

HARBIN LOW NEEDED TO make a decision. Well, two decisions actually.

The most pressing one was who to follow. He could go after the Tinker and the blue-haired Amazon. In a split second he dismissed that option. The pair had orders to pick up some engine part, nothing exciting except being swindled by a corrupt seller. To be expected on Ten Selva. He could trail the captain, who'd given no indication of where she was going. Or he could follow the muscle head, the navigator, and the old man who'd said he'd found the *Celeste*.

Harbin almost snorted out loud at the idea as he stepped out of the bar into the metallic air. The sun glared like an angry orange eye in the particulate sky. He slid his gaze sideways as Delphi stepped out after him.

She scanned the street. "Which way, boss?"

An innocent question, but her tone told him she'd probably heard exactly what he had. Which made his second decision more complicated: did he tell Halcyon Koning about the *Celeste*?

He jerked his head left to where he could still see the statuesque Amazon's blue hair. "Follow those two. See what they're up to. I'll follow the men." Delphi peered at him for a second, then pulled her scarf up over her mouth, only half covering the jagged scar on her cheek that she refused to get fixed. Tugging her cloak about her, she headed after the women. Harbin watched her for the first 20 paces before turning to follow the four men.

The Celeste. A treasure ship said to be loaded with the most precious remnants of an opulent but dying civilization. Brilliant gems, rare metals, art that people had already killed for. But the greatest prize was the tech of the ship itself — legend said the Dominion's interstellar civilization was built on the priceless tech of the other eleven ships.

If those tales were true, and this frumpy man had actually found it, Harbin could be a rich man. As long as he didn't tell Halcyon and managed to take it for himself. But not telling Halcyon meant a price on his head if she ever found out. He'd never had dreams of freedom from his reins, but now a glimpse of a life of leisure on Passalida shimmered in his brain like a damaged vid of a bygone era.

Yes, Harbin Low had a decision to make. But instead of making it, he focused his attention on navigating the crowded market street, staying out of sight while keeping the beefy pilot and pale, skinny kid in view. They were both tall enough that their black hair was clearly visible over most of the crowd. Harbin himself was short, shorter than he should have been at least, spending his early years as a malnourished orphan on a grungy Lazarette station.

A commotion up ahead drew him out of his reveries. He sighed. The fuss centred around his quarry. Echo Eris, what passed for a sheriff in this god-forsaken hellhole, harassed the navigator. Harbin wrinkled his nose. The locals might have seen her as a refreshing dose of order in their red-tinted chaos, but Harbin recognized her for what she was — a jumped-up bully with a self-made badge.

When she spoke, her voice reverberated, and the din of the crowd diminished, letting him hear some of what she said. His jaw clenched. He needed them free if they were going to lead him to the treasure ship.

Harbin's cheeks flushed. He realized he had no choice after all: he needed them to lead to the *Celeste*. And he needed Halcyon's name to keep them free: he didn't have the connections to go after such a prize on his own. Besides, he owed his life to Halcyon; a treasure ship was a small price to pay. He ducked into a doorway and tapped a message into his comms. Halcyon wouldn't be pleased if the *Lyra's* navigator was locked up by a virago. She wanted her own revenge on that ship and its crew. He peeked out, and a few seconds later the woman abandoned her pursuit.

He jumped when his comms notified him of an incoming call. *Her* ringtone.

"Hello."

"Why are you helping the crew of the *Lyra* get away from a brutal sheriff?"

Harbin swallowed. Halcyon had been clear that she wanted them dealt with in a most unpleasant manner, and he was still happy to oblige. But Harbin needed to know if the man told the truth; and he was sure Lady Koning would want to know too.

He shrunk further back into the dark door and brought his wrist close to his lips. "There's a man with them who claims he's found the *Celeste*."

Silence hung in the doorway for so long he looked to see if his comms were still working.

"I know," Halcyon's voice finally said.

Harbin jerked his head up, scanning the crowd out on the street. *How can she know?* He had a hard time believing that Delphi had said anything, even if she'd had a line to Archon Koning, but it was the only option that presented itself.

Unless Halcyon had already known. He stared at the red dust swirling at his feet. *If I'd tried to keep the knowledge to myself....*

"Harbin?"

"Yes, I'm here. Just making sure no one is listening."

"Do you have a secure location on-planet?"

"We're staying at the Paradise Inn." He, Delphi and a couple of the crew had taken a runner down to the planet, to be incognito in a way parking a Barracuda class starship in port wouldn't allow.

"Good. I have someone I want you to meet."

The comms winked off, and Harbin blinked at it. He rarely enjoyed Halcyon's introductions.

12: TINK

WITH A FORCE OF will she didn't know she possessed, Tink managed to keep her hands at her sides and her expression neutral as she peered across the counter at Elsbeth Aron. Maybe the fingernails she dug into her palm gave her strength. She slid a sidelong glance at Kandi, who feigned nonchalance as she picked up and put down random bits and bobs from around the counter.

"Our supplier, he takes a long time." Elsbeth gave her a look that tried to say 'forgive my slowness, I'm an old woman', but Tink knew a con when she saw one. "One more day. Come back tomorrow." The woman grabbed her son's arm as he tried to disappear into the back. "Iyan can keep you company, show you the sights."

He shot his mother a wide-eyed look as his face reddened. "This is Ten Selva." He leaned close to Elsbeth and continued with a whisper. "There are no sights."

"Speed is critical." Tink's words were clipped despite her effort to stay at ease. Iyan, the shopkeeper's son, appeared uncomfortable himself, shifting from foot to foot, hands clasping and unclasping, eyes lifting to hers before jerking away. She almost felt sorry for him, except her current mood didn't allow space for anything but annoyance. She fixed her gaze on Elsbeth.

"Aiy." The woman clucked her tongue and drew random patterns among the parts on the counter, not meeting Tink's eyes. "Speed is more expensive."

"Iyan." Kandi drawled the name as she leaned over. She rested her forearms on the counter, her biceps framing her breasts, which threatened to pop out of her tight top. "Your name is so lyrical." Kandi flicked her eyelashes, and Tink almost snorted despite her annoyance.

Iyan's flush turned scarlet. "It's the name of a famous musician."

"His father named him." Elsbeth waved a hand towards her son. "I would have chosen an engineer."

Tink watched as Iyan's lips pressed together, and his hands clenched at his side.

"Do you play music yourself?" Kandi's voice dropped, becoming husky, as her fingers inched towards Iyan's. His eyes widened and his mouth gaped. He looked at Tink like she would save him.

Tink smiled, then turned to his mother. "Delays get deducted off the estimate. Tinker rules."

"Who taught you such things?" The woman scowled at Kandi before returning her attention to Tink.

Tink narrowed her eyes and laid her fingertips on the countertop. "My uncle. He also said, if a Tinker can't deliver, look elsewhere."

"Bloody Emmon Bell. Had no loyalty."

"You're a Bell? Emmon's niece?" Iyan's flush had disappeared, taking with it some of his natural colour, leaving his cheeks the same shade as a viridian fish's belly. He squinted at her.

Frowning, she shifted her attention back to Elsbeth and away from his scrutiny. "Any way we can get the part now? We have a perishable cargo. And I still have to fix the ship once I get the thing." She didn't shift her focus when the nuts-and-bolts curtain rustled and Iyan disappeared into the back. *Apparently, he doesn't like Emmon for some reason, though he's not old enough from them to have met.*

"For you, I'll call our supplier, see if they can rush it." Elsbeth sighed and reached her hand forward, and Tink pulled hers away. "But as I said, it'll cost you. He's no Tinker." Elsbeth started picking up the items on the counter and placing them carefully in a bin beside her, all the while carrying on a litany about the shady business practices of those who weren't clan. Tink didn't know if the woman counted her in that number or not. She was about to snap, so she turned to tell Kandi they should go. As if she heard Tink think of her, Kandi stepped close to the counter, and pulled herself up to looming height.

"Why are you stalling?" Kandi's voice was hard as her attention finally settled on Elsbeth.

"I—"

The nuts-and-bolts curtain rattled, and Iyan reappeared, holding a package. He swallowed, gaze flicking between the three women before finally settling on Kandi. "Your part."

"Iyan!" Elsbeth's face went red. "Wha...." She looked at Tink then at her son. "When did that come in?"

Iyan peered at his mother. "This morning, when you received it from the shop down the way. Right before you told that Manta boor someone had been looking for just such a part."

"What?" Kandi glowered at the woman. Tink had to grab her wrist to stop her from reaching over the counter.

"What?" Elsbeth pulled herself up, though she shared Tink's diminutive stature, and her chin jutted out. "I have my son to think about."

Iyan scoffed as he handed the package to Kandi. "You weren't thinking of me. You were thinking of your gambling debts and future sales of core spikes to the Mantas."

"Thanks, for the part and the information," Tink said as Kandi turned toward the door.

"Hey, you still have to pay for that!" Elsbeth reached out but pulled her hand back a second later, quailing at Kandi's expression.

"You mentioned something about a Tinker's discount?"

"So I did," Iyan said with a smile that lit up his face. "Since we're almost family, consider it a gift." At that, his mother's eyes bugged out, and her mouth opened and closed. Then she turned on her heels and disappeared through the curtain, muttering something about 'no son of mine'.

"Do you have the other part I asked about?" Tink asked.

"Right." The man reached under the counter. "This was actually harder to come by." He handed it to her, his long fingers brushing her palm.

She peered at it then smiled up at him. "What do I owe you?"

"Nothing." He shook his head. "Consider it payment for my mother," he continued when she started to object.

"Maybe come visit some time." He jerked his chin over her shoulder to where Kandi stood waiting by the door, a small smile on his lips and a flush on his cheeks. "Bring her along."

Tink nodded then followed Kandi out the door. "I think he likes you."

"He's in lust with me." Kandi snorted but glanced over her shoulder even though the young Tinker was definitely not her type. She turned back, her gaze falling to the small contraption in Tink's hand. "What's that?"

"A key component of an Amazon's stave."

"I'm not an Amazon."

Tink's lips quirked – she could almost hear Kandi's eyes roll.

13: Rebeka

R EBEKA GLARED AT THE crates that filled the hold. She swore they chittered and rattled more than they had yesterday. If they didn't get to their drop-off in time, they'd have a ship full of bugs to feed. And they barely had enough food for themselves.

Out of need, she'd broken her cardinal rule: no live cargo. She wanted to curse Sera but knew she couldn't blame her former comrade for her current financial difficulty. Unlike Sera, she was a fighter, not a businesswoman.

With a huff, she turned away from the cargo, peering out at the dusty port. "Cass, time check?"

"Local time or ship time?"

"Never mind." Rebeka saw a blue head striding towards the ship, and a few seconds later Tink materialized from the crowd beside Kandi. Her engineer wasn't smiling though, and Rebeka's heart sank.

"You couldn't get it?" she asked before Tink even set foot on the gangplank.

"What?" Tink squinted at her. "No, I mean yes. We got it but the Aron woman sold us out. Someone was interested in our whereabouts and whatfors. Mantas."

Rebeka frowned and scanned the port. "Why would the Mantas be interested in us?"

"No idea." Tink flicked her finger over the tablet in her hand, as Kandi followed her in and dropped the package she'd been carrying on the floor inside the cargo bay. "Careful!" Tink gently moved the package out of the way. "I don't want to have to find another one of those."

"Well, it looks like we can get out of here anyway." Kandi jerked her chin towards the shack that passed as a customs house.

"Finally." Rebeka turned to see what she looked at. "Barnacles!" Alek and Ish were flanked by Dustan and his apprentice. "Get ready for trouble," she said over her shoulder to Kandi, then strode down the gangplank, stopping at the bottom with hands on her hips.

"What the hell are they doing here?" Rebeka asked Alek, before turning her glare on Dustan and Fennick. Alek threw up his hands.

"He saved my skin," Ish said.

"No." She stared at Dustan.

He held up his hands. "I said nothing. I figured the least I could do after saving Ish from whatever passes for a jail on this hellish rock is to see him safely to your ship." He cast his gaze around. "And what a fine ship."

"Flattery will get you nowhere, especially onto the *Lyra*."

"Come on." Ish tipped his head sideways and copped his best begging cat expression, but Rebeka had seen it too many times before to be taken in. "Least we can do is offer them a ride."

Rebeka shook her head. "You don't know him. If he helped you, it's because he wants something from you." Her gaze turned to Fennick, the assistant, whose attention was focused on the warehouses at the edge of the port landing area. Her eyes narrowed as she followed his gaze. "And you usually end up paying more for his help than you expected." Her voice tapered off as she noticed movement across the port.

"Rebeka, you wound me." Dustan held a hand to his chest in a dramatic flourish.

She opened her mouth to speak when something zinged off the metal beside her head. It only took her a second to realize what it was. She dropped into a crouch and dragged Ish with her. "No, the pulse rifle being fired at us will wound you."

Kandi crouched beside her while Fennick ducked behind the gangplank, his eyes still trained on the warehouses. The location the shots had come from.

"What have you gotten me into this time, Dustan?" she muttered before turning to Alek. "Get to the bridge and get this ship ready to take off." He sprinted to do her bidding as another shot skittered off the sand. "Ish—" she started, stopping when she heard him swear. Blood welled up from a graze on his arm. "Go with him. See if there are any slip points nearby."

"But we can't—"

"We can. It's just dangerous."

"Really dangerous." Ish grimaced but he ambled after Alek, while Rebeka crab-walked back to join Kandi and Tink further up the ramp.

"No more dangerous than Manta guns," she muttered.

Kandi had a blaster trained on the warehouses. "Poseidon's pox, it's too far."

Rebeka peered in the direction of the shots. She couldn't see any glints of metal, and only made out vague forms in the shimmering heat. Then the heat turned to dust devils.

"They're on skimmers," Tink said, her goggles pulled over her eyes. "Headed this way."

As if to underline her words, another volley of shots scorched the *Lyra* and the sand around the ramp.

"They're terrible shots." Dustan still stood at the bottom of the ramp, unharmed by the hits or the shrapnel.

"No, they're not." Tink's voice was low, drawing Rebeka's attention. Tink flipped her goggles up when she looked her way. "They're Manta. If you haven't been hit, they're missing for a reason."

Rebeka glared, wide-eyed, at Dustan as she felt the whine and rumble of the *Lyra* firing up. "Everyone inside now." Dustan started up the ramp, followed by Fennick. Rebeka pulled her blaster and pointed it at her ex's chest. "Not you."

"You'll leave us to be torn apart by the Mantas?" His eyes were big and sweat sheened his forehead.

Stepping closer, she brought the blaster right under his chin. "What do the Mantas want with you?" she hissed.

He opened his mouth but whatever he planned to say was forestalled by a howl from Fennick. The young man dropped to the gangplank, grasping his thigh. Blood seeped through his fingers.

"Fennick!" Dustan ran down the gangplank and dropped to his knees, pressing his hands to the man's bloody leg. "I'm sorry. It's okay."

Rebeka closed her eyes for a second, then opened them and huffed at Dustan. "Kandi, get your med kit," she said over her shoulder. Then she scuttled down the ramp to join her ex, scowling at him. "Help me get him on board."

X MARKS THE ... WHAT'S THAT?

14: TINK

TINK BANGED THE LATERAL stabilizer with a hammer, then felt bad when a hiss sounded from the other side and a streak of grey scampered across the engine room, before shooting out the door and down the hallway.

"Grim!" She huffed, letting out all the pent-up air in her lungs. "I'm sorry." Reaching her free hand behind her head, she worked it down her neck and across her shoulders, kneading as she went. But the tight muscles refused to yield.

The ship shimmied again. On the bridge, Alek was still fighting to keep them ahead of the Manta ships lurking amongst the ring of the gas giant and the moons where he'd hidden them. But the *Lyra* wasn't pleased, so Tink gave her a love tap or three. She lifted the hammer to strike again. *If I hit the sweet spot....* She bit her lower lip.

"Have you tried a gentle touch?"

Tink almost dropped the hammer on her foot as she spun around at the strange voice, but some part of her brain had the forethought to hold onto a weapon. Memories of her battle with the treacherous Severn Lynch perhaps.

The treasure hunter's assistant stood in the door, leaning against the jamb. His disheveled, black hair jutted out in all directions, and his face was pale as an alabaster beetle. His hand went to his thigh, and he winced as the ship shivered again.

"Fennick, isn't it?" The man nodded, and Tink turned back to the engine. "You shouldn't be here when we're dodging pursuers."

"I woke up ... the painkillers wore off." His voice was quiet, and she had to strain to hear him over the whine of an unhappy ship. "Didn't know where anyone was. Didn't know where I was." He cast his gaze around. "Nice engine. Need a hand?"

The ship bucked, and Fennick made a muffled sound. She glanced at him. When she saw him slumped against the wall, she put down the hammer. "No, but I think you need one." She slung his arm around her shoulders and stood up. "You should be back in the medbay." At her full height, the lanky man was still half slumped. Tink exhaled and almost gave up, but his other hand went to the wall, and he took a step forward.

One step at a time, they made it to the bottom of the stairs. Grim trailed them, having decided to forgive her for startling him, at least enough to sniff at Fennick's legs and try to trip her. She glared at the short staircase. "Oh, my industrial chain ratchet for a lift."

"There you are," a voice behind her said, then Dustan stepped up to Fennick's other side. "I was worried when I didn't find you where we'd left you."

Tink craned her neck, trying to examine the man around the torso between them. Rebeka's husband. Father of her child. Tink frowned. *The captain has a daughter. But the*

Lyra *is her family*. First Emmon, Taggard, Elise and Tink, then the other crew who'd come and left over the years. Anger burned in Tink's stomach and up her throat at the captain's lie of omission.

A cough drew her attention. "I don't think all three of us will fit up the stairs." The wrinkles around Dustan's blue eyes creased as he peered at her.

She was quiet for a second then nodded. "Come around this side so you can support his injured leg." Once Dustan had Fennick's weight, Tink stepped away. As she followed them up the stairs, she realized that the ship's movements had calmed down. Either they were surrendering or Alek had managed to elude their pursuers.

She almost bumped into Dustan, who'd stopped a step shy of the landing. Tink looked over his head to see Rebeka glaring down at them, hands on her hips.

"Into the common room." She jerked her chin in the direction of the space that served as their meeting room in addition to being the kitchen and recreation space.

"But Fennick needs to lie down." Dustan's voice rose, almost turning it into a question.

"He can lie on the chesterfield." The captain strode ahead of them, not waiting for any further arguments. There was nothing for it but to follow.

Entering the room, Tink saw the rest of the crew already gathered. Meaning Alek had eluded their pursuers and Rebeka was confident enough to leave Cass in charge of the bridge.

Tink helped Dustan get Fennick to the chesterfield, laying him down and propping his head up with a pillow. Fennick let out an 'oomph' as Grim jumped up on his stomach and started kneading.

"Sit." Rebeka nodded at one of the hard dining chairs. She watched Dustan while she went to lean on the cargo bay window. Tink took a seat beside Alek on the opposite side of the table, from where she could watch both Dustan and Rebeka.

Kandi knelt beside Fennick, placing her hand on his forehead and taking his pulse, and Ish plopped down in the reading chair she'd vacated.

"Don't get comfortable," Kandi said without looking at him.

Rebeka stared at Dustan, and a hush descended on the room. "What have you gotten us into?" she asked, her voice quiet and even.

"Nothing. It's just an expedition to uncover a bit of lost history. Like so many before." He cast his gaze around the room, stopping at Ish. "A legend, a mystery, and a map."

The captain crossed her arms over her chest. "There's something you're not telling me."

Tink scoffed and mimicked her posture. "You're one to talk about secrets. A husband?" She waved a hand at Dustan. "A daughter? You never found time to share that little tidbit?"

"I—" Rebeka's scowl deepened.

"Don't be too hard on her." Dustan peered at his palms. "She'd never have left Juniper if she didn't think it was to protect her. If she didn't tell you about her, it was to keep her safe." He looked up from his hands. "Me, on the other hand, well, I was easier to leave out. I wasn't much of a husband, and now—"

"We don't need to go into the details of the dissolution of our marriage," Rebeka said, and Tink realized there were still some secrets she was keeping. "We all have things we'd rather keep to ourselves." Her gaze sharpened on Tink, as if to remind her that she'd kept Tink's own secret for years — that she wasn't just the *Lyra*'s engineer, but also its owner.

The knot in Tink's chest loosened a little. She inhaled deeply, and when she let it out, she forced her shoulders down. "What *have* you dropped us in?" she asked, shifting her anger towards Dustan. "How much danger have you put my ship in?"

"I have no idea." Dustan examined his hands again. Fennick coughed, and the archaeologist looked sidelong at him. "Really. I'm just on a quest to solve a mystery. Like many times before."

"Another treasure hunt," the captain said. "I recall they always involve trouble. So, what is it this time?"

He shifted his attention to Rebeka as he squirmed in his chair. He tried looking at Tink then moved his gaze to Alek when she scowled at him. Apparently, he didn't have much more success with Alek as his gaze returned to face Rebeka's glare.

"The Mantas." Fennick fidgeted on the chesterfield, dislodging Grim as he sat up.

"Fennick!" The word came out as a curse as Dustan turned to glare at his assistant.

"Tell them." The young man's voice was quiet, wan to match his pallor. "Besides the danger we're putting them in, not telling them isn't getting us anywhere."

"What about the Mantas?" Alek shifted forward in his chair, his biceps bulging as he clenched his hands into fists.

Dustan glared at his assistant, then pressed his lips together before he finally shrugged and turned back to Rebeka. "We got the treasure map from Ariadne Ossif."

"The leader of the Mantas? She gave you a map to the *Celeste*?" Rebeka strode forward and placed her hands on the table, looming over Dustan. "She wouldn't give her mother a glass of water."

"Well, by give, I mean—"

"You stole it." Tink stood up and placed the capsule from Kandi's stave on the table so she didn't crush it. Without the distraction, her fingers tapped against her thighs.

"You stole the map to the sole remaining lost treasure ship from the leader of the most powerful gang in the galaxy?" Alek's words gave voice to the dread that crept through Tink's stomach. She'd heard of the Mantas but knew little about them. Apparently, he knew a bit more.

"We...." Dustan glanced at his assistant. "I procured it without her knowledge or agreement."

"Oh, I would say she knows." Rebeka's voice rose, causing Grim to jump and hiss. The cat stalked across the floor as she continued. "Give me one good reason we shouldn't just drop you off on the nearest chunk of rock and be done with it."

Dustan's cheeks reddened, but he just rolled a shoulder. Instead, it was Fennick who answered.

"Now that you're involved, you won't be done with it until the ship is found." The young archaeologist's face was pale. "Or you're dead." He winced and pressed a hand to his thigh.

"They'll never let you be. Even in the deepest dungeon or furthest anchorite, they'll find you."

Arms crossed in front of her, Rebeka glared at Dustan. "If we did, at least we might have a chance."

Ish sat forward in the reading chair, elbows on his knees and his eyes shining. "What's the harm of seeing where this map leads?"

"Are you serious?" Kandi settled on the armrest beside him. "You do remember the gun fight we just fled?" She raised a hand. "I vote rock."

Ish rolled his eyes but didn't respond. His gaze fell on Tink. Before their previous adventure, she'd always deferred to Rebeka as the captain; now that they knew she owned the ship, she hoped they didn't expect her to make the call. Even if the captain's past with Dustan clouded her judgment, Tink didn't entirely disagree with her assessment.

She sifted through the possibilities. There was a chance the *Lyra* could go down in history as the little ship that found the greatest lost treasure. But being blown to bits by the Mantas was more likely, as well as there being a distinct possibility of getting thrown in jail.

Rebeka shook her head. "A Dominion jail sounds like a good option over the Mantas, but I'll settle for you just not being on this ship."

Tink glanced at Alek as he shifted beside her. His face was grim, and his jaw clenched.

"I don't like this," he said. "But I won't leave anyone to the mercy of Ariadne Ossif."

"What do you say?" Dustan looked at Tink.

Rebeka stepped away from Dustan, hands coming to her hips. Even Tink shrank in her chair. "This is not a democracy."

"But...." Dustan waved a hand towards Tink, glancing between Rebeka and her.

Tink's eyes narrowed, and her lips pulled down. "I think...." She looked from person to person. Even Grim peered at her expectantly. "I think I need to go fix the slip sail while we have the chance."

15: HARBIN

Harbin's steps slowed as he walked the dim corridor towards his room. Despite the Paradise Inn's false advertising, it was still the best of a bad lot. The small runner he brought down to the surface didn't have enough room to sleep in. So, he and Delphi had taken rooms in this hovel, the nicest of the hovels in Excelsior. On the nightside, a *Barracuda* class ship might have been able to pass without much notice. But on the dusty dayside, it would have been the target of keen interest. And the fewer people interested in Archon Koning's business, the better.

So, he found himself in this dingy hallway. The door to his room was closed and still locked according to the panel, but the space between his shoulder blades itched. Something was off. Scanning the hall, he caught Delphi's expression... she sensed it too. The light at the far end of the hall — flickering before they left — was completely out now, but the one closest to him still shone, casting his shadow onto the floor.

Drawing his blaster, he powered it up as he stepped sideways and placed his palm on the panel by the door. When it slid open, he glanced around. On the surface, the room seemed the same as he'd left it. Dark, spartan and silent. But a scent hung in the air. *Flowers and spice.*

"Lights," a voice said from the darkness, and the room responded even though it was supposed to be keyed only to Harbin. As the lights came up, they revealed a pale, thin man with spindly limbs, long black hair, and eyes a shocking shade of blue. As he rose out of the only chair, it called to mind the cargo spiders on the station where Harbin lived as an orphan before Halcyon Koning found him. A shiver ran down his spine.

"Who are you?" Harbin asked. At a whine by his ear, he paused and slid his gaze sideways to see Delphi train her charged blaster on the man. Turning back, he added, "And what are you doing in my room?"

The man cocked his head, exposing blue veins underneath the pallid skin as his hair slipped from his shoulder. "I thought Halcyon told you to expect me." His gaze flicked from Delphi to Harbin.

Harbin's lips pressed together. He wasn't some neophyte, easily conned into revealing secrets because someone knew a nugget of the larger truth. "Who are you?" he repeated, even though a niggle in his brain told him he already knew the answer.

The man opened his arms, his long fingers uncurled, in a gesture of peace, though the smile on his face was edged with a sneer. "You can call me ... mmm, Ray ... Skate."

Harbin's eyes narrowed, and he suppressed a frown. "So not your real name."

"You know how she loves her codenames." *Ray* lifted his hands in a shrug and his chin tipped up.

To give himself time to remember where he knew this man from, Harbin strode over to the bottle of aged whiskey he'd opened earlier. But the glass he'd left beside it was gone. Turning, he noticed it on the table beside the chair the man had been sitting in.

The man's gaze followed his. His shoulder moved, almost like a shrug. "You have good taste. But perhaps you should call Halcyon before your friend takes my head off."

Harbin glanced from 'Ray' to Delphi. His cheeks flushed, knowing the man was right. "Take him into the hallway for a moment. If he tries to leave, shoot him."

The intruder's calm smile infuriated Harbin when the man walked past and led Delphi into the hallway rather than vice versa.

Harbin did a quick scan of the space and found no new bugs beyond the ones he'd neutralized when he'd first taken the room. Then he pulled out the proper comms unit — he wanted to see Halcyon Koning on the other end. He rang her up, tapping his fingers on the table as he waited for the call to connect.

"What?" Her voice spoke but the screen was still black.

His frown deepened. "I had a visitor."

"Yes, I told you I had someone I wanted you to meet."

"He calls himself Ray Skate. Not his real name."

"I know. But Ray is the name we agreed on. He's a slippery eel, even though anyone who needs to know who he is, does." Her face materialized out of the blackness. Sharp lines in a harsh light, she looked like a spectre. But she was still beautiful...viciously beautiful.

"I wasn't expecting him to be waiting in my room — my sealed room — when I got back." He rubbed his chin, still feeling where her fingernails had recently dug into the flesh, so deeply they drew blood.

"He's eager. And resourceful." An eyebrow lifted. "Admirable qualities."

"How do I know he's the man and not some impostor?"

Her throaty laughter bordered on a cackle. "No one would dare impersonate him. And even the most powerful cartel heads know better than to mess with a person of interest to me."

The cartels. Harbin's stomach rose in his throat, and he tasted bitter bile. Like the recoil of a pulse rifle, how he knew the man's face slammed into his brain. *Ray Skate* was the leader of the Kraits, the second most powerful cartel in the Dominion. And rumour had it he was bent on making his cartel *the* most powerful.

"I see the cogs have turned." Halcyon's keen eyes peered at him from the comms screen.

He swallowed. "Why did you want me to meet him?"

"He shares an interest in the *Celeste*, and in procuring information I want. Work with him for now." She ran jewelled fingers down her neck, silver-painted nails barely brushing the thin skin. "But watch him. Tell me what he does. And if he steps a toe out of line, I'll hand him over to the Mantas in bite-sized pieces."

Harbin opened his mouth to speak but the screen blinked out. His nostrils flared as he breathed in and out slowly. Finally, he opened the door, admitting Ray and Delphi again.

His Second's eyes narrowed, as she slid her gaze from the gangster to Harbin.

He gave a sharp shake of his head and turned to the man. "It appears we're to work together, *Skate*." As Harbin held out a hand to seal the deal, an emotion flickered over Delphi's face before she managed to marshal her features.

Ray stared at his hand for a minute before offering his fingers to shake. "Mmm, your skin is surprisingly smooth. For a military man." The gangster arched an eyebrow and smiled when Harbin tried to pull his hand away, only to find it trapped in an unexpectedly strong grip.

"Please, my friends call me Ray."

"I'm pretty sure your friends call you no such thing. And I am certain I'm not your friend. However, my boss thinks we should work together."

Ray laughed, like a hyena on the hunt. "I'm glad Halcyon made you see sense." He leaned so close Harbin smelled the sweet whiskey on his breath. "I'm the key to this pursuit."

Harbin shifted back, letting Ray step past him.

"I hope so. *Archon Koning* also said if you fail her, she'll feed you to the Mantas in pieces." Harbin was proud he mostly kept his amusement out of his voice.

Skate stopped, pausing as he half turned back. "I'll be in touch." The humour had left his voice. He started forward again.

Delphi's sharp eyes followed the gangster out the door before finally sheathing her blaster. Harbin and his second stood in companionable silence for a minute before Delphi broke it.

"What does Archon Koning have to do with this?" she asked, not looking at him.

16: TINK

TINK RAN HER HAND through her hair, strands of which were plastered to her cheeks. She'd replaced the directional wave sensing coil in the slip sail with Kandi's help, while Ish and Fennick watched their vitals from inside the ship. Now that the *Lyra* could slip normally, Ish had gone back to the bridge, saying something about deciphering Dustan's map and looking for slip points that might lead them away from here and towards there, wherever 'there' was.

This left Tink and Kandi alone in the cargo bay, cleaning up after the spacewalk. As she wiped the sweat off her neck with a cloth too meagre for the job, she glanced up at Kandi, who had stripped down to her skivvies.

The tattoos along her back and down her legs were clearly visible. Kandi had been bare skinned — a proper Antaran warrior, with a body only decorated by scars — when she'd come on board the *Lyra*. Since then, she'd added tattoo after tattoo. Despite having been around for them all, they told a story Tink couldn't read.

"If you keep staring, I'm going to think you're interested in my old offer after all."

Tink's cheeks flushed as she recalled meeting Kandi for the first time, before she signed on as a member of the crew. The Antaran had propositioned her through metal grating, blood dripping down her sweat-sheened face, as Tink watched the fight, eyes wide and mouth agape. Tink had been horror-struck at finding a blood sport in progress out in the open, barely off the station promenade. She'd declined the proposition, but Rebeka had offered Kandi a job when the fight was over, seeing something in the woman who won when she'd been told to lose.

Tink blinked and focused on pulling on her jumpsuit. "So, your stave." The skin around her eyes tightened as she thought. "I picked up a part for it from Elsbeth. Well, Iyan."

Kandi stilled and was silent for a few seconds. "Okay."

"I didn't tell him what it was for." Tink's forehead wrinkled. "Are all Amaz ... Antaran staves made like yours?"

Kandi shrugged, looking over her shoulder as she zipped up her top. "Yeah. So far as I know."

"Hmmm." Tink cinched her belt then dragged her boots from under the bench.

"Why?" Kandi pulled her leggings on.

Tink peered at her crewmate as Grim jumped down from the crate he'd been resting on and wound his way around her legs. "It's just ... different. The design is unique. And there's one part...." Her eyes narrowed as she pictured the capsule and the wires twisted through it.

"If you can't fix it, I understand." Kandi's tone said she told the truth, and it wasn't just a ploy to get Tink to try harder.

"I didn't say that." Tink reached down to scratch between the cat's ears, and Grim rewarded her by purring and rubbing his chin on her shin. "I'll figure it out. It just might take a little longer than I thought." She tucked a wayward curl behind her ear, then huffed when it drifted back in front of her face. "So...." She paused. "This treasure hunt."

"What about it?" Kandi sat on the bench to put on her shoes, and Grim ambled over to her, abandoning Tink. She extended her fingers to pet his head.

Tink shrugged. "I dunno, do you think it's real?"

"I don't much care." Kandi grabbed her weapons belt and strapped it over her hips. Tink noticed it now held two blasters, not the usual one. It also held an extra knife. "Except that it's brought us to the notice of some powerfully bad folk who'd as soon blow us from the sky as ask us about our historical research." She stood up, ready to go.

"Can you pass me my tool kit?" Tink jerked her head to the box at Kandi's feet. She took a deep breath. "And what about the captain being married with a kid somewhere?" she blurted out.

The other woman shrugged. "We all had lives before we arrived here. Even you, Tink." Kandi handed her the box. "What is your first name anyway?"

Tink scowled at Kandi. She hated the name her parents had given her. She told herself her distaste was because it was so pretentious to be named after the mythical first artificer, but a little voice called her a liar, whispering she hated it because they'd been the ones to give it to her. Stardust addicts both until they died and left her an orphan.

Kandi smiled, the skin around her eyes crinkling, before the smile fell. "And we all have secrets."

Tink opened her mouth, wanting to ask what Kandi's secret was, but she snapped it closed as the other woman turned on her heels and strode out of the cargo bay. Grim padded up beside Tink, and they both watched her go.

17: Rebeka

REBEKA SAT IN THE reading chair, letting Ish and Fennick's excited discussion about lost treasures and unsolved mysteries wash over her as she flipped through the novel on her tablet. Although she paid little attention to their words, she could tell the apprentice archaeologist was smitten with her navigator.

Through half-closed lids, she shifted her gaze to Dustan, who smiled as he glanced up at the two men from his tablet. She let out a sigh, hoping her ex didn't plan to use Fennick's obvious interest in Ish to manipulate her into doing what he wanted. It would be a major departure from the man she married — he'd always been single-minded in pursuit of his oddball theories but never ruthless. But they'd both changed. If he did, he'd find himself disappointed. From what she'd seen, Ish's tastes ran more to burly beefcake than willowy nerd. She blinked when Ish graced the young apprentice with a broad smile.

Abandoning her reading, she shifted her attention to her ex. *Not quite ex*, she reminded herself. He bit the end of his stylus as he turned his attention back to whatever he was working on. His jawline was slacker than the last time she'd seen him. His scruffy beard was the same, but there was salt in amongst the pepper. His hair fell over his face in the same way. He brushed it back in a move that made her stomach flutter, just to have it fall again as he wrote something on his screen. She exhaled and turned back to her story with a shake of her head.

Half a minute later, a laugh from Fennick and the scrape of a chair stopped her from sinking into the story again. Dustan stood and walked around the table to crouch between the two men. Rebeka's focused sharpened but otherwise she didn't move.

"If you're keen on solving puzzles, check this out." Dustan glanced between them, then pulled out a sphere he could barely cup in his hand. In size, it reminded Rebeka of the balls he used when playing catch with Juniper when she was a child. But that was the only similarity. Rebeka shifted forward without conscious thought to peer more closely at the blue orb. At her movement, Dustan's gaze slid her way.

She swore she caught a familiar twinkle and squashed the flutter in her stomach. She met his gaze only long enough to grace him with a frown before returning her attention to the sphere.

It wasn't a uniform blue. As Dustan tipped it back and forth, swirls writhed on the opalescent surface. The colour shifted from a deep grey slate to a vibrant aquamarine to a milky sky blue. And there was a shimmer to it, like it had a thousand stars trapped inside.

Rebeka blinked. "That's pretty. What is it?"

Dustan stood and peered at her for a few seconds, then quirked his eyebrow in that way he used to when they were just married. "It's the map."

The flutter returned, travelling from her sternum to deep in her gut. She suppressed it with a shake of her head. Her lips pressed tight together. He'd gotten them wrapped up with the Mantas, and all because of fools' gold, or the gem equivalent. "It's a bauble."

"No, it's not any old bauble." Fennick reached into his bag and withdrew a slender tube. "Watch." He held out his hand and, after a second, Dustan dropped the orb into it. Fennick held it up with just his fingertips.

"Careful." Dustan's fingers flexed towards the orb.

"Of course." The young man flicked his eyes to Dustan then returned to the sphere. He placed the tube near the bottom, and Rebeka realized it was a light.

Ish apparently did as well. "Cass, turn off the lights in the cargo bay and common room."

The lights winked out and darkness blanketed the space for a second before the light in Fennick's hand flicked on. Then Rebeka gasped and stood. She turned a circle but stopped when dizziness threatened her balance.

Pinpoints of light spattered across the ceiling and walls and were reflected in the window to the bay. They varied in brightness, and, although uneven, they had an order to them. Dunstan came to stand beside her as she tried to take in the sight.

"There *are* a thousand stars trapped in there." She hadn't meant to say it aloud, but she caught Fennick's ghostly smile in the small halo of light. She craned her neck, taking it all in.

Dustan's hand ran down the back of her arm. "It reminds me of that night on Arcus 7." His voice was quiet with a whisper of melancholy. Rebeka glanced at him, a half smile on her face. She remembered the night as well, naked under the stars. He leaned close. "We should talk. I need—"

Her cheeks warm, Rebeka pulled away and turned back to the pinpoints of light, trying to make sense of them. But there were too many — she couldn't map them in her mind, and she couldn't make out a star chart she recognized. A handful of the spots were brighter than the others, and in a rainbow of hues as opposed to the stark white of most of the points. One, bright red, pulsed larger than the rest. Rebeka's fingers twitched, wanting to reach out and grab it.

"So, the map is a literal star map?" Ish asked, and he lifted his hand to run through them. Pin pricks of light danced on his shadowed face as Fennick shifted towards him. "Which one marks the location of the *Celeste*?"

"That's the puzzle." Dustan's voice said into the darkness as Fennick's light went out.

"Cass, lights please." Rebeka blinked when the lights came on, harsh after the starlit darkness.

"There's a pattern to the coloured points but I haven't been able to work it out yet." He turned his face to meet Rebeka's eyes, his hand still on her elbow. His other hand rubbed his eyebrow — he always did that when he was thinking.

"Spit it out," she said, but her voice was soft.

"I sent the information to Juniper."

"What?" Rebeka stepped back, pulling her arm free.

"But—" Fennick gaped at Dustan.

"Encrypted. Our own personal cipher."

"You got our daughter mixed up in this? With the cartels after you?" The chair squeaked as Rebeka shifted to put it between them.

"The daughter I raised likes to know what her old man is up to. And she has the keenest cryptographic and paleocartographic mind I know. She's a smart cookie. Which you'd know if you been around when she was growing up."

Rebeka's fingers curled and uncurled against her thigh. "I—"

Dustan held up his hand. "I know. You did what you thought you had to to protect us." His shoulders rose and fell as he sighed. "And I honestly don't blame you for it." Running his hands through his hair, he reached for the orb, and Fennick placed it gently in his palm. "She's one of the few people who I both trust to help with this and who might have something useful to add." Turning the sphere, he peered at it before turning his gaze to her. He shifted his eyes from her to the orb and back, and his lips scrunched.

"What?" Rebeka's suspicions rose again. Her hands came up to her hips.

"I wasn't just interested in your ship to catch a ride."

Her arms crossed over her chest and her eyebrows pulled together. "So, you admit it wasn't just coincidence that you found me."

"Oh, it was a coincidence. A very happy one... but it put another idea in my head."

Rebeka's jaw was tight, and her words clipped even to her own ears. "Which was?"

"In lieu of Juniper's aid...." He glanced up. "Your ship has a CASS-ANDRA." Returning his gaze to her, he continued. "One of the most powerful, creative AIs ever birthed."

Rebeka snorted as she breathed in while laughing. "And you think she can help solve your enigma." She leaned forward, her hands resting on the edge of the table. "Sorry to disappoint, but the rumours of the Cass's powers are somewhat exaggerated." She looked sideways. "Sorry Cass."

"Captain? Is there something I can do for you?"

"No, but maybe you can help Mr. Key with mapping a star chart."

"Certainly, though Ishmael is a talented cartographer."

"I know." Rebeka lay a hand on Ish's shoulder, and his hazel eyes turned to her. "If you want to help him in his wild goose chase, feel free. I know you won't let it interfere with your duties."

"Of course not, Captain."

Rebeka flicked her gaze from Ish to Fennick before settling back on Dustan. Despite the intervening years, she still saw the man she'd married, the man she'd abandoned along with her daughter for their own welfare. The marriage had been his idea; he'd always been the more unconventional one. Given the bumps they'd had in those years, she wondered if she'd still be married to him if she hadn't had to make a living to support Juniper by working on sketchy ships amongst shady reprobates, all while enduring the harassment of the army's bioengineers. She gave her head a small shake — no, they'd have killed each other long ago. "Keep me informed."

"Wait, we need to talk." Dustan reached out as he stood. Then the ship shuddered, and the sirens started.

18: ALEK

W HERE'S ISH?" ALEK SAID when feet stomped onto the bridge behind him, not taking his eyes off the screen in front of him. The split display showed fore and aft views, but he couldn't see what had hit them.

"Here. Out of my way." Ish almost tumbled into the seat beside him. "Bleeding Hades, what happened?" he asked as he buckled in.

"No idea." Alek's teeth ground together as the ship bucked, and he fought with the stick. "Can we slip?"

"Something is hitting us." Rebeka's voice vibrated with tension, and he heard the snap of her own harness. "But there's nothing out there." Anger seeped into her tone, echoing Alek's own frustration. "Sit down," she snapped, and Alek spared a glance over his shoulder. Her husband and his assistant crowded into the doorway to the bridge.

"You might want to listen to her. It's going to get—" The ship shimmied, and he turned to focus on the images cycling over the display. Snow in the lower left corner told him one of the portside rear cameras had been taken out. Not that it was doing much good anyway.

"Slipping while being shot at is not great." Ish already had his navigation holodisplay up and was flicking through its ripples. "But I'll see what I can find."

"Sit over there," Rebeka said. Movement in Alek's peripheral vision told him she'd pointed to the jump seats to his left. "I'll see if I can find anything on the scans, but..." There was a pause. "Kandi. Bridge. Now."

"You found something?" Alek's stomach clenched at the thought of what might come out of nowhere, guns blazing.

"What? No, Kandi's just better at seeing ghosts in space. Cass, analysis."

"I'm scanning the space in our immediate vicinity. So far, I detect no anomalies."

"Could it be a ship with one of those shrouds?" Ish glanced at him then returned to plucking at the display in front of him. "Nearest slip point is...not near enough."

"Cass detected the last shrouded ship we encountered." Alek tugged at the stick, but it fought back. "Besides that's expensive tech — how many can there be?" The ship juddered, sending its backend sideways. His elbow slammed into his armrest. He stabbed a button. "Tink, something is wrong with the starboard thruster."

There was a pause then her hollow voice came over the comms. "Yeah, it's been shot." A moment of silence followed. "Best guess without going on yet another spacewalk ... torpedo with a plasma discharge." There was a rumble over the comms, broken by garbled cursing. "Something fried the circuits."

"What the hell?" Kandi came onto the bridge. Her stomp was unmistakable. "I do one spacewalk, and you all get us into trouble."

Alek smirked. "Sometimes you make trouble; sometimes you have it thrust upon you." The smirk fell. "This would be the latter." He hadn't known Kandi for long, but he was pretty sure she was like him: always up for a bit of trouble but wanted to face it head on. "Any insights on what's hassling us?"

"There's nothi—" She cut off so quickly, Alek thought for a moment she'd been shot, then his rational brain kicked in: if she'd been shot from outside the ship, they'd all be dead from sudden decompression. "Cass, what's that?"

"What are you indicating, Kandi?"

"That. No, there. Argh!"

Alek heard a hand slap something but had no attention to spare to suss out the source. The ship skittered sideways again, and he fought to keep it going the direction he wanted.

"I see, Kandi." Cass' tone was calm and even. "The lights that are there then not there."

"What are you two rambling about?" Dustan said. Surprised, Alek glanced at the man; he'd forgotten he was there. Next to him, Fennick's pale skin had taken on a green hue; the young man looked ready to vomit.

"There's a ... stop doing that," Kandi muttered. "There! There's a ... oh, a bleeding fast ship. A bunch of them. But as soon as Cass pinpoints one, it disappears."

Ish swiped the holodisplay away and leaned forward. "I ... wow."

"What?"

"I'd heard a rumour, back in my nav seal refresher class, but I didn't believe it."

"What?" The captain repeated Alek's question, but the word carried more edge and less curiosity.

"Slipper ships."

"What?" Rebeka asked again.

"Ships that can make their own slip points." Ish shook his head. "Kind of like the Sisters' jump gate. But the rumour was about Dominion Leviathans, not Manta clippers."

"Oh, Hera wept!" Rebeka's curse filled the bridge. "Shrouds, now ships creating their own slip points. Enough with the new tech already."

At that moment, a flash of light filled the display. When it cleared and Alek stopped blinking, clipper parts were scattered across their forward field of view. Thumps told him more were hitting the shields. With time to breathe, he scanned the other views on the display.

"We have company." Kandi's statement was superfluous as a silvery ship rolled over them, shooting at a clipper that was no longer popping in and out of the slipstream.

As the sleek ship spun to shoot at the clipper again, Alek caught the name on the side. "The Marrazo." He whispered the name as a red snake of dread writhed in his gut.

"If we get out of this, Dustan, I am going to kill you." Rebeka's voice echoed in the suddenly quiet bridge.

The sirens stopped, and Alek realized a minute had passed without the ship being hit by a charge — the recent arrival had driven off their attackers. Still, he felt like he'd been punched.

Their external comms crackled. Alek glanced at Kandi, who had her hand poised over the call button. She glanced at the captain, who, after a second, gave a crisp nod. He turned back to the screen to face their rescuer.

"Hail, *Lyra*." The viewscreen shifted to display the caller. A lean man with dark hair, pale skin and a long, narrow nose filled the screen. Hands clasped in front of him, he had a slip of a smile on his lips. "You looked like you needed some help."

"We were managing." The captain stood, even though Kandi hadn't turned on their bridge cameras. "But thank you for your assistance."

"Were your cameras broken in the attack? I'd like to meet face-to-face the valiant crew that would stand up to a pod of Manta clippers alone."

"We're just a little rattled is all. Not looking our best. Give us a sec." Rebeka turned to Tink, who'd appeared in the doorway to the bridge and was staring at the viewscreen.

The captain made a motion with her hand, and the light by Kandi's head blinked off, indicating they weren't broadcasting anymore, even though they could still hear him.

"We might be able to offer help in your repairs," the man said. "Looks like your starboard thruster sustained damage."

Alek's back muscles tensed, and he shook his head.

The captain mirrored the movement.

"Letting Ludovicus Visi or his crew on this ship is a bad idea," she said.

"You know who he is?" Dustan hissed, a hand to his chest. "I thought only criminals and those who fight them would know who he is."

"And which one are you?" Alek said. Obviously, Dustan knew the man as well.

"Permission to come aboard." Ludovicus' image quirked an eyebrow, as if he knew they were debating what to do.

"We *could* use help with the thruster." Tink huffed then squared her shoulders as her lips pulled down into a frown.

Alek saw the conflict in her eyes. "I agree it's a bad idea to let him on the ship." He shifted his attention to the captain. "But pissing off the leader of one of the most powerful cartels when we're limping through space might be a worse one."

Rebeka eyed the viewscreen. "No. I don't think we're going to get out of this without giving Visi what he wants." Her gaze slid to Dustan, who tugged at his tunic. "Straighten up and prepare to be boarded."

19: TINK

TINK'S CHEEKS FLUSHED, AND her pulse ticked rapidly. She glared at the man standing in the airlock when the door opened. He was supposed to be some kind of gangster, and yet he'd delayed the whole fiasco by insisting his engineer inspect the airlock conditions. Even Customs and Trade inspectors didn't do that.

Scrutinizing my ship. Her fingers clenched around the handle of her wrench. She examined the man. He was tall but thin, skeletal. *I could take him*.

"Put the wrench away." Rebeka stood beside her but didn't look her way as she spoke, the words quiet. She kept her eyes facing forward, towards the airlock.

Tink pressed her lips tight together but did as she was told as her face flushed even more. Her anger abated a bit as a twitter of fear snaked through her belly when the interloper's gaze flicked from Kandi to Rebeka before pausing on her.

"Hmm." He stepped out of the airlock into the cargo bay, his hands tucked into his sleeves, like some kind of monk. Tink couldn't tell if he meant the noise as appraising or dismissive. "A Tinker, on a little ship like this."

Dismissive then. Tink opened her mouth.

Rebeka gave a subtle shake of her head. "Welcome aboard, Mr...?"

Tink's teeth clacked as she snapped her mouth shut. Her uncle Emmon's words echoed in her skull: don't speak in anger, it always says more than you intend. Instead, she inhaled and exhaled, practicing the calming techniques Kandi taught her.

The man arched an eyebrow and smiled. "I doubt you'd have let me on your ship if you didn't know who I was, but I'll play this game. Ludovicus Visi, at your service." He bowed deeply towards the captain, his arm crossing over his waist and his long hair falling over his shoulder. He glanced towards Tink as he straightened. The look made her skin crawl, and she shifted towards Rebeka.

"And I doubt I had a choice." The captain's arms crossed over her chest. "But since you're here, we might as well get comfortable." She swept an arm towards the stairs.

Visi tipped his chin to her and stepped forward, then shook his head as his engineer reached an arm into his tool kit. "Stay here."

Rebeka's eyes narrowed and shot a look at Kandi, who nodded and took up a position leaning on the rail as the captain and Visi started up the stairs.

Tink waffled for a nanosecond before following the captain to the bridge.

Once on the bridge, Visi took up a commanding position in front of the viewscreen. His gaze trawled the room. "Quaint." His nostrils flared, and light glinted off a small gem set into the side of his nose. His eyes lingered on Ish as his lips stretched into a smile, which Ish half-returned before shifting back in his seat, a frown forming on his face. Tink wanted to hiss at Ish to take care, but she suspected that would just fuel the gangster's fire. The man turned to Alek, where the smile fell, replaced by something more predatory.

"You. You're familiar." There was hardly any change in his posture or face, imperceptible to most, but Tink saw his eyes slide sideways towards her and Rebeka before returning to Alek. His gaze passed to Dustan and his assistant. Grim, nestled in Fennick's lap, let out a snarling hissed and arched his back before skittering his way across the bridge and out the door, sounding like an Andoran asp the whole way. Visi's lips pressed thin as he watched the cat flee, then his gaze settled back on the captain's ex. "Dustan, you look well."

Rebeka glared at her ex at that, then returned her attention to the cartel leader. "So why is Ludovicus Visi on my ship? I doubt it's an interest in old cargo ships."

Again, his gaze flicked to Tink before returning to Rebeka. His left shoulder lifted in a lazy, dismissive shrug. "What can I say? I have a soft spot for the underdog." He lifted his hand in an arc, waggling his fingers, the nails coloured jet black with silver sparks to match his tunic. "For quaint old ships." His gaze slid to Ish. "And pretty things."

Alek made a sound somewhere between a cough and a snort, and Visi's sharp eyes turned to him. The fist clenching Tink's heart eased a fraction as he deflected the gangster's attention.

Alek spread his arms. "I'm pretty and quaint. Not very talented but definitely an underdog." His smile was goofy, lop-sided, but the skin around his eyes tightened.

"But not nearly as useful." Visi cracked his neck and shifted his gaze back toward Rebeka. "Perhaps you should screen your crew a little better."

"We vet the crew fine." Tink stood on tiptoe to speak over Rebeka's shoulder. "Interlopers we have a harder time with." It turned to a mumble as she sank back down, regretting drawing attention to herself as his gaze, sharp as an Agrippian hawk, homed in on her.

"I don't think you're here just to see this relic of a ship." Rebeka waved a hand around the bridge. Tink nudged her in the back with an elbow, but the captain ignored her. "But if all you're looking for is a tour, I'm sure Tink will oblige." Rebeka turned to look at her, her eyebrows raising, and Tink stared back with wide eyes.

Visi held up a hand, and Tink noted his fingers were almost as long as hers. "As you say, I'm not here on a social call. It wasn't a happy coincidence that I showed up to save you from those Manta clippers — something I will pay a price for, just so you know." His hands pressed to his chest, one over the other. "You have something I have a vested interest in." Visi craned his neck around to peer at Dustan, who shrank back against the panelling. "Or should I say, he has something."

"Dustan?" Rebeka's voice was hard as her head spun to peer at her ex. Tink's gaze followed.

"I, uh...." He rubbed his hands together.

"Dustan." The captain's tone shifted from her angry voice to her annoyed one.

He ran a hand through his unkempt hair. "Um, meet my angel."

"Oh, you idiot." Tink didn't realize she'd spoken aloud until Rebeka shifted her gaze from her ex to Tink.

As Rebeka turned back to Dustan, her hands came to her hips. "What she said."

Visi's hand came to his chest. "Really, captain. Here I am, being polite, and you malign me."

Dustan's cheeks flushed but he stood up straight and tugged his rumpled tunic down. "I needed an investor. He wanted a mystery." He waved his hand towards Visi, almost hitting Alek.

"I don't think it's a mystery he's after," Alek muttered as he jerked his head away.

Dustan scowled but focused on Rebeka. "I know you never understood my passion for history. Thought I was chasing ghosts in the sky. But now that I have a real lead, how can you still not get it?"

"I got...." She stopped and glanced around. "We can talk about this later." She waved at Visi. "Right now, we have your angel to deal with."

Dustan opened his mouth then snapped it shut, turning his attention back to Visi. "She's right. Although I appreciate your help with the Mantas, why are you here?"

"When you fled Ten Selva, without so much a word, Mantas on your tail, I wanted to make sure you were okay." Visi spread his arms wide. "But I see you're in good hands."

Tink almost opened her mouth to say Visi could have him. But the man made her skin crawl.

"Yes, he is," Rebeka said.

"I told you I'd let you know when I found something." Dustan shifted, glancing between the floor and the gangster.

"You haven't?" Visi's expression stayed neutral as he tipped his head to the side.

Dustan shook his head back and forth slowly. "No."

Tink glared at him. He made it sound like a question, like they had something to hide. And even she knew you didn't let the leader of the Krait cartel think you were hiding something from them. Not if you wanted them off your ship.

An uneasy silence hung in the air for a few long seconds, then Visi gave a little nod. "Well, then. I guess I can return to my ship."

"Let me show you out." Tink stepped forward. Rebeka glanced at her but didn't protest.

"Maybe I should—" Alek started to stand.

"No." Rebeka's hands dropped to her side. "I need you at the helm. The Mantas might still be around."

Tink stepped back to let Visi go ahead of her. He started forward then paused. "Where are you going next?" he asked, though Tink couldn't tell if he addressed the captain or Dustan.

"I—" Dustan stopped when Rebeka pinned him with a sharp look.

"Nefti Station." Cass' calm voice came over the comms, and Tink's eyebrows pulled together, though she was glad to see the captain kept her expression neutral.

"Nefti?" Visi asked.

Rebeka's hands tucked into her back pockets. "It's the closest jump gate." She nodded at her. "Tink, see our guest safely off the *Lyra* and back to his own ship."

Tink once again indicated for Visi to lead the way. But he didn't move.

"When you get to Nefti, visit Zebrafish Mercantile if you need anything. Give this to the proprietor." He walked around the cockpit and handed Rebeka a small disc embossed with a striped snake — a Krait, his personal insignia if Tink had to guess. She held it with her fingertips, as if it might explode. "My credit is good."

Then Ludovicus Visi finally looked at Tink for a second before preceding her off the bridge. She breathed a sigh of relief to follow him and see him off her ship.

20: Rebeka

"N EFTI STATION." REBEKA SHOOK her head and fixed her gaze on Dustan. It served as shopping mall to the stars, where the rich and the famous could by anything for the right price. Which was why, even though nominally a Dominion jump gate station, it was also home to all manner of pirates, from freelance freebooters to professional privateers and everything in between. No wonder Visi had contacts there. She tipped her head to the side. "Cass, why did you tell Visi we're going to Nefti?"

"It's the closest jump gate, Captain."

Rebeka's nose wrinkled. "There are a handful of other gates almost as close."

"This is the fastest route to the red planet."

"The what?" Dustan stepped up beside her.

"From Mr. Keys' map."

"To Nefti then." Dustan's grin crinkled the corners of his eyes, and sent a flicker of heat through Rebeka's gut.

She reminded herself she was angry at him and forced a frown onto her face. "Again, you don't get a say."

"But ... the *Celeste*."

Her hands came to her hips as she peered at him. Realizing what she was doing, she clasped them behind her instead. "Is solving this mystery worth your life? Juniper's life?"

He waved at the blank viewscreen. "This is the history of the galaxy. Of the Dominion. Going back to the Exodus."

"And beyond." Fennick shrank back as Rebeka glanced at him.

Dustan nodded. "And beyond. I have a real lead."

"A fancy marble and a red dot is your great lead?" Rebeka's voice rose. She sighed and forced herself to speak at a normal volume.

"You don't understand. I need to do this now or never. I—"

"How about never?"

"Captain." Kandi frowned at her console. "Communique from Visi's ship. Manta clippers on their long-range sensors."

Rebeka huffed and glared at the viewscreen. "To Nefti then." She spun on her heels and stalked up the stairs into her ready room. A grey streak ran past her — Grim had returned. She dropped into her seat and reached for the drawer with the whiskey but paused when she saw Dustan had followed her. He closed the door, and she opened the drawer, pulling out two glasses.

After pouring a couple of fingers into each, she slid one across the desk and leaned back. "It's not that I don't get it. It's your life's work."

"No." Grabbing his glass in one hand, he pulled the guest chair to her side of the desk with the other. "It's not that," he said as he sat down, sounding weary. "This isn't about personal glory, or even proving I was right to those pompous asses who head the Imperial Academy."

"What is it about then?"

He peered into the whiskey for a long second without taking a drink. His eyebrows still twitched when he was thinking. When he lifted his gaze to meet hers, a storm raged in his blue eyes. "If we can understand the rise of the Dominion, how the first Emperor seized power in the upheaval of the Exodus...." He glanced around, and found Grim, who rubbed against his leg.

"What?"

"Maybe we find a way to dislodge some of that power."

Rebeka inhaled sharply. "You're a rebel?" she whispered. It seemed ridiculous. He may have played the dashing, adventurous archaeologist for women and reporters, but he'd always been law-abiding for all that. But those words were treason.

Dustan snorted. "Hardly." He took a sip of whiskey. "There've been rebels as long as there's been the Dominion. There've been coups and cartels." He peered into his glass again. "And none of it has made a difference."

"I'm the one who has issues with the authorities, as well you know." Rebeka rubbed the spot just above her left breast. "You're the rule follower, despite what your self image might say."

Dustan shot back the rest of his whiskey, then coughed. After he'd cleared his throat, he caught her eyes. "You never met my mother."

"I thought she died when you were young."

He nodded, clutching his empty glass. "But I remember. I remember when they came. The door bursting open, hauling her outside. They dragged her into the dust."

"They?" Rebeka's eyebrows drew together. "I thought it was Pilgrim's Phage."

"A little lie my father's family came up with to ease the shame." He shook his head. "She dared to say the Emperor wasn't ordained by the gods, that the Dominion was built on lies."

Rebeka leaned forward, placing a hand on his knee.

He met her eyes for the first time since he began his story. "I was a rule follower so they would stop watching."

"I'm sorry."

Dustan put his glass down too hard on the desk and stood up, sending Grim skittering behind her chair. "I need to tell you something." He paused and his eyebrows waggled again.

"Spit it out." Rebeka stood, pushing his glass across the desk.

He ran a hand through his mussed hair. "I... I didn't endanger Juniper's life — she's too smart, that one. She wheedled it out of me."

"That's it?" She shot back the rest of her whiskey, relishing the burn in her throat. Putting the glass down, she shifted and wove her fingers into his hair.

Dustan glanced up, meeting her gaze. "No I ... I'm—"

Snaking her hand behind his head, Rebeka leaned in and pulled him close. She felt his sharp inhale as she planted her lips on his, tasting whiskey. His stubble grated against her chin, and she pulled away a few centimetres.

"You need a shave." She shifted forward again, at the same time Dustan pulled away, stumbled back.

"I should go. We should think before going down that road again." His shoulders slumped and he shuffled out the door.

Rebeka's eyes narrowed. For a moment she pondered going after him. But last time she'd pursued him, she'd ended up married. Instead, she slumped into her chair and leaned back as Grim jumped up on her desk and started cleaning himself.

21: ALEK

"WHY ARE WE HERE?" Alek scanned the Esplanade of Nefti Station. Under the arch of glass looking out onto the stars, this was the only tier where reputable citizens let themselves be seen by other reputable sorts.

The arcade sparkled. Golden railings rose from black and blue tiles which led to glass-fronted stores, gilt with more gold.

His skin itched. Rebeka had told him to wear his best. Tugging at the embroidered button placket of his long jacket, he wondered again why he kept this cladding of a former life. He sensed Rebeka shift to look at him again.

"If you keep checking me out, someone's going to get the wrong idea," he said. He dropped his hand and looked sidelong at her. She was in starched navy pants with a red stripe down the side and a sharp pleat in the front, topped with a short jacket replete with brass buttons. *Reminiscent of a marine's uniform.*

She snorted. "I don't think there's much likelihood of that, though I'll admit you clean up nice. I never would have guessed you had any dress clothes in the little case you brought with you." She arched an eyebrow. "And certainly not something so swank."

"I know how to pack." Alek tugged at the high collar of the starched jacket. In a muted azure, it was one of the few colourful pieces of clothing he still owned...and the only other dressy piece besides the navy pants.

She swatted his hand as he moved to adjust his jacket again. "Stop that, or people will think you don't belong here."

"I don't. Stop avoiding the question: why are we here?"

"Because Ludovicus' contact is here."

"That doesn't really answer the question. Why are you trusting him enough to get in touch with this contact? And why bother with the—" He waved his hand at himself and his garb.

"I told you, we need to look like we belong." She held up a hand to forestall another question. "Since we have to wait in line at the gate anyway, we might as well see what this person has to offer. Maybe we can get something useful out of the gangster's interest in our lives."

"Or they might stab us in the back."

"That's why I have you." He stopped his scan of the promenade to peer at her with a raised eyebrow.

"To take the knife?"

Rebeka scowled at him. "To watch my back. Kandi would be better, but she insisted on checking our shields and measly weapons." She looked at her wrist pad, checking their location. "How do you know Visi anyway?" Her tone was even despite the landmine of a question.

"Pardon." Unprepared, the word came out flat, without the question that should have been there.

"Visi. He seemed to know you. Strange for the paths of a junker pilot and the leader of the most powerful gang to cross."

"The Kraits are the second most powerful." Alek examined the catwalk that ran along the other side of the arch while sparing part of his brain to come up with acceptable answers. "Just because he knows me doesn't mean I know him."

"It may not, but in this case...." The statement tapered off.

Rebeka clearly had some experience getting people to talk. But he had experience not talking; she'd have to do a lot more than questions and leading sentences.

The image of her pummeling him to soften him up popped into his head. "But I imagine getting blood on the tiles is frowned upon." He didn't realize he'd muttered aloud until the captain replied.

"Huh? What do bloody tiles have to do with it?"

Alek shook his head. "Just thinking if there's trouble. They'd probably make us pay to clean the floor. Give me the Bowels any day."

"You're probably right." Her fingers twitched on her blaster. "But you're not squirming out of the question that easily."

Alek opened and closed his mouth, in an imitation of a fish, casting his gaze around as he tried to come up with something to say. Fate was on his side. "Isn't that the place we're looking for?" He nodded at the shop right in front of them, windows stylishly dark, the only sign on the front an abstract symbol — you'd only know what was inside if you knew what was inside.

Rebeka frowned at her wrist. "Yup."

Alek had never been so glad to enter a store. Until he stepped inside.

A tall woman with a large halo of tight curls stood behind the counter. Black tattoos cascaded down the brown skin of her arms, left bare by the vest she wore. Her biceps popped, starkly defined, as she leaned on the counter. The scar that bisected her throat was pale pink and clearly visible in the wide V-neck. Her lips, shellacked in shining black, lifted into a predatory smile.

Iniko Zev. A huff of breath escaped Alek's mouth. Also known as Zinnia, his contact in the Laurentian Brigade.

He gave a quick shake of his head, more for himself than her, but the look Rebeka gave him told him she'd seen it. She didn't say anything and turned her attention to the woman behind the counter, who slid her gaze to the captain. A smile lifted her lips but didn't reach her calculating eyes.

"Rebeka Mino. Long time, no see."

Alek's neck muscles flexed as he forced himself not to twist his head around to look wide-eyed at the captain. He kept his mouth shut as he focused on Zev.

"Yes, Iniko. That was intentional."

"You wound me." Zev placed a hand on her chest, its vicious nails painted the same black as her lips. Those lips pressed together as she looked between Rebeka and Alek. "You're the ones Ludo sent. How'd you get mixed up with him?"

Alek's eyebrow arched, impressed by her straight face. She turned her back on them, and he shifted his head to peer at the captain, watching for some hint of how she knew Zev, but she steadfastly ignored him. Instead, he loosened his blaster in its holster.

"Oh, you won't need that, Alek," Zev said without looking back. "If I'd wanted to kill you, I would have electrocuted you when you walked in the door." When she turned back around, she graced him with a smile. One hand held a data cube, the other, a box. "Besides, any friend of Ludo's is a friend of mine...whether I like it or not."

"Good thing I'm not his friend." Alek kept his hand on the blaster as he tried to untangle her truths from her lies.

"What do you have for us?" Rebeka stepped closer to the counter.

"Exactly what Ludo requested: detailed star charts for this sector of space and beyond, along with known criminal activity. And all the records of the Imperial Astroarchaeology Academy...?" She placed the data crystal down on the counter then opened the box with a flourish. "And this is a special little gift."

Alek's jaw clenched and his stomach churned at what was inside: a disperser. Illegal everywhere in the Dominion, forbidden even to the army, which always had the latest death-dealing tech. Even the Legion squirmed at the way it tore flesh apart, molecule-by-molecule. Your only hope was that you'd quickly pass out from shock. Even when he'd had encounters with the Mantas, dispersers were only whispered about, a step too far even for criminals.

"I don't know that I want his gifts." Rebeka didn't move to take either item. "I expect they come with strings attached."

"Smart Rebeka." Zev shrugged. "You can take them or leave them."

The captain scowled. Alek scowled. Iniko Zev smiled. She looked like she enjoyed seeing him squirm, which she probably did, payback for being the one who'd given her that scar along her neck.

Finally, Rebeka stepped forward and scooped up the cube, leaving the weapon where it lay. Zev glanced at it then at the captain. "And he suggested you might need some bug food." She handed Rebeka a chit as the captain opened her mouth to protest. "Take this down below to Martin's Market. They'll sort you out."

Alek swiped the chit, tapping it to his forehead. "Thanks." He glanced at Rebeka. "Unless you're going to take the disperser, we should go." Turning on his heels, he stalked to the door, only opening it when he heard her following him.

Stepping outside, he took a deep breath.

"So, if you won't tell me how you know Visi, maybe you'll tell me how you know Iniko Zev?" Rebeka asked, staring straight ahead. When he hesitated, she continued. "I need to know if you're a danger to my ship."

"How would me knowing her be any more of a threat than you knowing her?"

"Because I know how I know her."

Alek pressed his lips tight as he rolled his shoulders back. "We fought each other in the Arena once." An acid worm ate at his stomach as he told a partial truth to cover a lie.

Rebeka finally turned to him. "You fought in the Arena?"

"Maybe once."

"You never fight just once."

"No, you don't." He clenched his jaw tight, unsure how he'd answer the next question. But the next question didn't come. "That's how I crossed paths with Visi as well."

"We should get back."

Alek blinked.

Rebeka swiped the chit from his hand. "But first we should get some bug food. Damn Sera."

Alek swallowed, forcing his jaw to relax as she strode ahead of him.

"Don't think we're done with this conversation," she said over her shoulder.

22: Rebeka

Rebeka shifted in the chair again, thinking longingly about her lounger and the lava-tube aged whiskey in her cabin. But Dustan wasn't in her cabin, and despite his sidelong smiles, and the flutter they caused in her belly, he wasn't going to be. Not again. Her lips pursed. No, he sat in the common room, transfixed by a scroll of data on his tablet. So, if she wanted to watch him, she needed to be there too.

Ish had them deep in the stream, slipping away from Alpha Dianus, the most populous planet in the sector. Full of well-excavated ancient ruins and ultra-modded biohackers, Rebeka hoped to stay well away from it. Despite the shine he'd taken to Ish, Fennick sat beside Dustan rather than hanging out on the bridge. The young man seemed to shadow her ex wherever he went, fussing over him like he was an old man. A cough punctuated her thoughts, and Fennick patted Dustan on the back. Rebeka snorted. Dustan *was* an old man.

She glanced out the window into the cargo bay as movement caught her eye. She felt a rumble in her chest as Grim, who was nestled in her lap and kneading her stomach, revved up his purring. Down below, Alek and Tink had removed outer layers and were slicked with sweat. In between crates of bugs, the pilot appeared to be teaching Tink some moves of a martial art Rebeka was unfamiliar with. Her brow furrowed — she thought she knew them all. He snaked an arm between her bicep and torso, causing Tink to laugh. Two seconds later, he was on the floor.

Rebeka smiled. "Good for you," she whispered to Grim's head. Then Tink, flushed and smiling, offered him a hand up, and Rebeka sighed. Alek had too many secrets. "Don't do it."

"Do what?" Dustan asked, looking up from his tablet. He had it connected to the data cube from Iniko Zev, which sat between him and the orb on the table.

Rebeka flushed at being caught talking to herself. Well, the cat. Shrugging her shoulder, she reminded herself that Tink would be angry at Alek again soon enough. "Cat digging his claws into my leg."

Grim made a noise like he was going to cough up a hairball and arched his back before settling again. She picked up her own tablet and resumed reading. Earlier, she'd ditched the book on great tacticians in favour of a romance full of heaving bosoms and turgid members. Everyone had a vice. But even her vice wasn't holding her attention, and she once more found herself peering at Dustan, whose hair flopped over his face as he glanced between the tablet and the orb. So far, the data cube hadn't yielded results. Perhaps because she'd refused to let them feed the contents to Cass — there was more than one way to bug a ship.

Footsteps in the hall announced the arrival of Tink and Alek. Tink paused as she entered, her smile turning to a frown when she spotted Dustan. But she made a beeline for the kitchenette, followed closely by Alek.

Rebeka watched them over the top of her tablet. Tink's curls were a mess, and strands stuck to her face. Thankfully the blush had disappeared, so maybe it was just the flush of victory. She filled a bottle with water, as Alek reached around her for a cup to fill with coffee.

The ship shivered, hitting some turbulence in the stream. Both Alek and Tink were used to it and went about their business, but Fennick raised his head as his face went a lighter shade of pale.

"Why does your ship do that?" Dustan asked, staring at the orb. "Is there something wrong with your engine?"

Grim growled from Rebeka's lap as Tink sat down at the table, across from Dustan, and glared at him.

"The ship is fine. It's actually so fine it's sensitive to ripples in the stream."

"Huh." Dustan didn't look up from whatever he was working on.

"It would be even more fine if it hadn't been attacked by Manta blasters and clippers."

Finally, Dustan raised his head, and lifted his hands. "I apologize."

"Sometimes sorry is not enough." Rebeka laid her tablet down on the armrest and a second later wished she hadn't when the ship bucked, sending the tablet skittering across the floor. Alek picked it up and returned it to her as Kandi's voice came over the comms.

"Ish says we're in for some turbulence — a convergent Colombo flux, he says."

"Should we strap in?" Rebeka tucked her tablet beside her.

A moment of silence followed. "Nah, says it should be fine."

"Should be." Dustan snorted and shook his head.

Ish's voice took Kandi's place. "Never navigated through one before, but we're trained for them. I'll let you know if anything changes." The comms when silent, and Rebeka debated telling everyone to buckle up regardless.

She made up her mind when the ship rattled through some ripples, causing her teeth to chatter together. Once that passed, she opened her mouth to give the order but never got the chance.

Without warning, sparks filled her vision and swirled around her. Ribbons of light snaked through the air then disappeared. Her stomach heaved and she grabbed the armrests to keep from falling out of the chair. Blinking the dizziness away, she noticed others were also having problems. Dustan's knuckles were white from grabbing the table, Fennick had turned a green shade of pale, and Tink looked on the verge of vomiting.

The *Lyra* shuddered. The orb in front of Dustan flashed vivid blue before rolling across the table. Dustan lunged after it, with Fennick mimicking his movements. Instead of catching the thing, their heads collided, and it clattered to the floor.

It split into two halves.

In a flash of light, a new field of stars spangled the common room. A rainbow of dots marked some solar system or another. None of which Rebeka recognized.

"Cass." She clenched her jaw tight as the earlier ribbons of light cascaded to the ground in a wave. "Can you scan this?"

"Scanning."

"Ish. Kandi. What the hell just happened?"

"I...." Ish started then faded away.

"Give us a second, Captain," Kandi said. "Ish, look at me."

Rebeka felt a worm of fear in her stomach as the silence dragged on. It was one thing to be caught in regular space without a talented pilot; it was another to be caught in the stream without a navigator. Cass might do in a pinch, but from what little Rebeka knew, they were deep. Deeper was faster, but deeper was more dangerous.

She assessed the people in the room. They all seemed to be recovering, including Tink who shook her head and rubbed her temples. Dustan cradled his split-open orb in his hand. She saw it was hinged on one side, like a jewelled egg, though she'd detected no seam.

"Captain." Ish sounded drained.

"I'm listening."

"We passed through an anomaly."

"What kind of anomaly?" Silence descended again.

"I don't know. Something in the flux. There are a lot of strange things in the deep."

"Cass, do you have anything in your data stores?" Rebeka asked.

"Scanning."

Rebeka stared at the orb, which flashed a pale purple. The pulse almost seemed in time with her heart. Spots of light covered Dustan's face, and she craned her neck to look at the ceiling. This new starfield was still there. Grim grumbled as she dislodged him so she could stand on tiptoes and reach out for the stars.

"There's nothing similar in on-board records." Cass' voice was calm. "Do you want me to access the Connect? We would need to go shallower in the stream."

"No."

"No?" Dustan's voice rose an octave. "I need to know what just happened."

"Do you want *everyone* to know what just happened?" She pressed her lips together, and he shook his head. "Do you think the people who are after that map aren't tracking every signal sent from this ship? Every message, every tap into the Connect, every ping?"

"Captain." Even over comms, Kandi's voice was pitched higher than usual. She was either worried or wanted something. "I'm detecting some sort of signal. A beacon." There was silence as the comms cut off for a few seconds.

"Kandi?"

"Cass says it's words, but it's a language she doesn't recognize." Kandi's tone deepened. "And it's coming from inside the ship."

"Cass?"

"Captain. I've also pinpointed the red dot."

Rebeka imagined she heard an edge of excitement in the AI's words. She shook her head, trying to clear the fuzziness she still felt from the anomaly. "Red dot?"

"The planet in Mr. Key's star chart."

Rebeka glanced at the ceiling — there was no red dot this time. This chart displayed some other place.

23: TINK

TINK HANDED ALEK THE cup of coffee she'd brought him at the captain's behest. Now that they were nearing the red planet, he refused to let anyone else fly them in. Even though Cass said it was uninhabited, not even any colonies or mining outposts. Besides, Ish served as their backup pilot, and he was sleeping off the effort of slipping them into the system. At least that's what he said. The sounds from his room didn't sound like sleeping to Tink.

"Thanks." Alek raised his mug towards her.

She blinked, refocusing. His eyes were bruise-tired, and his lips tugged into a frown. She heard the cracking when he arched his back in a stretch. He rubbed his neck with one hand, exposing the edge of a scar.

Tink pressed her lips together, recalling the marks across his torso. *How does a pilot collect so many scars?* She let out a heavy sigh... she didn't like so many secrets on the ship.

Nodding, she started to leave. An itch in her stomach made her pause and shift her gaze to the viewscreen, where they were passing a seafoam ball shooting jets of ice into space — a large moon that orbited the fifth planet in the system. They headed for the fourth.

She examined the moon. According to Ish, there was a slip point nearby and another close to their destination, in addition to the one they'd come in through. *Unusual*, he proclaimed, squinting at his holodisplay, before leaving the bridge.

"I know I have a sexy back." Alek turned to cast a lopsided smile her way. "But I'd rather you sit and stay a while."

She grimaced and turned to go. But instead of leaving, she found herself curling into Ish's chair. She could review the acoustic sensor readings for evidence of the beacon's source from here as well as anywhere. Tapping into Ish's console, she sipped her coffee. It almost ended up down her front when Grim jumped into her lap, the bauble on his collar clinking softly.

"Be careful." She ran a hand down Grim's back before glancing at Alek. "I know Cass said the system is unpopulated, but any sign of anyone else around?" she asked as she scrolled through the last few hours of spectrograph data from the ship, filtering out the hum and hiss of the engine.

"No." Alek shook his head. "At least, not yet."

She peered at him. "So, you could go get some sleep." On the viewscreen, a grey, pock-marked planet, desolate and barren compared to its moon, emerged from the far side of the frosty orb.

He shook his head again. "Nah. There's dangerous lumps of rock around."

"Hurtling through space thousands of klicks away." She flicked a finger at her display to remove the sounds of the crew.

"They could jump out at us. They're sneaky like that." He slurped his coffee and smiled at her. She tipped her chin down and gave him a disbelieving look. He shrugged. "Okay, I don't trust that we won't meet up with trouble and need to make a quick getaway."

"Now *that* I believe." She smiled at him over her mug. "But I thought 'Trouble' was your middle name."

"Danger's my middle name. But either way, I'd rather make it than find it."

She took a sip of hot liquid to cover her snort. "So, what would you do with your share?"

"What?"

She jerked her chin towards the viewscreen where they were passing the rock world on their way to their destination — the red planet. "The *Celeste*, assuming it's real. What would you do?"

"You first."

She rolled her eyes. "Give the *Lyra* all the TLC she needs. Get the plasma manifolds scrubbed. Replace all the flex capacitors. Repaint the entire hull." She pulled her knees up and tucked her feet under her. "Your turn."

Alek shook his head.

"Yes, I shared mine. Now, you." She waved at him over her mug. "That's how it works."

He held up a hand. "Give me a chance to speak." He looked at a patch on his console, where the lights blinked a steady green, tapping it with his finger before turning back to her. "Nothing. I'd do exactly what I'm doing now." He peered at her with his blue eyes. "Pay those who want me doing something else to leave me alone."

She shifted her gaze away, back to the console. "Who wants you doing something else?"

"There's a line up."

"Okay, what do they want you doing?" Pulling with her fingers, she zoomed into a portion of the sonograph. Her eyebrows tugged together. "Huh."

"You okay?"

She glanced up and realized she been frowning. Peering back at the sonic map, she hovered her fingertips over it. "There are ... numbers." She grasped her mug in both hands.

"I thought the beacon was transmitting words."

"Yes, that's still there" She nodded, causing the colours on the display to waver and bleed together. "Cass can't make out what the signal says, even though she swears it's words. But there are also numbers." She paused, not wanting to put her suspicion to words: the numbers seemed an awful lot like.... "Coordinates," she whispered.

"And Dustan has listened? Fenn—" He stopped as the light on his console changed its flashing, pulsing in a different rhythm, the green shifting to yellow. His jaw ticked as he flicked it.

Tink frowned. "What's it saying?"

"Proximity sensor. But if there were anything around, Cass would be shouting at us."

Tink snorted. "Cass doesn't shout."

"You know what I mean." He glared at the viewscreen, as if that would reveal something. "Even a ship with one of these shrouds, she knows what to look for now."

"Cass?"

"Yes, Tink?"

"Is there anything around us?"

"No, Tink."

"Can you scan through the cameras, putting the images on the viewscreen?" Alek asked. He lifted a shoulder as he looked at Tink. "Just in case."

She squinted at the screen as images of the exterior flipped across it. "Nothing."

Alek shook his head slowly. "Nothing." He slid his fingers up the console, zooming in until a red orb hung in the centre, like a drop of blood. He flicked the proximity warning light again. "But there's our destination."

Tink's gaze was drawn from the screen to his console. She blinked as the warning light shut off, then turned her attention back to her screen and examined her would-be coordinates. Wherever the sound pointed, this planet wasn't it.

24: ALEK

S TOP FIDGETING." ALEK TURNED his head towards Fennick, though half his view was cut off by the side of his helmet.

"But it's so uncomfortable." The young man's gloved hand bumped the glass of his faceplate.

"It's not about comfort." Alek scanned the clearing where he'd landed the *Lyra*. There hadn't been a lot of options. The area near the target Cass had pinpointed was covered in trees and vines and needle grass...all an unnerving crimson. But someone, or something, had use the clearing before — a trail led off one side towards the target.

"But your AI said the air is breathable." Fennick's helmet bobbled again.

Alek stopped and turned full-on to face the young man in time to see his nose wrinkle and his lips tug back and forth. "And did you ever think what you might be breathing in?"

Kandi stepped up on Fennick's other side. "The eggs of Leishmann's lung borers." She shuddered.

"Taursa Epsilon hemorrhagic plague," Rebeka added.

"Pilgrim's phage." Kandi sidled past them to take the lead, keeping her plasma rifle pointed slightly down. "Just to name a few of the diseases settlers encountered on planets with breathable air." She glanced back, half turning. "Things that would make you wish you were dead."

Fennick stopped fidgeting with his helmet, and his hands dropped to his sides.

Dustan patted his assistant on the back. "Buck up. It's just a precaution. Nine times out of ten there's nothing to worry about." He stepped past Fennick to follow Kandi, and his assistant trailed him, shoulders slumped. "Well, maybe eight out of ten."

Rebeka looked at Alek. He motioned with his rifle that she should go first. Even through the faceplate, he could see the skin around her eyes tense slightly before she followed Fennick along the path.

And it was a path. A lighter groove worn into the red soil led between plants covered with dark crimson foliage and bright red vines. Every now and then a blue bud peeped out, the only thing that broke the impression of walking through a landscape soaked in blood. The groove led towards their destination: a rise in the tangle of plants where Cass had detected the only sign of unnatural construction on the whole planet. If it weren't for the AI's tech, he'd have no idea there was anything there. He scanned the area ahead; it was as much covered by plants as the rest of the planet. Except for the track. The thought of what might have carved out the line through the dark jungle made him heft the rifle up.

Even if the rise likely didn't hold the *Celeste*. Cass was adamant there was no ship to be found on the planet, more adamant than he thought an AI could be.

He opened a channel directly to the captain. "Why are we here? If the *Celeste* isn't?"

"You think Cass is telling the truth?"

"You think she's lying?"

"No, AIs don't lie. But they interpret."

"You think she's interpreting wrong?"

There was silence for a minute. "She is a Cass model." Another few seconds followed. "But no, I don't think the *Celeste* is here."

"So that leads me back to my question — why are *we* here?"

Rebeka paused, letting the others get ahead a bit. "If the map says the *Celeste* is here, Dustan won't give up until he's seen what's under that mound." She started walking again. "And however much I want to leave him on this rock to explore it himself, it means endangering others."

"Your daughter."

Ahead of him, the captain's left shoulder raised. "Juniper. Fennick. Even Ish."

"Who, by the way, was exceedingly pissed he wasn't allowed to come on this hike."

"I need a navigator more than I need you."

"Thanks. So, it's not that you need my muscle?" Rebeka didn't contradict him, and he cut the private channel. He needed to focus; as they neared the mound, it was clear that it wasn't natural. But neither was it a starship.

"So, where's the *Celeste*?" Rebeka asked, pulse rifle held across her hips, as she peered at Dustan. Given his experience with the captain, Alek wondered if she was holding the gun that way deliberately, so she didn't shoot her ex. "You said once we got here, we'd find the ship, and be free and clear of this mess you dropped us in."

Scanning the impenetrable jungle around them, Alek's irritation churned below the knot in his gut. He would have been a lot more frank in asking the question. Kandi stood on the other side of the small clearing they'd found at the base of the mound. She swept the tip of her rifle back and forth as she scanned the dark, dense wall of plants around them.

"I...." Dustan straightened from where he crouched, sweeping creepers from hewn rock, and held up a gloved hand. "I didn't actually say either of those things. Your Cass said this was the red planet in the star map." He glanced around and tipped his head as much as the helmet allowed. "You assumed the rest."

"You implied." Rebeka swung the rifle behind her, freeing up her hands. Instead of choking Dustan, she tapped the button on her helmet to comm the *Lyra*. "Tink, when can we take off?"

"But—" Dustan looked up at her.

The captain swiped her other hand across her throat, signalling Dustan to be quiet.

Tink shrugged. "It looks like the anomaly didn't damage any systems."

"Get the ship ready to leave and keep it primed."

"But we've barely explored." Dustan stepped toward Rebeka, and Alek shifted his rifle out of muscle memory.

"There's nothing here." Rebeka's hands went to her hips.

"*This* is here." Dustan gestured towards the stepped pyramid, cloaked in foliage. "Your Cass said it's not solid ... there might be a way in."

Alek grimaced. "You think someone parked the lost ship here, built a pyramid over it and left?" He couldn't stop the snort.

"This planet isn't on anyone's maps," Fennick said from where he kneeled at the base, inspecting the rocks Dustan had cleared. He'd pulled out a brush to clear dust off the surface, while his other hand clutched a tablet with a display full of graphs and numbers. The young man leaned forward until his helmet almost touched the stone. "This pyramid is an anomaly. A mystery."

"What have you found, Fennick?" Alek stepped towards the structure. Fennick straightened up, startled. Rebeka and Dustan stopped bickering to take a look.

"Uh, nothing. I won't know until we examine the playback in all frequencies." He reached a finger forward. "It's definitely hand-hewn, with primitive tools, I'd say. No laser cutters or plasma drills here."

Dustan turned back to the captain. "We can't just leave without exploring."

She peered at him. "Yes, we can." Alek watched the shoulders of her suit rise and fall as she took a deep breath. "Ish, any sign of our harassers?"

There was a long pause before Ish's voice came over the comms from the *Lyra*. "No, all quiet." He sounded disappointed.

Rebeka turned her gaze from Dustan to Alek. Through her visor, he could tell some inner battle raged. "Fine. We'll walk to the corners of this side of the pyramid. If we don't see signs that there's something more here, we leave."

"But the other side—"

"I can leave you here to continue exploring if you'd like." She shifted toward Alek. "You and Kandi take that direction." She jerked her chin towards where Kandi stood, though the movement was limited by her helmet. "Dustan and I will go the other way."

"What about me?" Fennick stood up, his eyes flicking over the jungle.

"Stay here." Dustan looked at the rock. "Keep clearing it."

"But I—" Fennick's eyes roved around.

"Cass has done a full scan." Rebeka hefted her rifle up again. "There's no one else here."

"Nothing alive except the plants." Alek patted the young man on the back.

Fennick looked at him wide-eyed. "Plants can be deadly. Venusian Tickleweed. Keplan Bindweed."

"We'll keep comms open." The captain turned to follow the rock wall the other direction.

Even though they hadn't gone far, the recycled air in Alek's suit was stuffy, ripe with his own stink. He took another sip of water from the nozzle by his lips. It was hot and he swore he tasted salt, though he tried not to think about it being made from his recycled sweat.

"Roll call." Rebeka's voice crackled in Alek's ear.

"We've been chatting all along." Alek arched an eyebrow. Then wished he hadn't as it dislodged the sweat pooled there, letting it run into his eyes. It stung, and the leaves on the vines went blurry for a second as he tried to blink away the burn.

"Humour me. Code says if we're separated, roll call every five minutes."

"Here," Kandi said.

"Here," he echoed. "No sign of anything but rocks and plants. Yet."

"Here." Ish's voice came across clear, and clearly annoyed. "Stuck on the ship while you're off adventuring."

"You can take my place." Even over the tinny comms, Fennick's words came across as a grumble. "I haven't been eaten by the plants yet."

"Discovered anything?" Dustan asked. There was no answer. Seconds ticked by "Fennick?" His voice rose, though it was hard to tell if it was concern or irritation.

"What?" The young man finally responded.

"Anything?" Dustan repeated. Clearly irritation.

"No." There was another pause. When the young man's voice returned, it was pitched higher. "But I ... it would be good if you could get back soon."

"He's found something." Dustan's voice was hushed, as if he were talking to himself.

"Have you, Fenn?" Ish's voice lifted.

Kandi turned to Alek. "Fenn?" she mouthed.

"I ... the rock—" Whatever he started to say was cut-off, replaced by a strangled utterance, half shriek, half howl.

The sound pierced Alek's skull, amplified by his helmet. He wished he could cover his ears.

"Fennick!" Ish's voice was almost as loud as the scream. "I'm coming."

"You're doing no such thing." Rebeka's voice brooked no argument. "Fennick. Fennick? Barnacles. Everyone back to the clearing." There was a rustle, and a second later, the captain's voice came over comms again. "Not you, Ish."

"Poseidon's pox." There was a squeak, a sound Alek recognized as Ish settling into his chair.

Shifting his rifle, Alek started back towards the clearing at a jog. A second later, he heard Kandi follow.

"Cass, keep tabs on Fennick." There was an edge to Rebeka's voice.

"Aye, Captain." There was a pause. "Captain, Fennick is no longer on the planet.

"What? Of course, he is. Scan the whole planet."

"I did, Captain, as far as my sensors can reach. I no longer see his beacon."

"Fennick! Talk to me." Dustan's voice was garbled, swallowed by a cough, but there was no reply.

When he glanced back at Kandi, Alek saw her expression was as grim as he felt. Hefting his rifle, he turned and started running.

Unwelcome Bedfellows

25: ALEK

WHEN ALEK ARRIVED BACK at the clearing, Kandi at his heels, he found the captain and Dustan already there. But not Fennick.

Rebeka scoured the edge of the clearing, shifting the vegetation with the tip of a long blade. Alek recognized the search: she was checking for signs that anyone ... or anything had passed that way.

"Fennick." Dustan slammed his palms on the lowest step. "Fennick!" A section of the steps was now cleared of dust and vegetation. It was almost the height of a man, and just as wide. At least if that man were Fennick.

Alek ran his finger over the grooves carved into the rock, tracing a pattern that seemed almost familiar.

"Sammi!" Dustan shouted, his face shining with sweat beneath his faceplate. "If you don't show yourself, I'll...." His words became quiet and trailed off.

"Sammi?" Alek asked, the name causing an itch in his ear.

Dustan blinked at him, and Alek saw the lines of worry etched in his face, even through the visor. "Fennick Sammi."

"Huh." Alek tried to dredge up where he'd heard the name before, but wherever he knew it from was lost in the mire of memory.

"What? It's a fine name. A bit unusual—"

"No. You're right. A fine name." He ran his gloved hand over the step just below waist height. "What do you make of this?" He traced the indentations with his index finger, a shape forming in his mind as he squinted at it.

"It's rock. Basalt of some type if I had to guess."

"I meant—" Alek started before Kandi interrupted.

"No sign of anyone else." She stepped up beside him. "Huh. A hand print." She reached her hand forward to the spot Alek had indicated.

He grabbed her wrist. "Is that smart?"

"It *is* a hand print, worn or carved it's hard to say." Dustan's shoulders sank. "How did I not see that?"

"You were distracted." Rebeka came to stand beside Dustan as he reached a hand towards the rock. "Don't touch it!"

"But Fennick is inside. Alone."

"We don't know that." The captain poked at the rock with the tip of her rifle. Alek rolled his eyes towards her. "Okay, that's a likely explanation for his disappearance, but we can't see him or hear him." Placing a hand on Dustan's shoulder, she forced him to look at her. "Neither can the *Lyra*. If we all go charging in there, we might all end up inside. With no way out."

"Right."

"Who knows, maybe Visi dropped in and whisked Fennick away." She scanned the clearing until her gaze settled on a large stone off to the side, and Alek guessed her intention. He slung the rifle over his back and followed her as she strode over to it. "Kandi, give us a hand."

With more than a little grunting and groaning, they shifted the rock so it was in front of the cleared patch on the mound steps.

Rebeka's visor fogged for a second as she huffed out. "Okay. On the count of three, Dustan, you place your hand on the palm print and then get out of our way. If that thing opens, we'll shove this rock in."

Alek placed himself on the far side of the rock and made a deal with his tetchy knee: if it didn't act up, it would get an extra dose of Cat's Paw cream.

"One."

Alek squatted behind the rock, and the captain glanced between him and Kandi as she crouched.

"Two."

Alek tried to find a decent grip that wasn't a jagged edge, then pulled his shoulders down, getting ready to lift.

"Three."

Dustan placed his hand on the imprinted stone. For a second, nothing happened, and Alek forced himself to exhale and take another deep breath. Then, in a blink, stone by stone, a section of the mound folded in on itself. His mouth dropped open, but he didn't have a chance to gawk.

"Now," the captain ordered. "Out of the way, Peanut!"

With a snarl from Kandi, a grunt from Rebeka and a groan from himself, they heaved the rock into the opening.

Alek shifted his rifle up, pointing it and its targeting light towards the darkness within, and took a step forward.

Rebeka's hand came to his chest. "Whoa. Kandi, stay here."

"What? That's bollocks."

"I want someone I trust watching my back." Her hand dropped from Alek's chest, and he frowned at the implication. She waved at the opening. "And if this thing closes, we need someone here to open it again." Glancing at Alek, she grabbed her rifle. "Me first, then Dustan. You bring up the rear." A few steps in and she was swallowed by darkness.

Alek cracked his jaw, trying to clear the wool from his ears. But it was no use — he still heard Rebeka and Kandi strategizing over the helmet comms, but the sound remained dampened, as if it travelled through water. Up ahead, he could just make out the outline of the captain at the front of the line. They were in a tunnel of some kind, the floor paved with the same stones as the rest of the mound. The bulk of rock overhead pressed down on his brain.

"Peanut?" Alek asked, trying to bring some levity to their situation, but he got no response, not even a 'shut it'.

"We should have tied a string around Kandi," Dustan said. His voice was clear, without wooliness. "To find our way back out again."

"We've been going straight." Alek glanced over his shoulder to where the square of light was still visible. "We just turn around."

"Do you know that? Besides, we might come to a fork in the road."

"Shush." Rebeka slowed. "Do you hear that?"

Alek cocked his head to the side, though it didn't make a difference in the helmet. He thought he heard running water. Then his comms crackled, followed by a sharp hissing static.

"Captain, can you hear me?"

Ahead of him, Rebeka held up a hand, her intention clear. *Be quiet.* His comms hissed again.

"Hello? Can you hear me?" Fennick's voice was rough, like his throat was raw.

"Sammi, my boy." Dustan stopped, and Alek almost bumped into him. "Where are you?"

"Inside."

"So are we."

"Not where I am. Keep coming. It's amazing."

Dustan started hustling down the tunnel, and Alek had to physically restrain him to keep him from bowling past the captain. She tapped the side of her helmet, and when her voice came through, it was quiet.

"How do we know that's Fennick, and not some ghost ... some artifact left by whoever built this?"

"Bah ... I—" Dustan stopped struggling and turned to scowl at Alek. "Fine. Speaking of nicknames...." He turned back to Rebeka as he tapped his helmet. "Fennick, what's your mother's name for you?"

"Really? Do I have to?"

"Yes." Rebeka's tone was sharp.

There was a long silence on the comms, and when Fennick finally answered, it wasn't with his usual light tone. "Mudpuppy."

"It's Fennick." Dustan grinned.

Alek felt a momentary twinge of sympathy for Fennick as he recalled collecting the water-loving insects as a child, during brief escapes to the river ... they where long-limbed with bulbous eyes and made a high-pitched chirp when startled, which happened a lot.

Rebeka inched forward. Alek glanced over his shoulder at the patch of light from outside — it was still there, now the size of his thumbnail. Turning around, the ghost of the light from outside stayed in his eyes. He blinked to get rid of it.

"Huh, it's not a ghost." The words were barely audible even to himself. Ahead of him, a square of blue light grew, resolving into a doorway. The captain stepped across the threshold then stopped, her helmet tipping back as she looked up, and Dustan almost bumped into her.

"A little warning next time," the man grumbled. Rebeka reached out and grabbed him, dragging him forward. "Oh."

"What?" Alek stepped through the opening to join them and felt like he'd emerged on another world. "Oh."

The mound opened into a pyramid shape, the sloping walls faced in a blue stone flecked with a mineral that sparkled as his light hit it. And in the middle sat a ship of shimmering chrome.

26: Rebeka

R EBEKA TORE HER GAZE away from the ship, forcing herself to scan the interior of the pyramid. Two waist-high pillars flanked the entryway they'd just come through, each topped with a polished spherical stone, about the size of a kora ball. She could have enclosed the milky white stone in the palm of her hand. But she didn't dare touch it.

"I thought Cass said the ship wasn't here." Alek's words were hushed.

"Well, she is a Cass," Dustan said, his tone giddy.

Rebeka didn't respond. Instead, she glanced around, noting similar pillars on the other two walls she could see. In front of her, a flight of steps led down to the floor. With both steps and floor tiled in the same stone as the walls, it made it difficult to tell where one ended and the other began. Between each tile ran a seam of golden metal. The tiles got narrower towards the centre, forming a web.

Even though it made her dizzy, she followed the seams inward. Towards the ship. And Fennick. Rebeka blinked, noticing for the first time the black obelisk that reached towards the nose of the craft.

Fennick knelt in front of the ebony spar. The young man glanced at them, eyes shining. "You found your way." He turned back to the black stone and the ship. "Isn't it awesome?"

Dustan hustled down the stairs before Rebeka could stop him.

"Dustan," she hissed. "You never had any discipline."

"You loved my lack of discipline once," he said without stopping or turning back.

Her nostrils flared. It didn't help that it was true. She resumed her scan of the interior as she started down the stairs, once step at a time.

"At least there's no one here." Alek stepped up beside her. "The only danger was Fennick's curiosity."

"Might still get us killed." Tapping her helmet, she swept her rifle left and up, lighting up the floor and wall. "Cass, you recording?"

"Of course, Captain."

Alek's exhale was audible in her ear, and she understood how he felt. Knowing the *Lyra* could still hear them, her own shoulders relaxed a fraction. Still, she glanced back to the opening they'd come through. She couldn't see the outside anymore but was glad they'd propped the door open and that she'd insisted Kandi stay outside. Turning back around, she scanned the space — she also didn't see the desiccated corpses of previous explorers hidden in the corners.

She stepped forward, continuing to sweep the cavern with her scope light, walking a wide arc to the left. She waved her hand to Alek to indicate he should do the same to the right, but he was already mimicking her movements in the other direction. The entrances on the two sides were visible, lit by some unseen light. She glanced back the way they'd come, and sure enough that entrance appeared identical. But as she approached the corners, they remained cloaked in shadows. The beam of her scope light made little dent. Out of the corner of her eye, it seemed as if the whorls on the sloped sides began to dance, but when she looked straight on, the lines were still.

She shook her head to clear the dizziness away, then continued along the wall. Sure enough, the far side had a door matching the other three. When she met Alek in front of it, he shook his head, indicating he'd seen what she had: nothing. She turned and headed towards where Fennick and Dustan both knelt in front of the obelisk, engaged in an animated conversation that seemed to be about the black stone rather than the giant ship in front of them.

"See this." Fennick's finger skimmed the surface. "I swear it's writing."

Dustan nodded. "Yes, but no known language." His shoulders slumped.

"No language known to *us*." Fennick placed his hand on Dustan's arm. "There is a difference, you know."

Dustan frowned, then opened his mouth. "I've—"

"Have you both forgotten about the ship?" Rebeka flicked her hand towards the silvery machine.

Dustan blinked and looked at her then the ship. "No. But there's no way in." He turned back to the obelisk. "This might be the key."

"Awfully big key," Alek said as he peered at the two archaeologists.

"Watch them." Rebeka held Alek's gaze as she jerked her chin at the pair. "Make sure they don't do anything stupid."

Alek quirked an eyebrow. "I'll try. No promises."

She turned away and started a circuit around the ship. The chrome sides rippled, reflecting the whorls and sparks from the walls. She reached out to touch it but pulled her hand away as the ripples seemed to undulate. Instead, she strode along the sides, looking for a seam that would indicate a door or access panel. When she met up again with Alek, her jaw ached from clenching.

"I'm sure we should put it in there." Fennick's fingers twitched as he waved his hand at a divot in the ebony stone.

"No." Dustan shook his head. "What if I don't get it back?"

"Then it wasn't yours to keep."

"Anything?" Alek asked, barely turning towards her.

"Nothing." Rebeka peered at the archaeologists. "What are they doing?" The words were barely out of her mouth when she noticed the orb in Dustan's hand, and realized it was a perfect fit for the divot in the obelisk.

Alek's hand lashed out to grab Dustan's wrist as the man reached forward. "Do you think that's wise?" Her ex scowled at her pilot, but he tugged his hand away and didn't reach towards the stone again. "We have no idea what will happen."

"Nothing, if we just sit here."

"Did you find a door?" Fennick glanced between her and Alek. Despite the cooler temperature in the cavern, his face was still flushed. "We have to try something." He slumped. "We don't know what to do next."

"Of course we do." She peered at the young man. "We leave and dump you two off on the next inhabited rock. You can find someone else to entangle in your schemes."

Dustan and Fennick both gaped at her for a moment. Then her ex moved more quickly than she thought he could, shoving the orb into the divot before she could stop him. She inhaled sharply, then forced herself to exhale slowly. The pyramid was so quiet she could hear herself breathing.

"Enough of this." She turned on her heel and started towards the door they'd come through. "If you want a ride—"

Thunk.

Her heart stopped as she froze. Slowly turning around, she expected to see a ramp descending from the ship. Instead, it shimmered. Rebeka swallowed against the bile rising in her throat. The walls around her rippled again, making her feel like she was underwater, and the ship ... dissolved. The chrome became pinpricks of light.

"A hologram." Alek's voice was a whisper.

"An exceptionally complex hologram." Rebeka blinked against the dizziness as flecks of lights swirled around her. As she did, an image began to resolve.

A wave of light-headedness hit her as she looked up. It felt as if she peered up into the night sky.

Dustan came to stand beside her, his shoulder touching hers. "It's a picture."

"No, a movie." Fennick stepped up to his other side, then gasped.

A ghost of a figure, reminiscent of a person, formed in front of them. Glancing around, she noticed more and more coming into being as the ceiling darkened. Soon they were surrounded by a host of glittering figures.

A starry ship flew in from the left and stopped above them, followed by another and another, like wasps to sugar. Each had a series of symbols on the side, but squint as she might, she couldn't make them out. All she knew was that the ships were nothing like the one that had filled the space when they arrived.

Rebeka flinched as the vessels started firing at them. Not at them ... at the figures.

"What the—" Alek started as he raised his pulse rifle up.

Reaching over, she pressed his wrist down. "Don't."

That's all she got out before the closest figure exploded in a rain of stars. For a second, she thought Alek had shot it. Then a howl rose from the host. A figure fell at her feet, and she jerked back a few inches as it dissolved back into flecks of light. In rapid succession, the other figures followed.

Dustan stumbled towards her. Catching him, she looked over his shoulder. The first ship was back, but smaller now that it was part of the movie.

"That's...." Fennick pointed at it.

"Our ship," Dustan finished as he straightened up and coughed into his sleeve. "The *Celeste*."

Rebeka watched as the ship sped away, pausing at a mesh of light. She gasped as she realized what it was: *the Wall*. The mesh disappeared, replaced by a starfield. Thirteen pinpoints stood out from the rest, brighter. Then the ship disappeared, and the sides of the pyramid turned back into night. Stars scattered across each face, while some still hung in the air — the thirteen stars. A red dot pulsed then disappeared. Further away, another pulsed green and grew larger.

She blinked to clear her vision and her mind. The other dots disappeared. Then she turned to Dustan. "Wait, what did you say?"

"It's the *Celeste*, clearly." He waved at the now empty space. The holographic ship hadn't reappeared. "The Desolation."

"The Exodus," Alek said.

"That's not the Exodus." She jerked her chin to the centre. "It's nothing like the sagas—"

"Captain." Ish's voice came over her helmet comms, the peevishness of earlier gone.

"Go ahead."

"You might want to get back to the ship, double-time."

"What's up?"

"Cass has detected ships in this sector."

Rebeka hissed in through her teeth. Other ships near an uncharted planet in an uninhabited system.... "Dominion or cartels?"

"Can't tell yet."

"On our way." Hefting her rifle, she turned to see Alek and Dustan already moving. Except Dustan was going the wrong way. "What are you doing?"

He didn't answer, just pointed to the obelisk. She sighed and turned back to Fennick.

"Come on." She jerked her head towards the door as stars started falling from the pyramid walls. Glancing at the obelisk, she saw Dustan tuck something in this pocket: the orb.

"Captain." Kandi's voice was loud in her ear. "This not-a-door is trying to close." A rumble reverberated under her words.

"But we have to study...." Fennick still sounded stunned. She grabbed his wrist and dragged him towards the door.

"No, we have to leave."

The young man only resisted for a second, following her when a chunk of ceiling fell. He paused again at the threshold to look back at the space.

She grabbed the neck of his tunic, her fingers entangled in the chain and pendant he always wore, and tugged. "If we live, maybe Dustan will let you come back. Unless I kill him first."

27: TINK

TINK FUTZED WITH THE sonographic analyzer on her tablet, both ear buds in to drown out Ish's arguments as to why he should be a part of the expedition outside. Some crazy impulse had made her think joining him on the bridge would stop the stream of complaints he'd broadcast over the open comms.

She grimaced. This was still better than what she'd been doing — hanging out in the cargo bay with crates of bugs which weren't as dormant as promised while she tried to optimize the spooler for the tentacles.

Tink shook her head and continued trying to tease some sense out of their mysterious beacon. The sound had settled into a whisper, but something still beamed it to the universe. Something on the ship. She glanced around. Her hopes that it had been Dustan and his orb were dashed when the group disappeared inside the pyramid. With their comms dampened and all signals routed through Kandi, the beacon had gotten louder.

So, she tweaked her analyzer again, trying to pinpoint its source. A high-pitched squeal repaid her efforts.

"Jacks!" She shoved the tablet away.

"What?" Ish waved a hand at his console. "Cass can't tell either."

Tink flushed, and her gaze slid sideways to Ish. She ran her hand up her cheeks to turn off the noise cancellation on her ear bud. But Ish glared at her, and his hand shot out like a snake, plucking the small piece from her ear.

"You weren't even listening." He threw the ear bud at her. "Ships headed our way."

"Sorry." She exhaled heavily. "I'm trying to suss out this sound."

"And?"

"And nothing. Warbles and whispers, I can't pinpoint the source. Except...." She bit her lip.

"Except?"

She inhaled and held her breath for a few seconds. She still didn't want to admit that the numbers woven into the signal were coordinates. She gave her head a small shake. "It's—" A screech pierced the ear that still had a bud in it. She tore the thing out and flung it to the floor.

The sound coming from the bud was still audible, the words now a roaring torrent. The ship comms crackled.

"Out of the pyramid." Rebeka's words were clear for the first time since they'd entered the ancient edifice. "Be ready to fly in five."

Tink glanced at Ish. "They're coming in quick."

Ish grabbed the secondary control stick at the nav station. Something in the ship squealed. "Why can't we teach Cass to do this?"

"We've tried." She grabbed her abandoned ear bud and tucked the pair in her pocket. "She's a worse pilot than you."

"Thanks."

"Any time."

He rolled his eyes at her then turned back to his console, running his thumb up a slider. The *Lyra* settled into a drunken hum punctuated by the occasional hiccough.

A thud echoed through the ship.

"Cass, what was that?" Tink peered at the viewscreen. Nothing moved in the multiple, red-soaked frames.

"I'm lowering the gangway, Tink." Her tone was entirely too cheerful. "The others are nearing the ship."

Tink flicked through the cameras, trying to pinpoint a rustle of leaves indicating the crew's path through the foliage. "You sure?"

"Of course."

Sure enough, seconds later, five figures in grey burst out of the bloody vegetation, just as the gangway touched the ground. More clangs and thumps echoed through the comms.

"Get us in the air." Rebeka's voice filled the bridge, even though she was still in the cargo bay. Tink peered at the screen that showed the gangway retracting.

Ish tugged the stick, and the ship whined.

Tink tapped her comms. "Um, maybe we should wait for Alek."

"Now." Rebeka made the word a command. A clink and a hiss followed, and Tink realized the ramp was up. The airlock was closed, and the team had started decon.

Tink flicked off the comms and arched an eyebrow at Ish. "Why do I feel like this isn't about the approaching ships?" Her eyes widened. "Jacks! The ships." She grabbed her tablet again and scrolled through the sensor data. "Ugh, it looks like those Manta clippers again." She zoomed in on an empty area of blank space ... too blank.

"Cass, what do you see here?" Even as she spoke it resolved into a Dominion cruiser. "Bleeding Hades."

"Maybe they'll deal with the Mantas?" Ish snorted at his own words, then tugged the stick towards him. The ship responded with a juddering tilt and roll.

"What are you doing to my ship?"

"If you don't like what he's doing, you could take his place."

Tink turned to see Rebeka enter the bridge followed by the rest of the crew and their two guests. Even Grim padded along behind them.

"And get out of mine." Alek tapped her shoulder.

Tink snickered and stood. "My flying is worse than Ish's." She flopped into her own seat beside the captain's. "Doesn't change the question."

"I'm getting us away from those ships."

"I think you need to work on your nav skills." Kandi woke up her console. "You're headed towards them."

"No, I'm headed towards that slip point." His right hand flicked towards the teal ripples of his holodisplay. "Phi 1°, rho 2, zeta 0.5."

"That's ... close." Tink stroked Grim as he settled in her lap. "I thought it didn't work well that close in."

"It doesn't."

Catching his sober expression, Tink stayed quiet.

"There's more than just the clippers and that cruiser." Kandi flicked through the screens on her Tac console, then cast one up on the main display. "It looks like our angel is back."

Tink scowled at the image.

"Slip point in 5...4...."

"Got it, Cass." Ish's fingers moved over the holodisplay.

In the space of a heartbeat, the ship dropped into the stream. Tink's stomach did its usual heave and roll. And then tossed and turned as normal space returned. The viewscreen displayed the ice moon they'd passed on their way in, but the ships hunting them had disappeared off the sensors.

"What the...." She dumped Grim off her lap as she scrabbled to unbuckle her belt. "Something must be wrong with the slip drive."

"Nothing's wrong with the slip drive." Ish ran his fingers through the holodisplay, flicking the ripples. "I blinked us."

"You what?" Rebeka stood up, crossing her arms.

"I took us into the slipstream and came out at another slip point within the system. Until we figure out what to do. Where to go."

"Is that even possible?" Alek craned his neck to peer at Ish.

"Obviously it is." Ish shrugged. "But then, this system is strange."

28: HARBIN

HARBIN SMILED AT *RAY Skate*'s scowl as the gangster flicked another bit of red foliage from his atmo suit.

"Are we done yet? We came. We saw. We found a mound. Common as mud." Skate picked something else from his suit. "Or bloody leaves."

"You're the one who insisted on joining us to explore the planet."

"No, I told you to go after the *Lyra*."

"Why, when they didn't find the *Celeste*?" Harbin stepped around a large rock to run the tip of his pulse rifle over the cleared patch of stone along the pyramid's base.

"What makes you sure of that?" Skate waved a hand at the same area.

"Because they would have had more mass going out than coming in." Liet shoved past the gangster to join Harbin. "Or there would have been two ships leaving."

"They'd have called their angel, wouldn't they?" Harbin lifted an eyebrow, suppressing a smile as Skate's expression went flat. Then he shifted his attention to Liet. "Report?"

"Other sides are all the same." She glanced back along the path that had disgorged them into this empty patch, then peered at the pyramid. "Except no clearing, no perpendicular paths." She crouched in front of the stones, a grim expression on the sliver of face visible in the profile of her helmet.

Harbin stepped back, frowning at the solid stone — not so solid, according to the *Argent*'s scans. "I don't like it, but we'll have to wait for the scientific team to get here."

"No, no scientists. And no waiting." Skate pressed his hand against the stone above Liet's head.

"That decision isn't yours to make" His voice shifted to a whisper, his comms directed to Skate alone. "Lady Koning won't leave this unexamined. Her team is already on their way."

Skate stepped towards him, jostling Liet as he did. He came so close his helmet almost bumped Harbin's. "The more people who know about this place, the more people to expunge."

Harbin snorted. "Lady Koning's people are the ones who do the expunging. She'll decide if this needs to be scrubbed or shared with the Dominion." He turned away from Skate to peer at the stone. "Hopefully, the scientists will have more success getting in," he muttered, forgetting the others could hear every word.

"If we can't get in, it's time to go after the *Lyra*. They could be a solar system away by now."

"Your pet archaeologist is still on board." Harbin squinted at the pyramid and pursed his lips. "But you're right, no use waiting. I'll leave a small contingent to guard the ruins, then we'll head out. Liet, head back to the ship and send Rao's squad, prepped to stay."

At his feet, Liet shifted. But it wasn't to stand. Instead, she reached out and pressed her hand into the stone.

"Liet." Harbin started to repeat his order when a rumble emanated from the pyramid. Stones fell away, like they were being swallowed by the hole that formed.

"How—" Skate eyed Liet.

"There was a hand print." She shrugged, the movement barely visible in her suit. "I put my hand in it."

Harbin squinted at his Second. He appreciated her initiative in a fight. Not so much in front of a mysterious mound on a forgotten planet. Skate stepped forward.

Harbin grabbed the man's arm. "What are you doing?"

"Going inside." The sneer was audible.

"You have no idea what's in there."

"Not the *Celeste*."

"Liet, you go first. Make sure there's nothing lurking to kill our guest. For some reason, I don't think Archon Koning would like that."

Liet's expression was unreadable before she turned and disappeared into the darkness. Skate trailed close behind.

Harbin turned to the two men from his crew and the woman Skate had brought with him. "You lot stay here, make sure nothing sneaks up on us." Pulling out his blaster, he followed Skate into the pyramid.

"Nothing." Harbin examined the interior. The blue malachite floors merged with the malachite walls — he felt like he was drowning in a sea of stars. Adrift in darkness. A part of him was grateful to find nothing there, though a small piece had hoped to end this snipe hunt.

"Of course, there's nothing." Skate's tone was imperious. "If there were something, the *Lyra* would have taken it."

"That's not nothing." Liet pointed her pulse rifle at the obelisk and the bowl of opalescent stones in front of it. The stones matched those on the pillars at the entryway.

Skate thrust his hand into the bowl. "This? This is nothing. Just moonstones." He plucked one out, turning the alabaster rock in the light. It did appear to be a rather ordinary white stone.

"Do you think you should just be picking things up in a hidden pyramid on a bloodshot planet?" Her scar wrinkled with her sneer.

Skate turned the stone in his hand, peering at it, then he slowly dropped it into his palm and flung it at her.

Liet dodged the stone and grabbed her blaster in one smooth move. Only reflexes Harbin had honed to perfection in the Dominion marines saved them all from injury.

Harbin grabbed her wrist, forcing her arm down. His eyes narrowed as he peered at the gangster. *Maybe I should have let her shoot him.* He sighed. "No, Halcyon wouldn't like that," he mumbled.

Skate smoothed the front of his atmo suit. "What did you say?"

"We should go." He focused on Liet, and she gave a sharp nod. "There's nothing here." Not waiting for Skate to agree, he spun on his heels and headed towards the door.

29: TINK

A SLIVER OF CERULEAN moon hung in the viewscreen, an entourage of rocky moonlets scattered around it. A hush that made Tink's skin crawl blanketed the bridge. Dustan got up from his jump seat... she wasn't the only one who was antsy.

She glared at him. "If your quest endangers my ship—"

"I have dibs on killing him." Rebeka didn't even look at her ex. "Alek, you're sure they can't see us here?"

Alek's head shook. "I'm not sure of anything right now. But I nestled us in the best hiding spot I could find until we decide what to do."

"What do you mean, 'decide'?" Dustan paced in the small space between the captain's chair and office. "You saw what was down there."

"No, I didn't." Ish craned his neck to glare at everyone in turn. "What happened?" He turned his seat around, elbows on his knees, chin in his hands. His eyes shone as he glanced at the crew who'd been outside. "Tell me everything."

"You saw." Rebeka jerked her chin at the viewscreen. "You were monitoring us."

He shook his head. "I saw your helmet cam video, but as soon as you entered that structure, it cut out. Just snow."

"Cass, do you have the video from the cams?" Tink tapped her tablet, swiping away the analysis of their mysterious beacon to pull up the ship data stores.

"Of course, Tink."

"Cast them onto the viewscreen." Ish swung back around.

As Cass complied, playing one video after another, Tink felt a burning sensation in her stomach. Like a thousand flightless fire wasps crept over her intestines, leaving tiny pinpricks of flame. She swallowed against the hard lump in her throat.

"It's gorgeous." Ish's awe infused his hushed tones. "Like a ship of diamonds." Then he straightened and his voice became harder. "I can't believe I didn't get to see that in person."

"It wasn't that great." Fennick slouched further into his jump seat as the vid from his helmet cam played on the screen. He kept his hands stuffed in his pockets, even when Grim jumped onto his lap.

"No, it's most definitely not great." Tink squinted.

"What do you mean?" Dustan ceased his pacing, coming to a stop in front of her. He waved his hand at the viewscreen, which was paused on the hologram dissipating in starfall. "It's wondrous. The hologram alone is a treasure."

"It's a weapon." Tink stared at the frozen image, the fire wasps turned to ice spiders.

"What?" Dustan's hands dropped to his sides.

"The star scatter, spreading to all those figures? A biological weapon."

"No, it ... the—" Dustan's cheeks went red.

"Cass." Rebeka stood up. "Repeat." She turned to Tink. "You're saying the *Celeste* is a weapon?"

She shook her head. "Whether it's the *Celeste* itself, or something it carries. Maybe it's just the specs for one." She pointed at the video, where the figures fell once more. "But that says weapon to me."

"Or it's just recounting history." Dustan turned from Rebeka to her, and back. "Nothing more sinister than that. There were a handful of figures. Maybe this weapon only killed 10 people."

Rebeka crossed her arms over her chest. "A weapon from the Desolation, and it only killed 10 people?"

"Captain." Kandi spun her seat around. "We're not as hidden as we'd hoped. Clippers inbound."

Rebeka sat back into the seat beside Tink. "I don't know what that hologram showed, but I do know all we'll learn sitting here is how good those Manta fighters are. Alek, get ready to fly. Everyone else, buckle up."

Alek shifted the stick, taking them closer to the blue-green ice moon. "Out of the solar system or back to one of your slip points, Ish?"

"Where do we want to go after?" He plucked at the waves in his holodisplay.

"What about Tink's coordinates?" Alek said as he glanced between his console and the viewscreen.

"Coordinates?" Rebeka craned her neck to peer at Tink.

Shifting in her chair, Tink glared at the back of Alek's head, then flicked her gaze to the captain, who continued to stare. She sighed. "The sound."

"The beacon." Dustan stepped closer. "Has your AI translated it?"

"I said buckle up." Rebeka shifted her regard to Dustan, but the reprieve was short-lived, and her keen gaze returned to Tink.

"No." Tink started to slouch but forced herself to sit up straight. "But there are numbers woven into it. A set of coordinates ... I think."

"Let's go then." Dustan shifted towards the viewscreen, as if that would make the ship move.

"Sit down, Dustan." Rebeka's tone was sharp. He hastened to comply, and she continued to stare at him until he slumped into the jump seat beside Fennick. "We have no idea where these coordinates lead—"

"Well, actually...." Tink leaned towards Rebeka, then caught her dark gaze and went silent.

"And we haven't decided to *not* drop you off at the nearest rock with breathable atmo.

"That would be the red planet," Fennick said, the words trailing off at the end.

Rebeka pursed her lips and turned to face the viewscreen. "We can discuss it later. Right now, we have bigger problems. Like getting away from those Mantas."

"And the Dominion cruiser following them." Kandi didn't turn from her station. "Should I plot a firing solution?" She paused then continued, her voice a sing-song. "Oh wait, our weapons wouldn't take down a gnat."

"Hey!" Tink stared at Kandi's back. "Emmon spent good ... medium money on the EMP."

Rebeka ignored them. "Alek, can you get us to the closest slip point? We'll figure the rest out from there."

Tink's stomach churned as the ship rolled around the moon, then suddenly slowed.

The muscles in Alek's neck tensed. "Not with that ship blocking my way."

"I don't think it was the cruiser that scared the Mantas away," Tink mumbled, slouching in her chair.

"Oh goody." Rebeka's tone was flat. "It looks like our angel is back."

30: ALEK

I'M SO SORRY, CAPTAIN." Ludovicus Visi's tone was calm, and his mouth formed a small smile as he peered at them from the viewscreen. Alek's eyes narrowed and the corners of his mouth tugged down – Dustan's angel investor or not, he wanted to get clear of the man asap. With hands pressed together in front of his chest, Visi would have resembled an Arcadian priest playing at sympathy if it weren't for the serpentine smile and the backdrop of a plush office on his own personal battle corvette. "That's all there is."

"Play it again." Rebeka's voice brooked no argument. Even though she'd already heard the garbled recording of her daughter's voice three times: *What is that ... a grave hides in the jungle ... Heaven's feet stand in a rain of death. Beware starfall.*

"Captain." Visi dropped his hands, splaying them open beside him, pretending at empathy. "It will do no good."

"Play it. Please."

Visi tipped his head to the side. Alek glanced back at the captain, noting the subtle signs of tension: lips pressed together, fingernails pressing into the handrail.

"Please." Dustan stepped closer to Rebeka, his gaze fixed on the viewscreen.

Visi glanced over his shoulder at someone who was off-screen, and the recording played again. Rebeka's gaze shifted slightly, barely sliding sideways. Towards Kandi. The Antaran craned her neck, tipping her head in a gesture that could almost be a nod. Alek pressed his jaw tight together to keep his realization to himself: Rebeka wanted the recording recorded.

As cover, he turned back to the screen. "You have no other information?"

Visi shifted his attention to Alek, his eyes tightening almost imperceptibly. He pressed the fingertips of his tented hands to the gleaming wooden desk in front of him. Alek recognized the grain, and that it would take an Archon's yearly income to afford.

"No. It came through the wire. People who know my fondness for history keep an eye on all the archaeological digs."

From over Alek's shoulder, the captain snorted, likely thinking the same thing he did: Ludovicus Visi's only *fondness for history* involved pillaging rare artifacts.

The gangster slid his gaze back to Rebeka. "I'm sorry to be the bearer of troublesome tidings. Perhaps it's not what it sounds like. But maybe we can take the opportunity to discuss business."

There was a beep, and Alek realized the captain had muted their transmission to Visi. "Kandi, anything?" Her jaw barely moved as she spoke.

"Not yet." The woman's blue hair bobbed as she nodded at the display in front of her. "But he's getting another transmission. Not via ansible."

Alek turned to face Rebeka, his back to the viewscreen. "So, someone close. Dominion or Mantas?"

She flicked her eyes to him but otherwise gave no acknowledgment.

"Captain?" Visi almost managed to keep his voice even, but even at a distance, Alek heard the edge.

With a scratch of her finger there was another beep. "There's nothing to discuss, Visi."

"How can you say that? You've been to the red planet's surface."

"As have you." Rebeka's eyebrow arched, and Alek swivelled to face the viewscreen, splitting his attention between examining Visi's expression and trying to plot an escape route: he wanted to know which way to go if they needed to flee. During the long silence that descended, flickering to his right caught his eye. Without moving his head, he tried to make out what it was. It only took a few seconds to recognize Ish's search for slip points. Ish had said they were rare on the stellar plane, and unstable this close to the centre of the system. But they'd already found two that led them in a circle.

Finally, Visi responded to Rebeka's assertion. "Yes. Quite the phenomenal building for an otherwise lifeless planet."

"Maybe it wasn't always lifeless."

"Imagine it. Untouched for who knows how long. Until you. With my interest in history, I'd like to see your recordings for myself."

Rebeka's lips pressed together, and her eyes flicked to Alek before she clasped her hands behind her, pulling her shoulders back. then she turned her gaze to the screen. "Certainly. Cass."

"Yes, Captain."

"Play the helmet cam recordings of the recon team, starting with Fennick."

As the recordings played, first the assistant's then Dustan's followed by those of Kandi, the captain and himself, a heaviness settled in Alek's stomach, like he'd swallowed a lump of clay. The sensation grew, filling his chest, as he watched an alternate version of events play out, one that bore little resemblance to his own memories. He swallowed against the lump in his throat as he forced his expression to stay neutral and to keep his eyes on the recording as it played beside Visi's face on the viewscreen.

"Again." That word had more harsh edges than it should, and it drew Alek's attention to Visi. The gangster's face was even paler than usual, his knuckles alabaster as he spidered his fingers on his desk.

"There's nothing more." Rebeka's voice was hoarse but even, her face a mask.

Visi's eyes narrowed. "I would hate to think you were keeping anything from me."

"Me too." The captain's gaze slid sideways, grazing Alek. She blinked and her focus was back on Visi. "Play it again, Cass."

The recording played again. Just as before, it deviated in key places from the events Alek had witnessed with his own eyes.

It showed Fennick pressing his hand to the stone and a door opening. Darkness ensued until he found his way to the centre of the pyramid, still stunning without a holographic ship. It showed Dustan arriving and almost tripping over himself in wonder at the cavernous interior, entirely empty except for the plain obelisk. The captain and himself followed with more subdued amazement.

There was no golden *Celeste*, no army of glitter, no orb tucked into the ebony obelisk. Only their hasty retreat at the arrival of the Mantas in the sector remained unchanged.

It was a seamless recreation of something that never happened.

"Perhaps your flawed AI made a mistake, didn't record everything." Visi brought his fingers together in front of him, pressing his index fingers to his lips.

"I don't make mistakes," Cass said. It almost sounded as if the AI sniffed at the end. Silence descended. Even the usual beeps and whirs of the bridge seemed muted.

"The map was wrong." Dustan frowned. "There was nothing there. Just some speckled pebbles and a black obelisk."

"I want to examine the recordings. In person."

"Of course. Maybe Dunstan and Fennick can bring them to you when we drop them off on the nearest habitable planet."

"Drop us off?" Dustan's voice squeaked.

"We have work to do."

"Work?" Visi sneered. "What work?"

"Scrounging up odd jobs is a job in itself." The captain's tone was back to normal. "Leaves little time to examine boring recordings of empty pyramids. But, with your keenness for archaeology, maybe you'll spot something we didn't."

"My thanks." The words were clipped, but the gangster tipped his head. "As you say, maybe I'll see something informative." Visi stood up, his face a mask of carven wax. "If you stop at Nefti Station, I can pick Mr. Key up there."

"I...." Dustan stood and glanced at Rebeka, tugging his tunic down. "I have some unfinished business here."

Alek breathed a sigh of relief that the archaeologist didn't mention the beacon. He was certain they wouldn't get out of there without Visi commandeering the ship if he had.

"Sex with your ex is not business." Visi held up a hand as Dustan shifted beside Alek's shoulder. "Besides, I don't care. I want those recordings and your research."

"But...I have another clue I can follow up."

"What clue?" The words dripped like freezing rain from Visi's lips.

"There's...." Dustan glanced around the bridge but was met with the collective scowl from the crew of the *Lyra* and fire in Rebeka's eyes. He peered down at the hem of his tunic, which he still held in his hands. Letting go and running his hands over his stomach, he continued, his voice almost a whisper. "There's the other planet, the green dot."

Visi's eyes narrowed as he peered at the archaeologist. "How do you know it's not another false friend?"

"I—" Dustan cleared his throat. "Juniper's research mentions a different pyramid, in a verdant jungle. I didn't think anything of it until...." He waved at the viewscreen.

"Another one?" Visi lifted an eyebrow. "And how will you get there if the *Lyra* won't take you?"

Alek glanced from Dustan to Rebeka. The captain looked as if she was about to flail her ex alive. Then a blip on the corner of the viewscreen, which still showed the space around them, drew his attention.

"Uh, captain?"

She focused her ire on him, and he nodded at the screen. Her lips pressed tight for a second. "Fine. We'll give you a ride to the next planet with actual inhabitants. You can pick him and his research up there."

"Maybe our angel would be so good as to keep that Dominion cruiser from disturbing Dustan's research so I can fly us out of here."

Visi's gaze flicked down to something in front of him, and his own lips thinned. "One more snipe hunt. Then I'm collecting what you owe one way or another. Remember, you owe me a ship." A slick smile bloomed on his face. "Take care out there. It's a dangerous universe. It would be a shame if something happened to the *Lyra* before I could collect." With that the screen blinked out.

"I guess he doesn't want the recordings then," Alek said as he glanced back at Rebeka.

"What recordings?" She slumped into her seat. "You mean the creative fiction Cass put together?"

"Yeah, that."

Silence blanketed the bridge. A Cass AI going off script was enough to make anyone nervous.

"Ish, Alek, can one of you get us far away from here?"

Alek half shrugged his shoulders, half rolled them. "I'm bound by the physics of normal space."

Beside him, Ish shifted. "This system is...." His fingers plucked at a convergence of ripples on his holodisplay.

"Unusual," Rebeka finished for him. "I know, you said. Have you found another slip point or not?"

"It's not so much a point as a...." His fingers twitched. "... seam." He turned to the captain. "But it seems to be following the laws of stream dynamics."

"Seems to?" Alek mouthed, and Ish rolled his eyes.

"There are laws to the stream?" Tink snorted.

Ish ignored her. "It's a downdrift. Teramaki theorized—" A klaxon blared, cutting off his next words, and the ship shuddered.

"Kandi?" the captain asked.

"Manta pulse cannon strafed our rear stabilizer."

Alek turned to refocus on the controls, taking them even closer to the green moon, slaloming through its companion moonlets.

"I guess our angel isn't going to keep them off our butts," she said. "Ish, how far to this not-a-point?" The ship rattled as another shot got too close.

"It's at phi 5°, rho 6, zeta 2."

"Let's go."

"But he said Teramaki *theorized*!" Dustan's voice rose an octave. "Theory."

"Most of stream astrodynamics is theory we haven't proven wrong yet," Ish said, as Alek caught his fingers moving out of the corner of his eye. "Alek, can you shake them enough to let me fly?"

"Are you sure?"

"We need to hit the drift at the right angle."

"I'll see what I can do." Alek tugged the stick, rolling them around a moonlet.

"Even then it'll be a bumpy entry. I suggest everyone buckle up."

A worm of doubt gnawed at Alek, hearing a question in Ish's tone. But if Ish said he could get them into the stream, Alek had little choice but to trust him. He jerked the stick, taking them around the backside of the next moonlet, then shot them out the other side.

"Slip...drift coming up in 10...9...." He pulled the stick closer, silently asking the *Lyra* for all she had. "Get ready to fly, Ish."

"Ready."

Alek kept hold of the stick, making sure Ish had control before he let himself release it. He squinted at the viewscreen. A ribbon of space undulated with the colours of Ish's display. He tipped his head to the side at a momentary fragment of music, then he blinked, and the ribbon disappeared. After that, he didn't have time to think as they hit the drift, and the ship shuddered.

31: TINK

GRIM'S PURR RUMBLED AGAINST Tink's tummy as she absentmindedly stroked his back with one hand while the other held Kandi's stave. She stroked her thumb along a certain spot on the grip, and one end collapsed into the hilt. Grim turned his head and hissed.

When she reversed the motion to expand it again, the opposite end collapsed. "You...."

Tink glanced at the table, scattered with pieces she hadn't yet found a home for while reassembling the device. The Antaran stave was a marvel of engineering. Almost like magic. But not quite. It reminded her of one of her uncle's many adages: at the heart of all magic is incomprehension and a willingness to believe. Tink wasn't sure she agreed, but she did believe in curiosity and engineering, and that she had all the parts needed to fix it ... plus one that didn't belong.

Her lips pursed, and she bent over the control circuit again as she picked up her plasma pen.

"Poseidon's pox!" Tink glowered at the stave as she sucked a finger numbed by a jolt of electricity. Her eyes narrowed as she pulled her finger out of her mouth. "We're doing this whether you want to or not."

She glanced at the door of the common room. She was still alone, so no one heard her mutter at the inanimate, disassembled object. With a huff, she leaned in again.

Almost as soon as she did, a shadow filled the doorway, and she glanced up. Her eyebrows tugged together.

"Hey, Ish." She straightened. "Shouldn't you be on the bridge? Given that we ...drifted...into the stream?"

He shook his head as he opened the fridge, peered inside then closed it again, empty handed. "Nah, Cass can handle it for a bit. We're in the stream now, however we got here. Alek is watching her."

"Have you ever done that before?"

He shook his head again as he stared into the cupboard. "No."

"Not even simulations in training?"

He closed the door, a bag of fried crickets in hand, and turned to her. His mouth opened then shut, and he twisted to grab a bowl. "No one has ever done that before," he said as he concentrated on dumping the bugs into the bowl. "There are no simulations."

"Really?" Tink stopped what she was doing, putting her tools on the table.

"So far as I know."

"I ... wow." She picked up her plasma pen again, then paused, tipping her head to the side. "Maybe don't tell the others that."

"Too late. Fennick knows." He shrugged. "Aren't you supposed to be figuring out what's generating the beacon we're transmitting?" He lifted a mug and raised his eyebrows. "Coffee?"

Tink spun the stave on her palm and nodded, gracing him with a big smile as she reached for the mug he held out to her. While she took a sip, he made one of his own then slumped into the chair opposite.

Grim promptly jumped off her lap and onto Ish's, turning circles and kneading his stomach.

"I know where it's coming from: us." She quirked an eyebrow and took a sip of coffee. "And I think we all know what caused it."

"But the orb went with Dustan into the soundproof pyramid." Ish scritched Grim's head.

"Just because it's not the thing transmitting it doesn't mean it didn't cause it."

"Fair enough. Then shouldn't you be working on how to keep it from broadcasting our location to the universe?"

She spun the stave in her free hand as she shook her head. "I don't need to figure that out. It stopped itself." She halted her spinning, putting the stave down. A frown tugged her eyebrows together as she clutched the mug in her hands and stared at the wisps of steam that rose from the surface of the dark liquid. "Which worries me more."

"Why?"

She lifted a shoulder. "What if it means the intended recipient got the message?" Ish was quiet, and she lifted her head to peer at him. He was busy scratching behind Grim's ears, and a small smile sat on his lips, as if he hadn't heard her. "What's up with you?"

He glanced up at her with a look like he'd been caught doing something he shouldn't. He quickly shifted his gaze to the bits and pieces scattered across the table. "Whatcha working on?"

"Don't try to deflect. You have something on your mind." She grabbed circuits and wires, tucking them into her toolbox. "Go ahead. I'm listening."

Ish snorted. "Do I need to go lie on the chesterfield?" She grimaced at him. He scrunched his lips then continued. "I'm just annoyed. I never get to go on any adventures."

Tink reached for the flux cable and transcoils and threw them into the box. "If it makes you feel better, you're critical to the ship." She picked up her plasma pen and waved it in his direction. "Almost as critical as I am."

"No, it doesn't. I swear, I'm more sheltered here than I was at home."

"At least here, you don't have your father looming over your shoulder, governing what you can wear, deciding where you can go, dictating who you can love." Tink stopped, her arm mid-reach. She'd seen the looks Fennick cast Ish's way, and had watched her friend respond, despite the studious young archaeologist being so different from his usual type. Who knows, maybe Ish's father would have approved of an Academy archaeologist.

She snapped the box shut and pulled the stave and her plasma pen closer. *If Ish falls in love, will he leave?*

Ish slumped in his chair, stuffing his hands in his pockets. "But if I'm never allowed off the ship, what does it matter?" His hair flopped down, covering half his face and making him look like a teenager.

"You're allowed off." Tink lifted her head, catching his scowl. "Just not in the jungle of some uncharted planet when we have gangsters pursuing us. In port, where we can find another navigator if you disappear."

He pulled a face. "Thanks. I feel so needed."

"Or get swept up in the throes of young love."

He rolled his eyes at her, a smile twitching the corners of his lips, but it was quickly replaced by a frown. "What I do in port is not love." Grim merruped, and Ish stroked him again. "And in a crew of 5, it's hard to find a man to come home to."

"Truer words...." Tink paused, trying to recall the last time she'd taken full advantage of shore leave. Instead, black hair and blue eyes flashed in her mind's eye, and she breathed in, down to her toes. Exhaling slowly, she tried to clear the image. "But I wasn't referring to the men in port." She smiled at him as his cheeks flushed.

He gave her a sidelong look, then pulled his hand out of his pocket. When he opened his fingers, a milky white stone veined with streaks of sparkling blue sat on his palm.

"What's that?"

"Fennick gave it to me. He felt bad that I couldn't go with them to the temple."

"The temple?"

"That's what he calls it. So, he brought a piece of it back for me."

Tink's stomach quivered. She told herself it was sympathy for the nascent flutterings of new love, not some ancient temple rock sitting on her ship. Her fingers inched along the table towards it. "Can I see?"

Ish stared at her for a few moments as he clutched it in his long fingers.

"I just want to check it out. With the specs." She pointed to the goggles perched on her head.

He lay his palm flat again and reached towards her. Her fingers hovered over it, but she didn't touch it. Instead, she flipped her goggles down.

As she cycled through lenses, her frown deepened and the fluttering in her stomach turned to a lump.

"What?" Ish leaned forward. "What do you see?"

Tink opened her mouth, before snapping it shut and cycling through the lenses again. Just to be sure. Then she turned to Ish, his face distorted until she flipped the goggles up. "Nothing." She peered at the object, not wanting to touch it. "It's the same in every view."

"So?"

"So, when I say nothing, I mean nothing. An absence of all things."

She started to say more when footsteps sounded in the corridor, and in a blink, Ish's fingers wrapped around the stone, and he dropped it in his pocket.

Dustin entered, trailed by Fennick. The latter glanced at Tink then Ish and blushed.

Dustin's hand hovered over Ish's head for a second, as if he was going to ruffle his hair. Instead, he patted Ish on the shoulder. "So, when do we get out of this stream?"

"Not a fan?" Ish asked as Dustin when to the coffee machine.

"He says it makes him dizzy." Fennick slumped into the seat next to Ish.

"It *does*." He sat across from Fennick and dropped his tablet and a hefty book – a real book – onto the table. "It makes my insides feel like they're on a fun ride."

"You're not the only one." Tink pulled her goggles off and rubbed her temples. Voices sounded in the hall, and a few seconds later, Kandi and Rebeka joined them.

Rebeka paused at the doorstep, staring at Dustin for a second. He was oblivious to her regard, already examining something on his tablet. Rebeka pursed her lips, then entered. "So, what's this clue you found in Juniper's research?" she asked, her back to Dustin as she made herself a coffee.

Tink watched him lift his head slightly as his eyes went wide.

"I...." he started. "There isn't one. I just said that to keep Visi off our backs." He flipped a page in the book.

"Our backs?" Tink turned her coffee mug around in her hands. "It's your back he wants."

"You're in this now." Dustin snorted, then his face fell. "For which I apologize."

"What he's saying is neither Visi nor the Mantas will leave us alone until one of them has the *Celeste*." Rebeka glared at Dustin from where she leaned against the counter.

"And the other is beaten into submission," Kandi added. "And let's not forget that Dominion cruiser wants a piece of us too."

"So, we find the *Celeste* or else." Tink peered into the dregs of her coffee.

"So ... let's make the best of it." Ish leaned forward. "What would you do with your share?" He jostled her with his elbow. "You have to have thought a little bit about it."

"Repair the portside lateral gyro." She nodded as she thought of all the work she could fund with a share of the treasure. "Replace the bilge tank filter."

Ish rolled his eyes. "That's so ... you." He draped an arm around her shoulders when she pulled a face. "And I love you for it. But there's more to life than this ship. Don't you want to travel somewhere in luxury? Go to Metropolis. Stay in a royal suite at the Luxe."

"That is so *not* me." Tink snorted and ran a hand over her oil-stained coveralls. "They wouldn't let me in the door."

"Not without cleaning the grease out from under your fingernails." Ish laughed and squeezed her shoulder.

"Besides, if we live through this, I imagine there'll be even more repairs I need to make to the *Lyra*."

The *Lyra* shimmied, and Tink grabbed the stave and her plasma pen to keep them from rolling off the table. The hum of the ship changed. A hiccough followed, and the queasiness in Tink's stomach settled. They were out of the stream.

She frowned at Ish. "Did you expect that?"

He shook his head and stared at the door. "Wouldn't be here if I did."

Rebeka tapped her wrist. "Alek, why are we out of the stream?"

Alek's voice crackled over the comms. "Cass says we're near Port Osoyoos."

Ish shook his head. "More warning next time, Cass."

"Of course, Ish."

He rolled his eyes. "She's getting worse. I won't be able to let her slip at all if she keeps this up. Another thing to add to your list of repairs — a checkup for Cass."

"You could buy a new ship," Dustan said without looking up from his tablet and the book he skimmed with his finger. He raised his head at Ish's gasp, looking from him to Tink to Kandi and Rebeka. "What?"

"The *Lyra* is more than Tink's ship. It's her home." Rebeka leaned forward to take a crispy bug from the bowl. "Mine too."

"So, what would you do with your share, Beka? Repair the—" Dustan waved his hand at the captain before turning back to his work, ignoring the thin line of her lips. "What was it? The bilge tank filter?"

"Yeah. And replace the coffee machine. Upgrade the fridge."

"Not go see our daughter?" He peered studiously at his book, though his finger didn't move.

"I doubt Juniper wants to see me."

"You don't know, you—" Dustan coughed into his elbow.

"What about you?" Rebeka grabbed a bug from the bowl. "And Fennick? What are your plans after this? Assuming you survive."

Dustan peered at his sleeve, then rolled it up. "Fund more research. Clearly."

Fennick shifted in his chair and stopped his reach towards the bugs. As Tink watched him, he lifted his head and saw her. He swallowed and grabbed a handful of the roasted bugs, glancing at Ish as he shovelled the snack into his mouth.

"What would you do, Ish?" he asked, the words muddled by crunching wings and carapaces. He swallowed and gulped a mouthful of water to wash them down.

"I'd help my mom send my sisters to the Academy at Exo. Then I *would* go to the capital and stay in the King's suite at the Luxe Palladium." He put his hands behind his head and leaned back, bringing his feet up to the table. "And watch the games from a noble's box. Dance at the Masquerade. And I would pay them so much they couldn't turn me away."

"Feet off the table." Fennick echoed the order that usually came from the captain's lips, and Tink had to suppress a giggle as she watched Rebeka's eyebrow lift. "And they can always turn you away."

Ish dropped his feet to the floor. "Yeah, I know. It's the bloodline you have, not the chits you carry."

"Or who you know." Dustan glanced around. "Sometimes it's who you know. I've watched the Imperial games from a noble's box. Overrated."

"Really?" Ish's mouth gaped.

"Kandi, how about you?" Tink asked before Ish could question Dustan about the games.

She shook her head. "Nope, never watched the games at the capital, or in a noble's box anywhere."

"I mean, what would you do?"

Kandi peered at her, her gaze falling to the widget Tink was futzing with: her stave. She shrugged. "Don't know. Maybe donate some money to the Sisters. You know, pay them back for caring for my brother." She stretched her arms up and back in an over-exaggerated yawn. "I'm knackered. I'm going to catch a catnap."

She scooped Grim up from the floor. The cat grunted but settled into her arms.

Tink took that as her opportunity to leave. She didn't want to listen to Dustan malign her ship ... or Ish make plans to leave it. Stopping at the kitchenette, she refilled her mug with coffee.

Rebeka came up beside her and grabbed another mug. "I should take some to Alek," she said, and Tink looked sidelong at her, taking note of the bags under her eyes and the tightness around her lips. "Keep him awake as we approach the station."

"I can do it." Tink reached for the mug.

The captain turned to peer at her, an eyebrow lifted. "From 'we should drop the cocky pilot off on the nearest rock' to bringing him coffee?"

"What?" Tink shrugged. "I won't be able to sleep anyway. Too much coffee already."

Hot coffee sloshed onto her hand when she spun on her heels and left, and she cursed silently.

32: Rebeka

"Tell me again." Rebeka scuttled around the bridge on her hands and knees. She grimaced — there were better ways to kill time waiting to go through the Osoyoos Gate to Nefti Station. Shaking her head, she tried to clear away the memory of Dustan's stubble on her breast...she was going to kill him when this was over.

Ish sighed. "There's nothing to tell. Tink said it just stopped."

Rebeka blinked, coming back to the present. "So, the source of the beacon is still here somewhere." Her simmering irritation — at Visi, at Dustan, at the whole snipe hunt — threatened to bubble over. It made her blood pound in her ears.

He shook his head, and his hair flopped over his eyes. "Tink can't find it. Cass can't either."

"Maybe Cass doesn't want to," Alek muttered. She shot a glare at him, but he remained focused on his console.

"It has to be here." She glanced up at Ish.

He stopped his chair spinning circles, and his fingers started tapping his thigh. He shrugged. "Maybe it was outside and got blasted...."

"Jacks!" She slammed her hand against the deck.

"You found something?" Kandi asked, as she scoured her half of the bridge.

Rebeka sat back on her heels ... or attempted to. On her way, her head whacked the underside of her own chair. "Poseidon's Pox!" She plopped her butt on the floor and rubbed the back of her head. Shifting to rest her forearms on her knees, she shook her head. "No. I just don't like this."

"So, we can stop?" Alek asked from the pilot's chair. "We've been over this bridge twice."

"*You* have not, fly boy." Kandi stood up and pointed a finger at him. "You and Ish got to sit back and relax while we crawled around on our hands and knees."

"We were plotting important route information." Alek picked up the mug beside him and took a glug.

Rebeka snorted as she stood up. "You mean *Cass* was plotting important route information."

"Yes Captain?" Cass' voice wafted over the bridge.

"Sorry, nothing." Rebeka slumped in her chair.

"Okay." Cass' tone was downright chipper.

"Wait." She sighed and gave her head a shake. "Did you find any evidence of a transmitter in your scans?"

"No Captain. I can keep scanning, but there is still no sign of the beacon's source on the ship. Unless there's some technology to hide it from me."

That possibility made Rebeka's stomach twist: there were too many people with too much impossible tech sailing the Black these days. If Manta clippers could create their own slip points, someone could slip a beacon or tracker into some out of the way corner of the ship without her knowing. Or hide it right in front of her. Her gaze trawled the bridge before settling on the viewscreen, which displayed the rippling blue jump gate of Port Osoyoos. And the long line of ships in front of them.

She jerked her chin at Alek. "Any ETA on when it's our turn to go through? And get your feet off the dash." She frowned at him. His bulky frame had to almost jackknife to get his feet up that high. "How do you even do that?"

"Mad skills." He waggled an eyebrow but dropped his feet and turned around. "No ETA yet." A red light blinked on his console. "In fact, it looks like someone wants to talk to us." He turned his head to look at her.

"No one talks to us." Ish scowled and sat down at his own console. "Our ship talks to their bot."

"Unless something is wrong." Alek looked sidelong at his console.

"Unless they refuse to talk to a Cass." Kandi pulled up a screen at her station.

"Unless someone wants to stop us going through." Rebeka ran through the possibilities, but there was nothing for it — they had to answer the call. "Let's hear it."

Alek tapped his console. "This is the *Lyra*, registration DLH-8789A."

"*Lyra*, please pull out of line," said a robotic voice from the gate keeper's command centre. "Prepare for inspection."

Alek tapped the light again and turned to Rebeka. "Captain?"

Rebeka absentmindedly trailed her fingers over Grim's back as he passed by her chair.

"Ships are leaving the Customs House," Kandi said as she sat down. "Headed this way."

Grim pawed at Rebeka's hand. As she pulled it away, she tugged her jacket down and sat taller. "Pull out." She pressed her palm to the comms on the armrest. "All hands, prepare to be boarded." Even though Tink was technically the only crew not on the bridge, Rebeka wanted to let Dustan know — she expected it was his fault customs officials would soon be crawling over her ship like bugs ... like beetles of indeterminate legality. Her stomach fluttered.

"Barnacles." She rubbed her palm on her forehead, then tapped the comms again. "Everyone but Alek, get to the cargo bay stat. Tink, bring blankets."

Ish tipped his head as he peered at her. She saw the second when he realized what she had — they had a cargo bay full of contraband bugs reaching the end of their stasis. "The insects. I'll get the secondary hold ready." He took off at a sprint, followed closely by Kandi.

Rebeka turned to Alek. "Stall them for as long as you can." Then she followed Kandi and Ish.

As she reached the stairs to the cargo bay, she met Tink lugging blankets, helped by Fennick. "Give me those," she said to the young man. He made to protest. "You're still recovering from being shot, while I'm an old war horse."

"Not really." He clenched the blankets tighter.

"Here." Tink thrust her side towards Rebeka, who graced her with a grimace but took the load.

Inside the bay, Ish had the panel to the smuggler's hold open, and Kandi was already sliding the first crate of bugs towards it.

Dropping the blankets on the floor, Rebeka headed to the second one. "Where's Dustan?" She kept her face neutral as she peered at Fennick. He stopped rubbing his wounded leg and shrugged.

"Here." Dustan strolled down the stairs. He'd cleaned up — showered even — and changed into fitted pants and a respectable tunic: the esteemed archaeologist. He filled out the suit well, but she already knew he was still fairly fit, despite the wrinkles and the rumples.

Rebeka squashed the fuzzy creature that wriggled in her belly. "Get your ass down here. You got us into this mess, you can help get us out."

He stepped up beside her and peered at the crate. "How do you know they're not here about your illegal bugs?"

She rolled her eyes at him and leaned into the crate. From inside came the hiss of rudely awakened bugs. Apparently, they were as cranky as she was first thing in the morning.

They'd just shoved the last crate into the overstuffed smuggler's hold — two holds actually, filling the gaps between the hull and the engine and utility rooms on either side of the ship — when she heard a thunk.

She tapped her comms. "Alek, I thought I told you to stall them."

"I tried. They're very keen to see what we have aboard this ship."

"Get those blankets over the crates then lock down the hold." She pointed at Dustan and Fennick. "You two, get back to your cabin. Make like paying passengers."

Dustan clasped a hand to his heart. "I offered to pay."

"Go." Rebeka's eyelid twitched. "Tink, with me." She headed towards the airlock. "Can you make it look like we had some difficulty opening our airlock?"

"I can make it so we *can't* open the airlock."

Momentarily tempted by the idea, Rebeka shook her head. "No, I want to get this over with and be out of here as soon as possible. If we can't open the lock, they'll just bring torches."

"And do a deeper search." Tink scowled at the window into the airlock.

Glancing over her shoulder, the doors to the hidden holds were still open. "How long?" Rebeka shouted.

"Five?" Kandi's disembodied voice said. "They are seriously pissed."

"You have two. Maybe."

Tink crouched in front of the airlock controls, screwdriver in one hand, some blue-lit widget in the other. Popping off the panel, she started mumbling, and Rebeka tapped the comms beside the airlock. "Alek, patch me through to the boarders."

"*Lyra*, registration DLH-8789A." A tinny voice crackled over the connection. "Umbilical seal is set. Open your outer airlock door."

"Who am I speaking to?"

"Not relevant."

"I just ... we're having a problem with the lock. Give us a minute."

There was a pause. Rebeka assumed the owner of the voice on the other side was ordering someone to scan the

Lyra. She glanced at Tink, who didn't look wholly convinced of her hack job.

The comms crackled again. "You have 30 seconds." The voice didn't need to say that at the 30-second mark, they'd get the cutting torches. Looking over her shoulder, she saw Ish and Kandi were out of the holds and setting the doors in place. Doors that looked for all the world like access hatches to grey water and cycler cleanouts...the most disgusting area on any long-haul ship.

"Time check?" Rebeka asked.

"Another minute." Kandi was tightening the latch by hand since Ish held the only ratchet.

"Done." He passed the tool to Kandi.

"30 seconds then."

"Ish, up to the bridge."

"But—"

"If they want to meet the crew, they need to ask."

"*Lyra,* open your air lock."

"Got it. We figured out the problem." She looked at Tink, raising her eyebrows.

"Aye, captain." Tink smirked. "The ... dip switch powering the ... clodpole is blown. Just a sec."

"The clodpole?" Rebeka mouthed, and Tink shrugged. At the sound of footsteps behind her, she turned to see Kandi run up the stairs.

"*Lyra,* open your door. Now."

"Got it." Tink disconnected her tablet from the door panel and closed it, and the outer airlock door slid open.

It was hard to tell for sure through the shiny faceplate on the Dominion soldier's suit, but he looked annoyed.

The soldier in charge — designated by the insignia on his black spacesuit — strode around the cargo bay as his lackeys searched the ship.

"Not a very good hauler if your cargo bay is empty." His voice rumbled through his tinted faceplate. He ran a gloved finger along a panel that needed to be cleaned. Rebeka frowned at Tink as the engineer shifted forwards from where she stood watch by the airlock, monitoring the tech trying to diagnose the "problem" that had prevented her from opening the door.

"That's why we're headed to Nefti station." Rebeka stood tall, hands behind her back. "Drop off our passengers and pick up our next load."

"And fix your airlock."

Rebeka tipped her head in agreement but stayed silent.

The soldier — Captain Gorse by his badge — glanced up at Dustan and Fennick, who stood at the top of the stairs being pat down by one of the other boarders, who'd just finished grilling them.

"A light load," Gorse said.

Rebeka snorted. "Then you have no idea how demanding two entitled, pampered academics can be."

With thudding boots, the other soldier came down the stairs and shook her head in her helmet, her lips pursing behind the visor. "They're travelling to Omalos, near Nefti. Academic research. Identities check out. A well-known — if slightly left-field archaeologist — and his assistant." She handed Gorse a tablet. Rebeka's eyes narrowed. Either the woman hadn't found Dustan's orb, or she didn't think it was anything important. Or her ex had hidden it somewhere; if so, she hoped he'd hidden it well, since a pod of customs inspectors still swarmed the ship.

Gorse swiped through the screens then started towards Dustan and Fennick. Just then a horrid hiss came from the portside smuggler's hold.

"Barnacles!" Tink stalked over to another panel, where she punched a series of buttons that Rebeka assumed did nothing. She hoped neither the soldier nor his minion knew much about the workings of a cargo ship. "Bleeding black water system. The flange is blown again." She glared at Rebeka with relish. "I told you." She waggled a tool at her. "We need to get it properly fixed, not just patch it." She swept the arm dramatically over the space, barely missing the minion. "Soon, this hold is going to be filled with shit. Again."

Rebeka frowned at her for a heartbeat before picking up the narrative, just as another hiss rattled from the hidden hold. "After the next job. When we have some money in the bank from those two." She waved at Dustan and Fennick. "For now, patch."

"That's what you said last time." Tink stabbed another button, and the hissing coincidentally quieted down. "You're not the one who has to crawl in there."

More pairs of boots stomped from the direction of the engine room, and the first soldier that appeared shook their head. Gorse continued to tour the cargo bay, coming to stand by Tink. Peering at the panel, he poked it. "A flange, you say?"

"I wouldn't do that if I were you." She glanced at Rebeka before returning her attention to Gorse. She shrugged. "Old ship, what can you do?"

"Hmm." He continued walking along the wall, towards the portside hold, and Rebeka's fingers itched to do something, but she kept them behind her back.

Boots thumped down the stairs. "Nothing in the crew quarters, sir. Pilot and navigator on the bridge. Amazon showed us around."

"Oh, she doesn't like when you call her that." Rebeka crossed her arms over her chest. "Maybe if you told us what you were looking for...."

"Illegal cargo." Gorse turned to his crew.

Rebeka shifted towards him, trying to psychologically nudge him towards the exit.

"We'd never traffic in contraband." Which was technically not completely untrue. The bugs weren't exactly illicit; they just weren't entirely legal either. They fell into a grey area, and their discovery would give the customs officers an excuse to tear the *Lyra* apart, bolt by bolt. And then they *would* find Dustan's orb. And, though she had no proof, every nerve in her body told her that's what they were after.

A raw exhale came from Gorse's ventilator. "Where is your final destination?"

"I told you." Rebeka's foot started tapping. "Nefti Station."

"After you pick up your cargo there?"

The captain's arms dropped to her sides. "That depends on—"

Then sound crackled in Gorse's helmet, and he stopped. His eyes slid to her before he turned away, tapping the side of his helmet. "Gorse." He listened to whoever was talking into his ear, his gaze flicking between the floor, her and Grim, who'd padded down the stairs after the soldiers. "But—" He nodded. "Yes sir."

Gorse stood up straight and looked around at his crew. "Move out."

Just then a loud spitting noise rose behind Rebeka. She stood stock-still, and Gorse turned to glare at her then peered over her shoulder.

"What was that?" He stepped past her, jostling her with his shoulder.

"I don't know," she said with all honesty as she turned around, though she knew it came from the hold. "A compressed air burst?"

He strode towards the hidden hold door, and Rebeka wracked her brain for an excuse. Just then something grey skittered out from behind the stairs. Grim, his back arched, danced forward, spitting and hissing at Gorse.

"Grim!" Tink reached towards the cat, who hissed at her then mrowled. After a second, he deigned to be picked up. "Be nice to our guests." She stepped towards Gorse, and Grim hissed again.

"Bloody cats. Vile creatures." The soldier sneered at Grim, and then turned on his heels and headed towards the airlock.

"You're done?" Rebeka asked, cursing herself for letting her annoyance seep into her tone. "We can get back in line?"

Gorse stopped. "You're free to go." Turning to her, he added, "Back of the line."

Rebeka opened her mouth to protest, but Tink elbowed her. Dustan and Fennick came down the stairs, and they all watched in silence as the customs crew cycled through the airlock.

When a thud let her know that their umbilical had disengaged, another rattling hiss sounded from the smuggler's hold. She reached over to scritch between Grim's ears. "You're getting an extra portion of kibble."

33: Harbin

Harbin's nose wrinkled as they emerged from the gate. Being back in the Green Zone, he swore he smelled the metallic tang of Ten Selva mixed with sewage.

"Where to, Sir?" Liet's shoulders moved as she swiped her hands across her console.

"After the *Lyra*."

"Sir? Shouldn't we ease off a bit after Gorse, let them think they're safe again."

A smile twitched on his lips. He liked the way she thought, and it would be his usual tactic ... but he wanted this over. His lips pressed together, and his eyes narrowed. "No. Hound them. Harry them. Force their hand."

A light blinked on his armrest: *Ray Skate*. He ignored it ... the man could wait. Did Ludovicus Visi really think that Harbin — a Dominion soldier, captain of his own ship, creature of the Archon Koning — wouldn't recognize one of the most powerful gangsters in the empire? The codename had been pointless when he'd first encountered Visi lurking in the darkness of his motel room and had even less purpose now. He snorted out loud, causing Liet to glance his way.

"Call me when we're closer." He strode to his room and closed the door, frosting the window as he did. Sitting down at his desk, he pulled up the map of the region. Selva, Archideus, Corican. And a glitter dusting of small ships between them all. He was sure that was only half of what was out there. The semi-legit ones. The rest had had their transponders altered, which would result in the ship and themselves being confiscated if they were caught.

He flicked the screen and shifted to the recording from the bug the Archon Koning had planted on Visi's ship, jumping to the man's last encounter with the crew of the *Lyra*. A smile crept onto his lips. "You'd think the man didn't trust the scavengers." The gangster's pale cheeks were blotched with red. Harbin took a sip of his whiskey, relishing the burn as it slid down his throat. Then the smile fell.

Apparently, the *Lyra*'s captain had had enough of adventure and of Visi's interference: it appeared she was trying to drop the treasure hunter and his assistant back where she found them. If she did that, he'd have to decide whether to follow the *Lyra* and make good on his promise to destroy it and its crew or pursue the archaeologist and his treasure map. He sighed. It wasn't his decision to make, and he already knew what the Archon would say. Halcyon Koning was, above all, practical.

He started the recording again, sipping his whiskey as he leaned back and listened. The rumpled archaeologist spoke. "There's the other planet, the green dot." Harbin sat up and paused the recording. He repeated the segment, bringing up his map of the sector beside it. He homed in on the academic, his mirth at Visi's discomfort forgotten.

A green planet. A jungle pyramid. "Huh, Aconitia."

He tapped his lip, then tapped his console. "Liet, plot a targeting solution on the *Lyra*."

"We'd have to drop the shroud to attack."

"I'm aware. I don't want to attack yet. I just want to know it's possible." He cut the comms and went back to watching Visi. His lips quirked into a smile again.

The screen went blank, a slate grey flecked with white stars. Harbin was left to wonder if Visi had connected the green pyramid planet to Corican V... Aconitia. A few seconds later, a light flashed on his console, accompanied by the beep of a pending direct message. Harbin stroked the console of the *Argent*, still appreciative of his new ship.

He watched the light blink for a half a minute, an eternity for him, and he was sure for Visi as well. Finally, he punched his finger at the slick black surface.

"Low here."

"You need to stop that ship." The voice held the sneer of command.

Harbin scrunched his lips. Maybe the gangster had also picked up on the location the old man revealed. "But why? They're headed into home territory."

"I don't have time for this."

"Halcyon says there's always time to be polite."

There was a brief pause on the other end, short enough that it could simply be inter-ship transit time. But Harbin knew it wasn't. He took a sip of whiskey and let the warmth suffuse his bones.

"Manta territory. Stop them." The tone was tight, the words clipped, and Harbin felt Visi's seething anger at that admission. "I'll send a crew to retrieve the archaeologist and his map."

"We're perfectly capable of taking him ourselves. And reporting back to Halcyon." This time the pause was obvious, and Harbin imagined Visi choking back his rage, his pale cheeks flushing like a cooked crab. The line went dead, and a trill of glee rippled in Harbin's gut.

"And now I know I'm right." They were getting close to the *Celeste*. And Visi had no intention of sharing.

He may not get to keep the riches from the *Celeste*, but he might get a little bit of the glory. At the very least, Halcyon might forgive him for failing her in not retrieving the boy from the *Leviathan* in his first encountered the *Lyra* and her crew.

As long as he could keep the ship and its passengers all going in the same direction.

The smile dropped from Harbin's lips, and he stabbed at his console. "Delphi, what's the status of that targeting solution?"

34: TINK

TINK SLAMMED HER SPANNER down on the phase inverter. It hadn't been damaged in the previous attack. Nothing had. The spanner slipped off the inverter and clattered to the floor. The noise hurt her ears and startled Grim, who'd been cleaning himself. He skittered behind one of the crates full of bugs.

"Grim." Her shoulders slumped as she sat back. Even the cat was on edge. "I'm sorry."

"I don't think that'll fix it."

Tink spun around in her crouch to find Alek emerging from below the stairs, his hair still wet from a shower. He lifted his tank top to wipe some drops off his face, giving Tink a glimpse of his torso, and its carved muscles criss-crossed with scars. Her cheeks flushed, and she grimaced at him.

"But it'll make me feel better."

"No, it won't." He ran a hand through his hair, shifting the damp strands back. It was getting long, like he hadn't cut it since coming on board.

"Besides, it's fine. Doesn't need fixing." Tink grimaced as she picked up her spanner and ran her hand over the inverter to see if she'd done any damage. Assured she hadn't done any damage, she put the spanner in her tool kit and shifted in her squat to face him.

He crouched in front of her, elbows on his knees, a long-sleeved shirt clenched in one hand. The muscles of his arms twitched as he found his balance. "What's bothering you?"

She arched an eyebrow. "Seriously?" She waved her hand at the universe then grabbed the nearest thing to keep from falling: his forearm. The skin was surprisingly soft, especially given the scars. She pulled her hand away, resting her fingers on the toolbox instead.

"If you're taking it out on the *Lyra*, it's something particular."

"I hit things all the time."

"You hit things with a purpose." His voice was low as he indicated the equipment with his shirt. "What would hitting that thingamajig accomplish?"

"Inverter." She shifted her toolbox in front of her so it sat between them, and then took a keen interest in examining its contents. "Nothing."

"So, what's wrong?" He reached his fingers out, as if to touch her chin, but drew his hand away when she lifted her gaze to meet his. He waved at the cargo bay. "The customs' inspection? Visi's technician on your ship?"

She shook her head. "Nah."

"You didn't seem keen on exploring some arcane, forgotten ... weird-ass structure. So not going on that little expedition isn't making you cranky like it is Ish."

She smiled. "No."

"So?" He shifted back to shrug into his shirt, and something in Tink's chest fluttered like a nocturna moth in the light.

Tink frowned as she tried to untangle her thoughts from her feelings. "Why are we going after the *Celeste*? Ludovicus Visi is just going to snatch it from us, whatever he says." She snapped her tool kit closed. "If there's even any treasure to snatch."

"Maybe we'll get scraps?" He shrugged.

"You know what they're after isn't history or exquisite art or even precious metals." She continued when Alek stayed quiet. "You've heard the theory as sure as I have: half our tech comes from these treasure ships. It's part of the mystique."

"So?" It was halfway between a question and a statement. Alek stared at the grating.

"So, if that hologram was true – what if *this* ship's treasure is a weapon of mass devastation? Of desolation." She glanced up as movement in the common room caught her attention. Dustan peered down at them. Reaching towards Alek, she placed her fingers on his forearm, feeling the tension despite his seemingly casual pose. "I don't understand the captain's change of heart."

"You should talk to Rebeka. I imagine it has something to do with guilt: she wants to save her daughter, even if her daughter doesn't need saving." His blue eyes met hers, and he lifted a shoulder. "But it's also your ship."

"Merrup." The grey cat's green eyes peered at her from the top of the crate beside her. There was a hiss and rattle from inside, and Tink skittered back.

Her adrenalin spiked, and her hand went to her chest. "Sweet Hera, Grim! Don't rile them up." She waited for the bugs to stop, but the hiss went on.

"We need to get those off the ship. They're waking up."

"We need to feed them." Alek stood up. "They're probably hungry." He held his hand down to her, and she took it, letting him help her up.

"If you want to reach your arm in there...."

"We don't have to get that close." He nodded and pointed to a hatch on the crate she'd assumed just exposed a status panel. "We have some pellets we can put in the feeders."

"Huh." She turned to him, raising an eyebrow. "How do you know about bug transport?"

"I'm a man of many mysteries." He smiled and started to walk away.

"Um, what about the bugs?" she shouted after him, then lowered her voice as the crate rattled again. Eying it with suspicion, she grabbed her tool kit and took off after Alek.

At the entry into the corridor, she bumped into him, bag in hand. He wrapped one arm around her to stop her falling backward.

"Careful." His blue eyes were stormy as they met hers.

Her hands came up between them, and she shoved him back. "You're the one who bumped into me." When his arm dropped away, she shifted her gaze to the bag. "What are you doing?"

"Feeding the bugs."

"Uh, as you say, I need to talk to the captain." She returned his smile as she danced around him to the stairs. That nocturna moth flickered in her belly as she took them two at a time.

"What are you doing?" Tink frowned at Rebeka, who was down in the pit with Cass' core exposed.

Rebeka glanced at her before returning her gaze to the circuitry. "Making sure Cass wasn't jostled too hard during the attack."

"Really? Cass has been through worse. We got away easy this time."

The captain snapped the cover shut, nodding toward her feet. "One of the footings cracked — we'll need to add that to the list of things to fix — but she seems fine."

"Has she run diagnostics? Cass—"

"Cass is always running self-diagnostics." Rebeka hopped out of the pit, patting the plex that glowed softly blue like fairy lights on a festival eve. "Aren't you, Cass?"

"Yes, Captain."

Tink didn't move, blocking Rebeka's exit. "What are we doing?" She stuffed her hands in her belt to keep from crossing her arms as she peered at the captain.

Rebeka tilted her head to the side, her eyes narrowing. "Fixing up the ship?"

"I mean the big 'what are we doing'. You wanted to dump Dustan off on the first airless rock. We've passed multiple candidates. Inhabited ones even. So why are they still on the ship? Why did you decide to take him to the next 'X' on his imaginary treasure map? And take us back into the orbit of Ten Selva."

"Aconitia doesn't orbit Ten Selva."

"Don't be literal — back into the Green Zone."

"Even a portion of a treasure would pay everyone's salary for months. Make all the repairs to the ship." The captain looked down at her hands. "Fund a retirement cottage between a river and a field of barley."

"It might... if it exists. If Visi lets us keep any of it."

"You think he won't."

It was a statement, not a question, but Tink nodded anyway. "You know he won't. And he knows we kept something from him."

"We didn't."

"Literal *and* pedantic."

"Okay, we don't know what happened to the recordings of the pyramid, how they were altered. We didn't intentionally keep anything from him."

"And you think that will matter to him?"

Rebeka didn't answer, instead her gaze slid sideways to look at Cass' core. Her voice was quiet when she spoke next. "*We* didn't keep anything from him. Cass did."

"Why would she, without orders?" Tink turned her gaze to the blue glow. "She's an AI."

"She's a CASS-ANDRA." Rebeka arched an eyebrow.

Tink pressed her lips together. Rebeka had always been tetchy about the AI, but Tink couldn't refute the fact that Cass had mucked with them. "That doesn't answer my original question – why are we still chasing mythical ships?"

She crossed her arms over her chest and stared at Rebeka in silence, forcing the captain to speak.

Rebeka stared back for a few seconds, then leaned against the wall. "I think Juniper is in danger. Whether it's from Visi or the Dominion, I don't know. I don't care." She peered at her hands, as if lines were a script she was reading. "If I can deliver the *Celeste* to him, give him what Cass knows. Maybe he'll give me her safety in return."

"But what if the ship does contain a weapon of biological mass destruction? If the hologram told the truth?"

"*Your* interpretation of the hologram." Rebeka shifted away from the wall.

"Come on, you saw what I did. You know it's a possibility."

"So what, we turn it over to the Dominion instead?"

"Obviously not." Tink's cheeks flushed.

"If we go after the treasure, we might end up with something. We can control the outcome."

Tink snorted then stopped herself. She'd never seen Rebeka so lost.

Rebeka shrugged. "At least, it'll give me time to come up with another plan."

"So, you'd give him this weapon ... or treasure, even if it means you lose everything. *We* lose everything." Tink waved her hand around, trying to indicate the entire galaxy. "I don't think your daughter would want that."

"You don't know what she'd want." Rebeka's voice rose, then dropped. "Neither do I." She stared at her feet for a few long seconds before lifting her eyes to meet Tink's. "All I know is, if I don't get him what he wants, he'll go after

Juniper. I'd give all the treasure in the cosmos if this can save her."

Tink peered at her mentor and friend, then reached out to wrap her arms around the other woman's shoulders.

After a few seconds, Rebeka spoke. "You're not a hugger."

"I know," Tink said into Rebeka's collarbone. "Take it while you can." She smiled as Rebeka's arms embraced her. A few long seconds later, Tink pulled away, scrunching her lips as she did. "I think I already have another plan." She glanced at the captain, whose eyes narrowed.

"I'm not going to like this, am I?"

"Depends." Tink stared at the floor. "How do you feel about pitting gangsters against the Dominion?"

"With us in the middle?"

Tink quirked an eyebrow. "What do you think?"

Let Them Fly

35: Tink

T INK SWEPT THE NEW circuit with the laser welder. She traced the lines perfectly from the one she'd pulled out of Kandi's Antaran stave. All the connections were solid. Snorting, she put the circuit back in the handle then flicked her wrist. Nothing happened.

Despite Kandi assuring her there was no magic to it, Tink was close to admitting defeat. She put the stave down, and her gaze slid sideways to the stone Fennick had picked up on the red planet.

Her scans said it was nothing — not even a rock. So, she'd applied energy to it. Thermal. Light at different wavelengths. None of it had made any difference so far. She pulled out her tuning forks and flicked her tablet to be an o-scope. "If this doesn't get a reaction from you, I'm getting my chemistry set."

Taking out the smallest fork, she tapped it on the table and alternated her attention between the rock and the display on the tablet. Nothing but the pure sound of the fork. Sliding it back in the case, she pulled out the next one and repeated the process: tap and observe. She'd gotten to the third fork in the set of five when she heard voices coming down the hall. She pulled out the next fork, then looked up to see Ish and Fennick enter the room. When Fennick saw what was in her hand, his arm dropped from Ish's back and his smile fell. The young archaeological apprentice was one of the few people she knew who looked more mature with a smile.

"Fennick, I said I'm sorry." Ish gave her a pleading look. "I've only shown Tink."

"The rest of us have a right to know what dangerous goods are brought onto the ship." Tink tapped the fork on the table. The line on the oscilloscope wobbled as Fennick slumped across the room to lean against the window.

"You said it was inert. How can it be dangerous?" Fennick stared out at the cargo bay, his hands leaving fingerprints on the glass. "What's he doing?"

"Feeding the bugs." Tink had seen Alek earlier, distributing pellets amongst the crates, followed assiduously by Grim. Her lips pursed — the insects were getting restless, demanding food more frequently — and they were nowhere near dropping them off at their destination.

"This stone is odd." She peered up at Ish from behind her specs as she put the fork away; it was too loud in the common room now. Instead, she pulled up the sound generator on her tablet and started adjusting the frequency. "And odd is dangerous."

"I'm odd."

"And you're dangerous." She gave him a lop-sided smile, then glanced over as Alek came in, trailed by Grim, and a few seconds later, Rebeka and Dustan.

Tink scowled and closed the sound generator, giving up on any more investigation for the time being.

"What's dangerous?" Dustan asked over the captain's shoulder, his hands on her hips. "Ah, Fennick's gift."

"Does everyone know?" Fennick's cheeks flushed, and he stared at Ish, whose hands raised in protest.

"I saw you pick it up in the video." Dustan leaned over the table to peer at the stone.

"It's just a rock," Fennick muttered. "Not even a piece of treasure from the *Celeste*."

"Here." Tink shoved the rock at Ish, along with the flexible wire cage and chain she'd made. "So, you can wear it...." Ish flushed and looked around. Tink's lips quirked into a smile. "To remind you of the mission you couldn't go on." He grimaced but snatched the cage and the stone from her.

"Speaking of the *Celeste*." Rebeka poured herself a mugful of coffee. "Tink has a question. Tink?" She leaned against the countertop, breathing in, her nose close to the dark liquid.

"What?" Tink glanced around at the assembly. "I ... why do all the rich and powerful want the *Celeste* when they don't know what's on it?"

"The tech." Dustan leaned against the fridge.

Ish's eyebrows pulled together. "But don't we have all the tech from the other treasure ships?"

"They know there's something different on the *Celeste*." Tink frowned. "How?"

"How would they know?" Fennick stepped forward. "*We* don't know what's there. Not for sure."

Silence blanketed the common room. Even Grim's purring went quiet.

Rebeka's words were muted when she spoke. "What else would draw the Dominion and the Cartels into open pursuit?"

Dustan coughed. "I think it would be wise to accept the premise that it's a weapon of sorts, as Tink says." He nodded at her, then turned away as the cough returned.

Rebeka's lips pressed together as she carefully placed her mug on the counter. "Did you know what it carried?" Her voice was quiet, and she didn't so much as glance at Dustan.

He threw his hands up. "No. I swear." A phlegmatic cough followed, and he covered his mouth with his elbow.

"It's true." Fennick slipped into the seat beside Ish. "He always just thought it was the last great treasure ship."

"You know me. I'm a coward in search of fame and fortune." Dustan looked at his palm, flexing his fingers. "But it's the only thing that explains the money Visi has loaned the expedition. It's something that will irrevocably shift the balance of power – or destroy it completely."

"Loaned." Rebeka's arms crossed over her chest. "But that's not the whole story, is it?"

Dustan glanced at her before casting his gaze around. His shoulders slumped. "Juniper's transmission. The code. She figured out where the *Celeste* is and what's on it."

"So, is it a weapon?" Tink asked.

"Where is it?" Ish's words tumbled over hers. "We know it's in the Corican system."

"No, your beacon says it's there." He nodded at Tink.

"It's not—" Tink started.

"Enough." Rebeka held up a hand. "Dustan?"

"The message was garbled. *What* it is wasn't clear. Just that it was something powerful that meant death on a massive scale." He glanced at Rebeka again before continuing. "Where it is ... Aconitia. Tanopolis, to be exact."

"The ancient capital? You're bloody kidding me, back where we were when this whole thing started?" Tink shook her head. "And a planet picked over by archaeologists and treasure hunters, who somehow missed the massive treasure ship in their midst?"

"It's not so popular with archaeologists anymore." Fennick's index finger drummed the table. "Everyone thinks anything interesting has been found."

"It's still a retreat for the decadent, the decaying rich." Alek's voice dripped with disdain.

Dustan ignored the commentary and continued. "What better place to hide something than in plain sight? So few people look at what's right in front of them."

"So, what do we do?" Fennick stopped crunching the bugs he'd been eating.

"We know the Dominion can tail us." Ish wiped his hands on his pants. "If we find the *Celeste*, so do they."

Alek shifted his stance, his feet moving a little wider apart as he crossed his arms over his chest. "That ship that attacked us. I'm willing to bet they're still tracking us."

"So?" Rebeka's eyes narrowed.

"So, what do we do?" Tink repeated as she held the captain's gaze.

"Go to Visi?" Dustan's tone didn't instil confidence.

"If you're worried about what the Dominion could do with this potential weapon, you should be terrified of what Visi will do." Alek's arms tensed, causing the muscles in his forearms to twitch. "Neither of them need any more power."

"Okay then," Dustan said. "As the Tinker says, what do we do?"

Tink watched as Rebeka gave her a small nod. She licked her lips before speaking. "Upset the balance. Pit the gangster against the Dominion and slip away while they're at each other's throats."

"He won't just let you give up the search for the *Celeste*." Dustan cheeks flushed. "He'll come after you. Even if I leave the ship."

"No." Rebeka peered at her hands before lifting her gaze to pass over the crew. "Tink means we go after the *Celeste*." Alek shifted in his stance, but the captain held up a hand. "At this point, they have enough information to eventually find it themselves. If we draw both Visi and the Dominion ship chasing us to it, they fight each other and...." She glanced at Dustan. "Just maybe then we can destroy whatever is on the *Celeste*."

"If it's data, Ish and I can deal with it." Tink wished she had a widget to spin. "If it's physical...."

"We get them to destroy it." Rebeka stared at her hands again. "And if there is no *treasure* left to claim, maybe we come out alive." With a sharp exhale, she looked up and her eyes met Tink's. "Any dissenting votes?"

"I thought you said this wasn't a democracy...." Dustan started but petered out at Rebeka's sharp look.

"In this case, everyone gets a say." Rebeka dropped her hands to her hips. "Just mine is the final say."

Alek raised his hand. "This isn't going to work, but I'm with you."

Ish raised a hand. "Me too. Kandi's not here, but I'm pretty sure she'll vote for a fight that screws both the Dominion and the cartels."

"Do I get a vote?" Fennick lifted his hand. Rebeka tipped her chin down, indicating assent. "I'm in. And not just because I've been searching for the *Celeste* since I was a boy."

"You're still a boy." Dustan smiled at Fennick's grimace. "I—"

"If you say *nae*...." The captain crossed her arms over her chest.

Dustan stepped up to her and placed his hands on her shoulders. "I was going to say I'm in. And not because of the treasure on that ship."

"Oh." Rebeka's arms dropped to her sides, and she cleared her throat "Tink?"

"It was my idea. I hope I'm in." She placed her hands on the table and pushed herself up before grabbing Kandi's stave and her tool kit. "If we're going to do this, I need to go make some incendiaries."

36: HARBIN

HARBIN SMILED. THE *LYRA* lit up like a beacon through the jungle canopy below. Red against green. The blip punctuated the quiet hum of activity on the bridge. He stroked the balustrade, then pressed his palms into its sleek plex.

After hounding the little ship for a bit, he'd let them get away. To think they'd escaped. To believe they were safe. Only to pop up and harry them again. Finally, he hovered over Aconitia, watching them fly towards the final resting place of the *Celeste*. Knowing the planet and its history from his tutelage by Archon Koning, he could guess at where its grave was: somewhere near the Tanopolis ruin ... but the remnants of the ancient capital sprawled under hectares of the jungle slowly consuming them.

"Head in for the kill, low and quiet."

Liet immediately set to following his orders with smooth efficiency.

He suppressed a smile at the thought of revenge for the dressing down he'd gotten from Archon Koning for letting the ship and her crew slip through his grasp in his first encounter with them. This time, perhaps annoyed at finding out the *Celeste* lay so close to her ancestral home, Halcyon finally gave him the go-ahead to take down the *Lyra*, regardless of how much Visi protested.

Harbin planned to scatter the ship to the four winds and bring her their heads on a platter.

His smile fell. She still wanted the ship intact, if not the crew. It held something — or someone — she wanted. "Scratch that. Prepare for immobilization and extraction."

Liet's shoulders shifted a little at that. "Yes sir."

A few moments later, a soft ripple told him the ship-paralyzing stun grenades had dropped away. A flutter of leaves hinted at their path through the canopy. There was no other sign to warn the *Lyra* of its impending doom.

A sequence of beeps and whistles tweeted from his comms. He'd come to know the pattern too well lately, and his frown deepened. "I'll be right back." He turned on his heels and strode into his ready room, closing the door and frosting the glass behind him.

Harbin tapped his desktop. "What?"

A pale face appeared on the screen, the cheeks blotched an ugly red. "Did I say you could engage?" Ludovicus Visi's voice was thin and pinched.

"I don't take orders from you, Visi. Sorry, *Ray Skate*." Harbin enunciated the man's pseudonym.

"No, you take orders from me." Another caller joined the stream, remaining faceless.

"Archon Koning." Harbin stood straighter. "Have you changed your mind?" He pressed his lips closed to keep from saying more.

"No." There was a pause in the darkness at the other end. "However, I want our friend to do his part."

"What do you mean?" The pale man's lips pursed, and Harbin's smile crept back despite his best efforts.

"You have too little blood on your hands." Halcyon's voice was flat, and it cracked in places like ice on a shifting lake.

The pale man snorted. "The blood of my enemies fills my veins." He gave a small, tight smile. For a second, Harbin wondered if he was being literal.

A chime sounded, and Liet's voice came through. "Grenades are locked on their targets. Orders, sir?"

Harbin shifted his gaze between the thin man and the void of Halcyon's view. "Disarm them." He stood up straight, hands clasping behind him. "Then pull back."

"Sir?"

"Those are your orders, Liet."

"Sir."

"We'll be your flusher." Harbin splayed his fingers on his desktop as he peered at Visi. "Get ready to hunt."

The pale man's eyes narrowed, and a thin smile stretched his lips. "I'm always ready to hunt."

For the first time, Harbin believed the man told the unadulterated truth. He reached to end the call.

"Just make sure you don't get caught in the crossfire," Visi said just before the connection broke.

37: Rebeka

"CAPTAIN." CASS' VOICE FILLED the silent bridge, and Rebeka winced, even though her logical brain knew their pursuers couldn't hear the sound, not over the noise of the ship itself.

"What?"

"Projectiles incoming. In 5...4...."

"Kandi, countermeasures."

"2...."

"Too late."

Rebeka flinched and grabbed the back of Ish's seat, even though she had no idea what headed towards them. Beside her, Alek clutched the armrests of his chair as a dull thunk echoed through the *Lyra*. She braced herself for the explosion, but none came. After a few more tense seconds, she lifted her head. "Cass?"

"The projectiles didn't detonate."

"Time-delayed?" She craned her neck to peer at Kandi.

"I don't think so, Captain." Kandi sat at her console, but turned towards the bridge, her head tipped sideways. "The impact ... they sounded like plasma grenades."

"You can identify ship-to-ship munitions by their sound?" Alek's eyebrows raised as he regarded the Antaran.

"Of course." Kandi straightened up. "Can't you?"

"I'm a little rusty."

"If you're finished, can we identify where they came from?"

"Already done captain." Kandi shifted back to her station. "An empty patch of sky."

"Another shrouded ship?" Rebeka's hands went to her hips. "How many of these things are there?"

"No, Captain," Cass said. "The source location is truly empty. Now."

"How did they know we were here?" Alek turned back to the viewscreen where scans from the system flicked past.

Rebeka grimaced. "We're not as stealth as we think, hotshot?"

"Ish brought us in so deep, he's still sleeping off the effects."

"A spy?" Kandi didn't turn from her console.

"Found the ship." Alek's voice ricocheted around the bridge. The viewscreen flicked, displaying another camera feed. "It's one we've met before."

"The *Barracuda* class vessel. The one that was harrying us across Corican."

"Permission to get the hell away, Captain."

"Permission granted." Rebeka sat back down and buckled in. "Cass, let the rest of the crew know."

Yellow lights started strobing along the floor, casting the bridge in a sickly hue as Alek took the *Lyra* straight up.

The ship paused as they cleared the canopy, and Rebeka's stomach lurched.

"What's wrong, fly boy?" The ship spun in a tight circle then straightened out, and bile rose in her throat.

"That." An oily black arrow of a ship hung in the viewscreen, as if suspended on wires. Meanwhile, the *Lyra* whined at being held in place.

"Is that what shot at us?"

Kandi shook her head. "Those grenades were Dominion. That's not. But it is charging up its pulse cannons."

"Get us out of here, Mister Wa." In response, the *Lyra* shot forward, towards the sleek ship. Rebeka's fingers clutched her armrests. "Speak to me, Alek. Why are we heading towards the threat?"

"Get under them before they can charge up." The *Lyra* screamed at going so fast, so suddenly, but she complied. Alek steered her straight towards the other ship, and Rebeka's hands clenched into fists. She recalled that she didn't really know their new pilot all that well. But she knew he had secrets.

The *Lyra*'s running lights reflected off the chrome hull of the other ship. At the last second, Alek tipped the nose down and slid under its belly, while Rebeka's stomach did a somersault. Behind them echoed the boom of pulse cannons hitting rock. Part of the viewscreen shifted to their rear cameras. Flames licked the forest and turned the underside of the silver ship orange.

"Let's try to not do that again, Mister Wa."

"I'll try, Captain, but we're far from clear yet."

Rebeka peered at the viewscreen. "Cass, identify that ship."

"Transponder says the *Espado*, registered to the Tala Corporation out of Garamond Prime."

Rebeka's eyes narrowed. She'd never heard of Tala but Garamond Prime was a notorious flag of convenience.

"Visi." Alek's voice was rough.

"That's not his ship." Rebeka scowled at the screen.

"You think he has only one?" Alek stated, and Rebeka had to concede that point with a nod he couldn't see. "Why is he shooting at us?"

"Are you saying you trusted him?" Kandi didn't turn from her console. Rebeka glanced over her shoulder at Kandi's screen to see her running simulations with their meagre weapons inventory.

"No, but he's supposed to be our investor." Alek glanced at her.

"Maybe he's come to collect." Rebeka pulled up her own console, tapping in a series of numbers. "Focus on flying, Alek."

"Yes sir."

Within seconds, a corner of the viewscreen shifted, displaying Ludovicus Visi. Rebeka saw Alek's head jerk towards it before he caught himself and turned his attention back to the main view of the landscape in front of them.

"Hello—" Visi barely got the word out.

"What the bleeding Hades, Visi?" Rebeka scowled at him.

"Captain, there's no need for profanity."

"There is from where I'm sitting. I thought you were Dustan's angel investor."

Visi tipped his head sideways. "I may be his angel. But I have a devil of my own whispering at my shoulder. It wants results."

"And you think shooting at us will get you that?" Rebeka's squint shifted from the feed with his head to the landscape on the main feed, marred with a smear of gunmetal grey. Her stomach sank. "Kandi, what's that?"

"*That's* the Dominion ship that dropped grenades on us."

Visi sneered. "And there's more where that came from if you don't give me the *Celeste*."

"We don't know where it is."

"Don't lie to me, Captain." Visi spat the words out, then frowned. His words were more measured when he continued. "You didn't come to Aconitia for a holiday, or to drop off those bugs in your cargo hold." Her gaze flicked back to his face at mention of their cargo, but she stayed silent as he continued. "I want it. Now."

Rebeka muted the line then tapped her console. "Dustan, get your ass to the bridge." Her voice echoed through the ship, and she didn't wait for a response before turning back to Alek. "Keep looking for an escape route, Wa."

"Absolutely. Sir."

Before long, hurried footsteps echoed down the hall, and Dustan tumbled onto the bridge. "Rebeka?"

"Visi is shooting at us."

"I—" Dustan's skin paled and he started to sweat when he looked at the screen. "But we have a deal."

"I suspect your deal is off." Rebeka opened the line to Visi's ship again.

Before she could speak, the man smiled. "You should really kill your video too. I told you I have my own devil to please. Strong and handsome, and much more powerful than you. And she has an armada at her fingertips. Not just some rust bucket with an outdated pulse cannon and a cargo of bugs." He glanced at the hands he held clasped in front of him, looking for all the universe like a beneficent monk, except for the slight tension in his lips as he pressed them together. Dropping his hands, he looked up at her. "That's why I'm shooting at you."

Rebeka killed the line completely. Her shoulders heaved as she took a deep breath. The ship lurched, dropping a hundred feet without warning. "Alek?"

"I have a plan."

The *Lyra* skimmed the treetops, heading towards the Dominion ship. "I don't think that will work twice."

"Concentrating."

Rebeka opened her mouth to censure him but, seeing the muscles of his neck and forearms twitch and bulge, she decided to discipline him for improper etiquette later. Instead, she turned to Dustan. "So, your angel is in the Dominion's pocket." Dustan shook his head, and she waved her hand to the screen even though Visi's visage had disappeared. "He said so himself."

Dustan held up his hand. "Not the Dominion. Someone within it."

Rebeka huffed. "Fine. Either way, our half-assed plan to pit them against each other just crumbled to ash."

The ship shuttered and spun to the portside as something hit their flank.

"Not quite fast enough, Wa." Kandi punched a sequence into her console. "Permission to fire, Captain."

"Fire at will."

"I'll fire our creaky, old pulse cannon as fast as it'll let me."

Tink stumbled onto the bridge, dressed in her atmo suit, helmet in one hand. Thrown into the wall by a hit to their starboard, she dropped her helmet to juggle the canister in her other hand. "I have an idea." Slumping into her chair, she thrust out a container full of tiny balls.

"Throw marbles at them?" Rebeka's eyebrows lifted.

"They're not marbles. They're Alassi Fire grenades."

Rebeka pulled away. "You have an open container of Alassi Fire balls on the bridge? Are you insane?"

Tink looked up from her container and shrugged. "Maybe. Wait 'til you hear the rest of the plan."

"Why do I think I'm not going to like this?"

The *Lyra* shuddered, and Alek cursed.

"What is it, Wa?"

"Nothing. Just got too close to the canopy."

"We have two ships after us, right?" The fingers of Tink's free hand clenched. "We need a wide dispersal weapon."

"So, what, we throw these out the cargo bay? That's not a good plan."

Tink held her fist to her chin as she shook her head. "No. Bugs. We feed them to the bugs. They're so hungry they'll eat anything."

"I—"

"Then we let them go." Tink released her fingers, splaying them in a starburst. "A flying minefield."

"You are insane." Dustan gazed at Tink with a look of horror. Rebeka didn't blame him.

The ship skidded through the atmosphere again and klaxons sounded.

"Portside hull integrity at 20%." Cass' tone was annoyingly calm.

Rebeka scowled at Tink. "How long do you need?"

"15 minutes. Less with help."

"I'll come." Dustan stood up. The horror still lingered in his expression.

"But you and bugs...." Rebeka remembered an incident with a teddy bear bee, a book and a broken window.

Dustan coughed into his sleeve then squared his shoulder. "If I'm eaten alive by hissing, ravenous insects, at least I won't have to suffer through this." He waved at the screen. "But after this, we have to talk."

"Woot! Bug bombs!" Tink strode off the bridge, before doing a 180 to collect her canister full of incendiary marbles. "It'll be fine." She patted Rebeka on the shoulder as she passed. "Bug bombs." She smiled and splayed the fingers of her free hand before leaving the bridge again.

Rebeka craned her neck to watch Dustan follow her. She slumped back in her chair. "I'm going to die in a swarm of fiery bugs."

38: TINK

ERE!" TINK SHOVED A bag of the combustible balls into Dustan's hands, which trembled. "They're fine. The oil won't ignite until I tell it to." She tipped her head side to side. "Unless, of course, we're hit by something that sparks. Or it gets too hot."

Dustan's eyes widened. "That's a lot of 'ors'." He paused as the ship shimmied. "Did you mention to our pilot the importance of not getting hit?" The usual tenor of his voice turned to a squeak.

"Of course, I—" Tink tapped her wrist. "Alek, try to not let them hit the ship."

"I'll try." The pilot's voice crackled.

"If you fail, we might go boom." She turned back to Dustan. "See. Sorted."

He swallowed and looked sidelong at the crate beside him which jumped and hissed like bara root in a frypan. "Not really. We still have to get the bugs to eat these things and fly out the door."

"Alek showed me how to feed them in the crates." Tink popped open the reservoir on the nearest one and dumped a handful of balls into it. She snapped it closed then jumped back as the crate rocked back and forth, the hiss becoming a snarl. "I think they're hungry?"

"And how do we get them out without releasing oil-filled bugs into the cargo hold?"

"One problem at a time, but I said I have an idea." Tink's lips pressed into a thin line. She did have an idea but didn't think he'd like it much. She didn't like it, given that it involved standing on the wrong side of the safety netting with the door open in the middle of a hurricane of weaponized bugs. "Just feed the bugs in these first six crates. It should be enough." She ran to the next crate and popped a handful of marbles into it. As she prepared to move to the next, the ship was hit, throwing her to the floor. "Barnacles!" She picked herself up, glancing at her throbbing knee. Her pant leg was torn, and pinpricks of blood dotted the skin. Looking at her hand, she saw the jar of mini bombs was intact and her grip solid. "Try not to fall, Professor." She swallowed. "We don't want little fire marbles rolling around the cargo bay."

"Thanks. I wouldn't have guessed. One more."

Tink glanced his way and saw that he was indeed almost done his side. She sprinted to the next one in her line, hustling to catch up. Container empty, her hands went to her knees, and she panted. Dustan joined her, sweat sheening his brow. His face was the colour of Merian clay, pale and pasty.

"You okay?" she asked.

He pressed his lips together and nodded. "Just don't like bugs." Looking back on the crates, he continued. "So, what's next?"

Tink didn't meet his eyes as she spoke. "We roll the crates into the loading area we're standing in." He nodded, and she mimicked the movement. "We raise the safety netting so they don't fly back in when they're released."

"Oh, I like the sound of safety netting."

Her eyebrows lifted and she looked at his feet. "We get into atmo suits, tether in, stand here and release the doors as we shove the crates out." She said it all in a rush before she finally looked him in the eyes. His mouth hung open and his face was a paler shade of grey.

"You're serious?"

She nodded, scrunching her lips. "I'm insane. But it's the only way. There's no time to hack the crates for a timed release. Once they're out, I blow them and hope those ships are in the right place at the right time."

Dustan stared at her for a second, blinking. "This is a ludicrous plan." He pointed at her, then turned around. "Where's my atmo suit?"

The *Lyra* took another hit, and the lights flickered.

Rebeka's voice came over the comms. "How much longer, Tink?"

"Ten minutes."

"You have five."

"Behind that panel." She nodded over Dustan's shoulder. "The one with a suit icon on it."

Dustan scowled as he opened the panel and pulled out the one-size fits all emergency suit. While he struggled into it, Tink rolled the crates into the loading area. Once done, she checked Dustan's suit then pulled her own helmet on.

"Ready to do this?" she asked, hopping up onto her toes to try to catch the handle of the safety net.

"No." Dustan stepped beside her and pulled the net down. After snapping it into place, she hooked Dustan's tether to the anchor on one side before attaching her own.

Slamming her palm onto the manual ramp release, the *Lyra's* alarms blared at her, informing her that the ramp was lowering while the ship was in motion. She tapped her other hand to the comms on her helmet, shouting to hear her own voice over the wind that howled around them. "Ready to release the bug bombs. Where are those ships?"

"Coming up hot behind us."

She could almost hear the smile in Alek's voice, then the ship banked, and she cursed him. Nodding at Dustan, she stepped up to the first crate on her side and pushed, one hand on the manual door release. Dustan did the same. As the crates cleared the ramp, a hundred angry bugs swarmed behind the ship. They made quick work of the rest of the crates, until there was only one left.

Tink let out a sigh of relief. Her shoulders ached, but she shrugged and gave the crate a shove. It didn't move. Coiling what little energy she had left, she put her legs and back into it. It didn't budge. Sparks filled her vision as something hit the back of the ship. Sparks were bad. She looked up to see an iridescent black arrow closing in on the swarm. Swallowing hard, she crouched down and pressed her shoulder to the crate.

"What's wrong?" Dustan's voice echoed in her helmet.

She shook her head. "It must be caught on something. We have to get it out of here before we can detonate." She felt his bulk nestled beside her.

"On three?"

"One."

"Two."

"Three." The word came out of her mouth as more of a grunt. There was the sound of metal grating on metal, but the crate finally slid forward. Tink fell on her face, her helmet hitting the grating. Dustan kept hold of the crate long enough to open the door.

She tapped her wrist. "Crates away, Captain. Preparing to detonate."

"Sooner is better."

"Aye aye."

Sparks cascaded over her helmet again, and she was sure she'd have holes in her suit after this. She glanced up at Dustan. "Time to get behind the safety net." She tipped her head down to look at her wrist patch, punching in the sequence to detonate the Alassi Fire-filled mine field of bug bombs. Smiling with anticipation, she looked up at the archaeologist, who hadn't moved. He still stood at the end of the ramp, facing her with a crate door in his hand. But he wasn't looking at her. He was looking down at the red blooming over his torso.

"Dustan!" Tink scrambled towards him, reaching him as he fell to his knees. She flinched as the first of the incendiary marbles burst and hit the ship trailing them. "Dustan."

Finally, he acknowledged her, looking up with his mouth slightly open. "Shrapnel's a bitch." He slumped to sit on the grating, pressing his hand to the wound. Judging from the amount of blood and the pallor of his skin, it was bad.

"Kandi, get down to the cargo bay!" Turning to Dustan, she pulled the door from his grip and threw it over the edge. "Come on. We need to get inside and close the ramp." When he didn't move, she got behind him. Hands in his armpits, she yanked him back, her sore shoulders protesting the weight.

"Bit busy at the moment." Kandi's voice was tinny in Tink's ear.

With another heave, Tink got Dustan far enough into the loading bay. "Cass, can you close the ramp?"

"The ramp should not have been opened during flight, Tink." Nonetheless, Cass did as asked.

Tink watched the ramp rise until she was sure it would close, then started to lie down on the floor. Then she sat up again with a start. She groaned as she took off her helmet and looked at Dustan's wound.

"Why didn't I pay more attention in first aid?"

39: Rebeka

"WHAT HAPPENED?" KANDI LEANED over the stretcher as Rebeka and Fennick dropped it onto the table in the medbay. The *Lyra* took an unexpected drop, and Rebeka's stomach heaved. She told herself it was the movement of the ship and not Dustan's grey pallor.

The ship shifted again, and Fennick's hands clenched the stretcher handles, and together they kept it from shifting. The assistant scholar had more muscle than she'd given him credit for.

Tink rocked forward. "Some piece of something hit him." She glanced from Kandi to Rebeka. "There were a lot of things bouncing off the ship."

Fennick turned away as Kandi peeled off the cut-open atmo suit. Even Rebeka grimaced at the frothy mix of pink, white and blue that coated Dustan's abdomen.

Kandi tsked and turned to Tink. "What is this?"

"I slathered him in styptic from the med kit." Tink shrugged her shoulders. "I'm not a medic. It was all I could think of." Her eyes glistened, and her head fell. "I just knew I needed to stop the bleeding and you were busy saving the rest of us," she added, her voice quiet. Her lips twisted, and she lifted her head. "Did I do something bad?"

Kandi shook her head, a strand of blue hair falling over her face. "No, I can work with this." She took her laser to the foam. "But when this is over, remedial first aid for everyone." She pointed at them with her free hand before setting to work again.

A hiccoughing sound drew Rebeka's attention to the man standing beside her. Fennick's face looked almost the same shade as Dustan's, except tinged with green. "Fennick, can you get Kandi the styptic Tink used?" The young man nodded then headed for the door.

"I'll go babysit." Tink pushed away from the table, rolling her eyes, then headed after Fennick.

Kandi looked at her, her eyebrows pulled together. "I don't need the styptic."

"No, but he needed to get away from this for a minute. Anything I can do?"

"Get Alek to calm down with the joystick."

Rebeka's head tipped sideways. "I think he has." She realized the ship hadn't dipped or turned unexpectedly since they'd dropped the stretcher on the table. She tapped her comms. "Alek, status."

"I think I lost their tracker drones. Bugs took care of the ships for now." There was a pause, as she heard mumbling between the pilot and Ish. "Just need to know where to go next."

"Right, about that..." Rebeka stopped as bloody fingers grasped her wrist. Dustan's brown eyes peered at her. His lips moved, but no sound came out. He winced and his fingers tightened as he glanced at Kandi before returning his attention to her. His lips moved again, and his hand went to his throat. *Water.*

"Right." She stepped over to the dispenser and returned with a mugful of water. When she lifted his head, Kandi glared at her.

"Not a good idea to move him, Captain. I don't know what's loose inside his gut."

His bloody fingers clutched at the air, reaching for the mug.

"I'll get you something to drink with so she doesn't yell at us again." Rebeka put the glass down on the table and went to the supply cupboard on the wall, cutting a length of tubing to fashion a makeshift straw.

"Stop moving or I'll knock you out." Kandi glared at her as she returned to the table. "Can you hold him still?"

Rebeka placed the straw in Dustan's mouth, and his lips closed around it. She laid her hand on his upper chest, making a pretense of holding him down.

Kandi reached for a sterilizer wand. Rebeka winced at the memory of its burn. She put some actual pressure on Dustan's chest. He winced and jerked against her hand, then spat the straw out.

"Tell'asim." His voice was quiet and hoarse, and Rebeka had to lean close.

"The abandoned capital?" Rebeka shook her head and placed her other hand on his forehead. It was hot. "Hush."

"Go to Tell'asim. It's under the hill at the centre. Tell Fennick."

"Why Tell'asim? It's a ruin."

"So was the pyramid," Kandi said but didn't pause in her work.

Dustan moved a shoulder, then stopped as a grimace passed over his face.

"Stop. Moving." Kandi scowled at Dustan then bent her head over the wound she was closing with dermatape.

"It's ... I found the clue in Juniper's notes on the treasure ships."

"Juniper's notes?"

His fingers gripped hers, the dry blood tacky. "Tsst. Not really Tell'asim. It's Tell-ta-sema."

Across from her, Kandi jerked back. Rebeka looked at her to find her staring at Dustan. "Tell-ta-sema." The words were barely audible. She glanced at Rebeka, her mouth opening before snapping shut.

"What? This nonsense means something to you?"

Kandi shook her head for a few moments, pressing her lips together. Then she huffed. "My Erivan is rusty — Ish would know better — but Tell-ta-sema. It means Hill of the Heavens." Her head tipped sideways as her eyes slid to her patient. "Celestial hill."

Rebeka peered at Dustan, whose eyes had closed, though his chest still rose and fell under her hand. "Bleeding barnacles." She tapped her wrist. "Alek, set course for Tell'asim. Park us somewhere near the centre." She went to close the link, then paused. "But out of sight if you can."

"Captain?"

"Pilot, set the course."

"Aye aye, sir."

40: TINK

I'M NOT LEAVING THE ship." Tink stomped her foot for effect, even though Rebeka, who was somewhere out by the monument, couldn't see her. The move sent Grim jumping into Kandi's lap. Kandi had barely been convinced to stay and protect the ship; she'd fought it until Rebeka mentioned she also had a patient to look after.

"We need your expertise." Rebeka's voice was thin over the comms.

"Why?" Tink grabbed the back of Alek's empty seat, her hands slick with sweat. Even in the ship, the humidity was unbearable. "What can I possibly do to—"

"We have a bug. We need you to deal with it."

Tink's eyebrows scrunched together as she muted the comms. Her mouth opened and closed as she turned to Ish. "A bug?"

"She's worried someone's listening," he said. "Not unfounded. Doesn't want to say what's really up."

Tink grimaced and opened the line again. "Fine."

"Ish, you too."

"Okay?" Ish stood as the line went dead. "Why me? I mean, I'm happy to get off the ship, but I don't know how I can help with a search for buried treasure."

"Tell-ta-sema." Kandi peered at him.

"What?" Tink picked up the package she'd brought for Kandi.

"Heavenly Hill?" Ish tipped his head sideways. His eyebrows lifted. "Ah, Tell'asim."

"Your people tend to be taught the old language, keepers of the faith and all." Kandi scritched behind Grim's ears. "Same as the Antarans, except as dealers of death, we don't tend to practice words as much. I imagine there's some writing even Fennick can't decipher."

There was a cough in the hall, and a few seconds later, Dustan half-stumbled onto the bridge. "I'm going with you," he said, one hand to his abdomen, the other pressed to the wall.

"Absolutely not." Kandi stood, dumping Grim unceremoniously on the floor. The cat mrowled his displeasure then flicked his tail, stuck his nose in the air and stalked off the bridge.

"You are not my keeper." He breathed in deeply. "I've spent my life searching for this ship. All the other finds were simply ways to distract treasure hunters from my obsession." He turned to Tink. "I'm going with you or without you."

Tink frowned, and looked at Ish, who simply shrugged. "I suppose I'm not the boss of you either." She sighed, running one hand over the box she held. She thrust it towards Kandi. "I tried. I don't know that it works."

Kandi took the box, her eyebrows pulling together in a question. When Tink stayed silent, she lifted the lid. Her mouth dropped open. Slowly, she reached in and pulled out the handle of her stave. "You did it."

Tink shook her head. "Not really." She scrunched her lips. "They're supposed to be able to do so much more. I tried to program it the same as it was originally, but I can barely make it open."

Kandi looked at her, eyes wide. "You shouldn't have been able to make it do anything." Putting the box down, she flicked her wrist. Tink jumped back as both ends of the stave extended.

"Oh. It didn't do that for me."

"Huh, maybe in time, we can train one to listen to you." Kandi swept it around as one end crackled with electric charge, a smile on her face. "But not this one. This one's mine." She graced them with a wicked grin. "If we're going, we should lock up."

"*We're* not going." Tink's voice was quiet, and she grimaced. "You still need to watch the ship."

Kandi growled but slumped into her seat.

Tink neared the base of what remained of the giant statue of Emperor Tan that sat in the centre of the ruins of Tell'asim. The path started to open up, releasing her from the dank and torrid jungle into a humid and sweltering clearing. She started to make out a line of pale stone columns, the colour of bleached bones, set into the rock. The rock itself was grey as dead flesh and worn to a smooth, waxy finish.

The scowl on Rebeka's face as the three of them neared the mausoleum of the long-deposed Erivan emperors told Tink all she needed to know. The captain was not pleased.

"He was going to come anyway," she said, guessing at the cause of the captain's anger. Rebeka's gaze flicked over her shoulder to where Tink knew Dustan followed, having heard his breath grow more ragged with every step. He still refused help from any of them.

"You didn't really expect me to stay in bed when my life's work was mere steps away."

"Yes, actually, I did." The captain scowled at him. Her hands came to her hips, but she dropped them as she turned to Tink. "Can you crack this thing?" She jerked her chin towards the base of the monument that bore the legs of Emperor Tan — a woman bore either the epithet 'the Magnificent' or 'the Terrible' depending on which side of history you belonged to.

Tink peered at the panel. "It's just a bunch of tiles." She arched an eyebrow. "Stone's not really my thing."

Fennick stepped up beside her, unrolling the scroll he held in his hand. "From the data available, I'm pretty sure we need to press certain tiles. Maybe in a specific order." His voice got louder and more clipped as he continued. "For sure, if you press the wrong things, it gets angry, and shuffles and resets." He ran his fingers over the tiles, something thousands of people before him had done, judging from the faded and worn glyphs, despite the equally worn and faded sign that warned of the punishment for touching any of the monuments: lose the fingers that defile the stone. "So, there must be a machine behind it, right?"

"Gears and levers." Alek removed a hand from his pulse rifle to pat her on the shoulder. "Right up your alley."

She threw him a grimace but didn't rise to the bait. "What about Ish?" She glanced at the navigator, who stared at the squiggles and dots on the unrolled scroll, which Fennick and Dustan held against the stone. "What do you need him for?"

"This is the original inscription." Dustan peered up at the legs. "Worn away now by air and water and time."

"And people," Tink added as she leaned in to inspect the tiles. A curl fell to her cheek, and she tried to huff it away, but it stuck to the sweat.

"We got our hands on a copy and translated it. But it still makes no sense."

Beside her, Ish trailed his fingers over the scroll, looking crisp and unbothered by the heat. "It's beautiful."

"I don't care about its aesthetics." The captain peered at the lettering. "Is it decipherable?"

"Everything's decipherable if you know the cipher." Returning his gaze to the scroll, he started muttering to himself in undulating syllables. For all Tink could understand, it might as well have been some alien tongue, so she turned her attention to the tiles.

Lowering her specs, she shuffled through until the surface was magnified and she could see the marks of previous attempts to pry the tiles away to reveal the mechanisms underneath. Other people knew the puzzle hid something. But judging from the fresh pockmarks on the hillside, it had yet to be found. Tink hoped it was the *Celeste*. Then this dangerous adventure would be over, and she could get back to her engine room.

Magnifying further, she tried to find any gap between the tiles. She failed, despite having the scratches of history to guide her. It was almost like it was one piece of stone. Almost. She flipped through her specs, testing all the lenses and settings to see if they revealed anything.

After a few long minutes, she stood up straight, arching the kinks out of her back. "I don't—"

"Ha, I have it!" Ish's face beamed with a smile. He pointed at the legs. "Take that Tan the Terrible. Think you're so clever."

"What does it say?" Dustan peered over Ish's shoulder.

"Booming but voiceless, I howl." Ish's voice echoed off the stone, reflecting the words, and his stance mimicked that of a Meropi actor, broad and overdrawn. His voice dropped theatrically. "Hard but formless, I roar. Tongued but toothless, I bite." His lips quirked in a lopsided smile, breaking the performance. "Small but boundless, I consume."

Fennick frowned. "Um, that's what we already translated."

Ish's smile beamed, and he squeezed the young archaeologist's shoulder. "But you need to read it in Erivan to hear the riddle inside the words."

"Enough suspense, Ish." Rebeka scanned the hillside, pulse rifle at the ready. "Let's crack this thing and get out of here. Or, if we can't crack it, just get out of here."

"Booming but voiceless, I howl." Ish peered over Tink's shoulder. Then he reached forward with a long finger and pressed one of the tiles that looked like a three-pronged turbine. "Air." There was an audible click and the tile stayed depressed.

"Hard but formless, I roar." He scanned the tiles and this time picked one that looked like waves.

"Water." Tink looked at her friend, slightly awed by this new facet to him. She'd always known he loved puzzles but riddles in ancient tongues was not something she expected.

"Tongued but toothless, I bite." He pressed a glyph that indeed looked like a delicate tongue. "Fire."

"Small but boundless, I consume." He pulled back. "Earth." His fingers hovered over a glyph with a series of dots, then moved to one with a flat line. "Hmmm. Maybe this one." He shifted to one with a series of triangles. "Mountains could be earth?"

Alek leaned over Tink's shoulder and pressed a simple circle. "Earth," he said as the glyph sunk into the surface. Tink held her breath, waiting for the puzzle to reset, but the tiles stayed depressed.

"Huh," Ish said beside her. "Earth."

There was a rumble and a large cracking sound as the whole wall slid into the ground, exposing the top of a staircase that led down into darkness.

"So, I can go back to the ship now, right?" Tink backed away from the abyss.

"No one is going anywhere," said an unwelcome but all-too-familiar voice.

Her shoulders sunk as she spun around to see Rebeka, her arms in the air, at the end of Visi's blaster.

41: ALEK

A LEK BROUGHT HIS RIFLE up out of instinct. The whine of the blasters held by the bruisers flanking Ludovicus Visi kept him from firing. Visi peered at him as if he were an interesting specimen in a menagerie — an expression Alek knew well.

"Tsk tsk." Visi's hands clasped in front of his tunic. "Really Mr. *Wa*, you need to learn better control. My men can drop you before you even have a chance to squeeze the trigger." His left hand flicked and the goon on that side stepped forward. "Drop your weapon, then turn around and lead us into Hades. Or is it heaven?"

Alek kept the rifle butt tight against his shoulder, peering at Visi over the scope. Visi snapped his fingers, and Alek tensed, expecting a blaster hole in his head. Instead, the bruiser lifted his weapon and pointed it at Rebeka's temple. Alek's breath grated against his eardrums as he considered his options. Then he realized he had no options.

Lowering into a crouch, he laid his rifle on the ground. He stood again, raising his hands as he did and placing them on top of his head.

"Good dog." Visi's lips twisted into a smile, and Alek's stomach soured. The man crooked his index finger over his shoulder, and another figure, clad head to toe in fuchsia, stepped out of the darkness. Thighs as thick and sinewy as a man-eating snake. A map of scars criss-crossed muscled arms, including the long, still-pink scar on her left arm.

"Sorcha." The word fell from Alek's mouth before he could stop it. Ludovicus' sister pegged him with her icy gaze — the only similarity between her and her brother. That and a deep cruel streak.

"Hello Alek." Her voice was low and serpentine. "It's been too long." She rubbed the scar on her arm.

"Not long enough," he muttered. The sourness in his gut turned to acid. It didn't look like she'd forgiven him for giving her that mark, though she hadn't had it removed ... she hadn't avenged herself yet.

Rebeka's eyes narrowed, and her lips tensed as she peered at him. "How—"

Sorcha sent a donkey kick into the captain's stomach. The captain glared at her as she coughed.

"Enough," Visi said. "We can all catch up inside." He tipped his head back to scan the sky. "Move."

Sorcha drew her blaster and pointed it at Alek's chest, a smile twisting her lips. "You heard him. Go in ... I'll be right behind you." She nudged him with the barrel.

Loath to turn his back on her, Alek nonetheless did as he was told, following Tink into the abyss.

The only brightness in the passageway came from Tink's flashlight and the lights on the blasters. The only sounds were their soft footfalls and the hushed rustled of their breath. There wasn't even the drip of water despite the humidity above them.

As they continued to descend, Alek started to see spots in his vision, and had the brief thought that there wasn't enough air down there to feed them all. Then one of the spots scurried across the ceiling.

"What was that?" Dustan's voice was weak but still carried in the confined space.

"Glitter bugs." Sorcha's breath whispered over the nape of Alek's neck, sending shivers down his spine. "If you eat them alive, apparently they're an aphrodisiac."

"It's not just glitter bugs." Tink swept her torch across the passage. "There are lights up ahead."

"What?" Sorcha muscled past Alek. "If someone—"

"It's another bleeding riddle." Tink lifted her flashlight high. Beside her, Sorcha aimed her blaster at the door.

"I wouldn't do that." Alek rested his hand on her forearm, exerting the lightest of downward pressure, despite the risk of the action to his own life and limb. "What do you think will happen if the blast ricochets, or brings the ceiling down on us?" She scowled at him but lowered her weapon.

"Ish?" Tink called over her shoulder.

"Yeah?"

Alek nearly jumped at the navigator's voice so close behind him. To cover his nerves, he pointed at the rock in front of them. "More words in your ancient tongue."

"It's not *my* tongue."

"What does it say?" Visi crowded in behind him.

"Speak the name of heaven's creator to enter and be amazed."

"Heaven's creator?" Alek peered at the unintelligible letters.

"Uranus?" Fennick's voice was surprisingly close.

"Tiamat?" Rebeka offered.

"Yanus?" Tink tipped her head to the side as she spoke.

"Tan." Ish spoke in a whisper, but the wall slid away, exposing a cavernous space beyond. And in the middle, surrounded by crates and cylinders, sat a sleeping spectre that twinkled red and blue in their lights.

"Tan?" Tink's nose crinkled. "I...." She tipped her head sideways.

"The maker of heaven." Ish swept his arm over the space beyond. "Of the—"

"The *Celeste*." Visi's voice held more emotion than Alek had thought the man capable of.

Staring at the ship, Alek knew it was true, even though he couldn't read the metallic letters on its iridescent side. The characters seemed familiar, like the Ancient Erivan his grandmother had made him study, but weren't any he remembered. The skin of the ship rippled in the scope lights, like mercury battled with oil.

"That's the answer, yes?" Visi turned to Ish, who nodded before turning to the stairs down into the inverse pyramid. "Oh, I think you should stay by me." Visi looped his arm around Ish's elbow. "You're a man of hidden talents. Speaking the ancient languages. Drifting into the stream."

Alek took a step towards the gangster, intent on showing him some manners. Then he felt Sorcha's blaster in the small of his back.

"Walk. Hands where I can see them."

Alek lifted his hands to the back of his head as Visi glanced at him, a sneer on his lips, before stepping down the stairs.

"Wait," Sorcha said as Visi's foot landed on the first step.

There was a thunk somewhere far above, where the ceiling was hidden by shadow. Visi froze as lights started to click on around the space. Alek held his breath.

"Second thought." Visi turned to his sister. "You and him go down first," he said, jerking his chin at Alek.

After a moment's pause, Sorcha prodded him with her blaster. Holding his hands high, Alek picked his way down the steep staircase, searching for anything he could use as a weapon. He tried not to get distracted by the legend parked in the centre. It still gleamed, even though it had been in this underground grave for millennia, its slate grey sides shimmering with iridescence as their torches and scope lights passed over it. It was a lot smaller than he expected a treasure ship to be. And locked up tight, not even a seam visible on its sides. But its resemblance to the hologram in the pyramid on the red planet was unmistakable.

At the bottom, Tink passed him and strode up to the ship. She placed her palms against its hull, pressing her ear to the metal, as if it were some breathing beast.

The whine of a charging blaster refocused Alek's attention. Ludovicus pointed his weapon at Tink.

"Hands off my ship."

42: Rebeka

I THOUGHT IT WAS *our* ship." Dustan stepped beside Rebeka. He didn't sound angry or upset. Rebeka glanced at him. *Resigned.* His skin was pale and waxen, and covered with a sheen of sweat.

Visi peered at Dustan, his eyebrow arched. "For an academic, you're not very smart." He turned his attention back to Tink. "Hands off."

Tink raised her hands. "But—"

"Captain." Kandi's voice came from Rebeka's wrist.

"Not now, Kandi." Rebeka's throat rasped as she tried to whisper, even though every word could still be heard in the silent, underground hangar. Considering they were below the massive stone monument, Rebeka craned her head back to examine the rock above them, wondering how they'd gotten the *Celeste* in here in the first place. But the ceiling of the inverse pyramid was lost in shadow.

"Yes now. You have incoming."

Rebeka stopped whispering. "I know. Visi and his gang are here."

"Oh, Poseidon's pox." There was a pause on the other end. "I don't mean Visi." More silence, and when Kandi came back online, her voice was strained. "The Mantas are here."

"Yes. The Mantas *have* arrived." A sinuous voice echoed from above.

At the sound of the new voice, Rebeka spun around and down into a crouch behind the nearest object large enough to be a shield. Her muscles hadn't forgotten their training, even if they protested the sudden movement. Not long ago, they'd have sprung into action without complaint.

She peeked over the top of the crate to get a better look at the black-clad fighters swarming down the staircase and around the overhead catwalk that ringed the pyramid. A pulse bolt hit the rock in front of her hiding place, sending sparks flying. As she ducked back down, she examined her makeshift shield: a crate coated in dust.

She scowled at Visi, who'd ended up beside her. "If you get me killed, I swear I will haunt your ass into eternity."

He smiled at her. "I don't doubt you would." Raising his voice, he continued. "Echo, let's make a deal."

"Echo?" she mouthed, squinting at Visi as she tried to place the name.

"Like you made a deal with these poor folks?" The woman's laugh momentarily lightened Rebeka's heart, until she realized she was caught on the losing end of this encounter whichever way she looked at it. The Mantas weren't known for letting bystanders live. "I don't think so."

"When did you start working for the Mantas?" Visi's question was smooth and hard as marble.

"They made me an offer I couldn't refuse."

"Wait a minute ... Echo Eris?" Rebeka glared at him, remembering the sheriff on Ten Selva. "She was in your pocket, wasn't she? Watching us."

"I wasn't watching you — I had Dustan for that." Visi shrugged. "And I didn't know she was in bed with them."

"Would it have made a difference?" Rebeka's fingers twitched, wishing she had her blaster.

There was a second too much silence. "Maybe. I needed to nudge you in the right direction so I could keep my name clean ... but I don't like divided loyalties."

Rebeka snorted at that, given his own situation of serving himself and serving the Dominion.

From a few crates away, Sorcha fired at the stairs. Another pulse bolt repaid her efforts. Rebeka shook her head, trying to dislodge the ringing in her ears.

Her eyebrows pulled together as she stared at the gangster. "Why?"

"What?" His top lip wrinkled.

"Why are you even after the *Celeste*? You don't need the money."

"You're right." He quirked an eyebrow. "But I *want* the power. Money only gets you so far."

Rebeka pursed her lips and turned to glared at the ship. A ship that couldn't hold much treasure. *If there is any treasure.* Anger flushed her cheeks. "There better damn well be," she muttered, turning around to face the crate. To her surprise, it wasn't locked. She popped the latch and lifted the lid, an action that earned another pulse bolt. This round hit the lid, which managed to survive the impact.

"Oh." Rebeka's hand came to her chest as her heart beat faster. "So there is." Her fingers fluttered over glittering gems and glistening metal.

"Close that crate!" Eris' voice held an edge of violence.

She snapped the crate shut and dropped behind it again. "Give me my rifle back." She stared at Visi, who shook his head. "Return our weapons, stick to the deal, and we'll help you fend off the Mantas." She crossed her arms over her chest and gazed at the *Celeste*. "Otherwise, I can sit here while they mow you down. All the same to me."

Visi shifted. His eyes narrowed as he peered at her. A chirrup echoed through the cavern: a fire launcher coming to life.

"Fine." He thrust her rifle at her, then tapped his ear and whispered. Glancing at Alek, she saw him grab a rifle from Sorcha with one hand while the other slid the blaster into his empty holster. Even Fennick had a blaster, she noticed, and looked like he actually knew how to use it. His shot a few seconds later confirmed that assessment, taking out the gangster who crept along the catwalk in an attempt to get behind them. And Tink had never surrendered her kit, which Rebeka knew was full of things incendiary and potent.

A splash of heat and clinging fire landed in front of them as Eris finally got a shot off with the fire launcher.

"Are you a good shot?" Visi asked.

"First in my class." She popped up over the top of the crate, took aim and fired, then dropped back down, all in the space of a heartbeat. Hearing the scream and thud as her target fell off the catwalk, she nodded.

"Take this too." Visi handed her a blaster, which she grabbed before he could pull it back. She had no idea where he'd been hiding the weapon, since he still had the one he'd held to her head in his hand.

As she took another shot, and brought down another target, Dustan scuttled up beside her. "We need to get on the ship." He poked his head up above their little circle of crates. Rebeka pulled him back down as a projectile skidded across the top. "They can't shoot at us in there."

"And how do you suggest we do that?"

"Your Tinker?"

Rebeka glanced at Tink, who crouched beside the adjacent pile of crates. She futzed with something Rebeka couldn't make out. Beside her, Alek took aim at Eris, but his shot went wide as a pulse bolt grazed his shoulder. He growled and dropped back down. Visi's sister — Sorcha — ducked as she re-charged her blaster. Blood oozed from a wound on her thigh.

Rebeka tapped her wrist, whispering. "Tink, if you have any tricks in that magic bag of yours, use them to open up that ship."

Tink turned to stare at her across the distance between them, tipping her head to the side while her free hand gestured towards the *Celeste*. Rebeka could only guess at what that meant: there were 5 metres of open ground between her and any cover provided by the ship. Then Tink ducked as a spray of sparks cascaded over the pocket of boxes where they'd taken refuge. She'd popped open the lid on one of them to give herself more cover.

Glaring at Rebeka, she picked up her bag and rose into a low sprinter's crouch. She rocked back and forth for a second before pushing off. Fennick tried to grab her as she passed him but missed. He tipped his head to the side, staring at Rebeka before inching around his crate to take another shot. A projectile hit the ground behind Tink's heels, going wide as the man who'd fired it tumbled to the floor, taken out by Fennick.

A few seconds later, Ish tore from his hiding spot to fling himself towards the ship. With his long legs, he almost caught up with Tink by the time they both skidded behind a strut. Rock chips and dust sprayed over them as the Mantas shots shifted focus to the area around the ship.

"Draw their fire away from the *Celeste*." Rebeka abandoned being quiet, raising her voice loud enough to be heard. They all doubled down on the Mantas on the catwalk. All of them except Fennick, who sprinted after Tink and Ish. There was a whomph, and the ground trembled. Chunks of rock rained down on them, and dust choked the air along with the smoke. Rebeka coughed and waved her hand to clear the dust away from her face.

"Fennick!" Dustan ran towards his apprentice, who lay sprawled on the ground. The dust from the impact of the grenade quickly settled, leaving the pair exposed.

"Zeus' bollocks!" Rebeka shouted. "There was a plan!"

"Really?" Visi arched an eyebrow. "Not much of a plan."

She scowled at him then sprinted to Fennick's other side. The young man moaned as she grabbed his other arm with her free hand and hauled him roughly towards the ship.

"What were you thinking?"

"I have the key." Fennick's head lolled back, and his skin was pale.

As they reached the strut, Dustan clapped his hands to Fennick's face. "Stay with us." He then ran his hands over the man.

"I'm fine." Fennick swatted at Dustan. "Just rattled." He stood up and yanked at the neck of his tunic, tugging at the arabesque pendant he always wore. He pulled it over his head and handed it to Ish. "The key."

Dustan stepped back. "The key? What are you talking about?"

Another resounding boom echoed through the cavern, sending a shower of sand and debris down from the ceiling.

"Now is not the time." Rebeka jerked Dustan down as he covered his head with his hands. "Tink, try that thing."

In the dust cloud that followed the grenade, Alek and the two Visi siblings scuttled to join them under the ship. Tink's gaze shifted from the newcomers to her and Fennick before she finally turned to Ish and took the pendant. Rebeka noticed Visi's eyes narrow as he watched it changed hands, and she momentarily wondered if he knew what the hell it was. But she was distracted from that thought by Alek slumping down beside her, his shirt sleeve soaked with crimson from the wound on his shoulder. Blood now actively seeped from Sorcha's bicep as well as her thigh, and she shifted her blaster to her other hand.

She scowled at her brother. "She's going to pay for this. This is my favourite vest."

"You only have one vest, sister."

"I know!" She stroked the shiny fuchsia. "And that woman destroyed it."

Rebeka's attention was drawn back to the staircase. *That woman* — Eris — had descended to the bottom and now hefted the fire launcher to her shoulder again.

"Now Tink! Now would be good."

43: TINK

TINK STARED AT THE pendant, trying to figure out how Rebeka expected her to use the delicate piece of interwoven metal to open a ship without so much as a seam, let alone a keyhole. More shots echoed behind her.

A woman's voice rose from the ruckus. "Because I'm a good person — and a gang war might be bad for my health — put down your weapons and I'll let you walk away."

"Lies," Alek said, a rough cough following his words.

"You learned your lesson," Eris said, the sneer audible in her tone. "You're not as dumb as your average muscle-head."

"I'm not a muscle-head. I'm a stick jockey."

"Enough. Come out and take your chances. Or stay and die. It's all the same to me."

Between the shooting, a whine arose: the grenade launcher spooling up, getting ready to fire again. She slammed her fist into the ship and howled in a mixture of pain and frustration.

A cry close beside her drew her attention. Ish clasped his left hand to his right shoulder, blood seeping through his fingers, and he tucked himself closer to the strut.

His wide eyes caught her gaze. "Just a flesh wound."

Tink punched the ship again with her free hand. "Open. Up. You. Bleeding. Ship." The ship remained impassive.

"I don't think that's how it works," Ish said, then muttered something in Erivan.

Frowning, she hit the ship again, this time slapping it with the hand that held the pendant.

The ship chirped.

Tink fell back onto her rump, catching herself with the hand that held the necklace, wincing in pain as the metal pierced her skin. Warm blood oozed from the wound.

"Umm." Lights lit up on the surface in front of her and a voice emanated from the ship. She dusted herself off as the ship repeated itself. "Gibberish."

Beside her, Ish hauled himself up to standing. "Not gibberish. Erivan." He left bloody fingerprints as he tapped at the surface and muttered to himself.

"Time's up." Eris' voice held an edge of glee as it echoed throughout the cavern.

The percussive force of the explosion knocked Tink off her feet. She threw her hands over her head as shrapnel and sparks rained down, ricocheting off the ship. After the worst of it, she lifted her head. A gangplank had lowered from the ship's belly. She reached behind her for Rebeka.

"Captain." She grasped at air. Rebeka wasn't where she'd been. She spun around "Captain?" Through the curtain of dust and debris, she spotted her crouched beside Dustan. Tink shuffled over to where the captain was trying to get her ex standing with help from Fennick.

As Fennick sat up, the blood covering his torso became visible.

"Fennick!" Ish knelt beside the young man, patting his chest.

"It's not mine." Fennick stared at Dustan, his eyes glistening.

Dustan knelt in front of him, clutching his abdomen. When he coughed, it was wet and pink.

"Dustan?" Rebeka grasped his face. Even Tink could see the man was in deep trouble.

"Leave him." Visi's voice was more commanding than Tink had ever heard it, and she almost wanted to follow. She turned to see him, already on the gangplank.

"No," Rebeka said.

"He's dead," Visi hissed. "Or as good as. You can see it as well as I can." His voice dropped lower. "We have to go. Now."

Ish spun to face the gangster. "We don't go without him."

Visi's eyes narrowed as he peered at Ish, and Tink's stomach twisted. His smooth tone returned. "Fine. Sorcha and I will go without you. Sorcha!"

Sorcha stopped shooting at the Mantas, leaving Alek's side to join her brother.

Ish stepped towards him and laughed. Tink gaped at him, but he ignored her.

"And just how do you think you'll manage without a translator?" As if on cue, the ship rattled off more unintelligible words. Ish smirked, hand on his hips. Then he stopped and dropped his hands. "Help us get him onto the ship, or I'll surrender myself to the Mantas."

"Ish," Tink said. When his eyes met hers, there was no waiver in them. He meant it.

"You're right, we need a translator." Visi grabbed Ish and dragged him up the ramp with him.

"Ish!" Tink ran up the ramp after them, pausing to look back at the captain. Alek and Fennick now carried Dustan towards her. A judder in the ramp forced her to turn around and find her balance. It lifted with her on it, then came to a sudden stop.

A muscled form filled the doorway. "Who has the key?" Sorcha Visi asked.

Tink opened her mouth then snapped it shut and stepped forward as the captain came up beside her.

Rebeka crossed her arms over her chest, blaster held by the hand facing Sorcha. "We do." Sorcha scowled then stepped back, clearing the way for them. Rebeka leaned towards Tink. "You still have it, right?"

Tink just nodded, clutching the pendant in her bloody hand.

The ramp snapped closed like the jaws of a predator. A predator they were now trapped inside of with one of the biggest criminals in the Dominion. Tink stood in some kind of central common area that bore no resemblance to a cargo bay, except for its openness. Delicate arches rose from both sides, meeting in the centre of the ceiling. The space was scattered with crates similar to those outside. Some appeared to be stasis units, still functioning after millennia, while others sat dark, any status panels long dead, and looked as if they could hold a treasury full of gold. There were what appeared to be cages. Empty cages.

Behind the entrance, openings on either side led down darkened corridors. In front, stairs hugging the outer walls led up. Visi glared down from the mezzanine. Ish stood at his side, his face serious. She wouldn't have wanted to be alone with Visi either, even if it was just a few seconds. Rebeka shifted to follow Sorcha, who took the stairs two at a time.

"Umm, Captain?" Tink tapped the captain's shoulder.

"What?" Rebeka sniped. "I don't want to let them get too far away."

Tink pointed directly in front of her where a flat patch of floor stood out in contrast to the rest. "There's a lift."

Tink walked onto the lighter rectangle, but Rebeka continued after Sorcha. Fennick and Alek stepped on beside her, Dustan still supported between them. The ship spoke unintelligible words. Her stomach sank, until Ish shouted down at them.

"Kari."

She looked up as the platform started to rise. Dizziness swept over her as she realized there were no walls or handrails on the lift. Rebeka reached the top the same time they did and stopped beside Visi.

"Clever." He frowned at Tink, undercutting his assessment, then continued forward.

Fennick stumbled getting off the platform, his face sheened with sweat. Rebeka moved to take his place at Dustan's side. Tink was shocked when Sorcha muscled her away and took Fennick's place, despite his protests.

Tink glanced at the captain, breathless beside her.

"I hope we make enough from this for me to retire."

"Retirement would kill you." Tink rolled her eyes at Rebeka. "If this escapade doesn't."

Rebeka pressed her lips together but stayed silent. Heading down the broad hallway, they joined Visi at the helm. Ish already sat at the navigator's station, still recognizable despite the intervening centuries.

"Key me." He turned to look at Tink, holding out his hand.

She passed him the pendant. "How is that thing a key?"

Ish leaned close to the console in front of him, then ducked and craned his neck, a look of consternation on his face. "I ... I don't know." He held his hands up.

Alek grabbed the pendant as he stepped into the well beside Ish. "I don't think you should have this."

"Hey." Fennick lurched forward. "That's mine."

"What I mean is, the navigator wouldn't be in control of the ship's power." Alek held the pendant in his hand as he ran it across the console that circled the pilot's pit.

"No." Rebeka reached for the necklace. "The captain would." She sat at what she'd obviously determined was the captain's seat, the station raised above and set behind the others.

"I don't think you're getting your necklace back," Tink said to Fennick, who now crouched at her feet beside Dustan.

The captain slid the pendant into some slot on her armrest. Lights lit up on consoles across the bridge.

Alek yelped as gloves of light enveloped his hands. His hair stood on end. "I think you turned it on."

"And you're not the captain." Visi stood in front of Rebeka, who glared back, not moving. Then Sorcha pressed the muzzle of a blaster against her head. The captain shifted her head slightly to peer at the woman, then stood up, letting Visi take the seat.

Tink sat at the station beside Alek, which she guessed was Tactical, looking at the controls in front of her. She jerked back, sitting upright.

"It's in Standard. Well, close enough."

"Yes, it is." Visi's voice cut like a laser scalpel. "You lied." He frowned at Ish.

The navigator shrugged. "How was I to know? Everything 'til now has been Ancient Erivan."

The ship rocked, and the lights flickered in a wave.

"What was that?" Visi leaned forward to peer out the window in front of them, a window that hadn't been visible from the outside.

Echo Eris stood facing them, hefting a grenade launcher onto her shoulder.

"I think she's intending to blast her way in," Tink said.

Visi scowled at her. "Anything over there that will deal with these insects once and for all?"

She scanned the panel and shook her head. "Whoever made this ship, it doesn't seem like they were too keen on deadly force. But—" She stabbed one of the buttons. For a minute, she thought it hadn't worked. Then the whole cavern shook, dust spreading out from them in waves. Even inside the ship, she felt like the breath had been knocked out of her.

Outside the window, the woman lay on her back, blood dripping from her nose.

"What was that?" Alek asked.

"Sonic boom." Tink's eyebrows lifted. "I need to get me one of those," she whispered at the same time the captain said, "Don't tell Kandi about that."

"Lifting off," Alek said. The ship juddered in response, and he canted his head. "Maybe." He shifted his hands over the strange controls, and the ship moved more smoothly this time. The ground shifted out the window, then the ship paused.

"Alek?" Rebeka asked.

"I ... I have no idea which way is out. It's not like there's a door—"

As he spoke, an ear-piercing screech reverberated through the shell of the ship, and dust fell on it from above, pattering like rain. Seconds later, there was another loud thwump and the *Celeste* rocked sideways, causing a grinding sound on the port side.

Tink tried to make sense of the console in front of her. Her hand went to her goggles, then dropped — they'd be no help with this. She pulled back as Ish reached over and pressed a button. A schematic popped up, hovering in the space over the console, showing the route to an exit.

"Go up it says." She turned to Alek. "We should see a door?"

A heartbeat later, a great tearing sounded, and light and dust spilled into the cavern. Apparently, Emperor Tan — or Emperor Tan's feet — had stepped aside.

44: REBEKA

"STOP FUSSING," DUSTAN SAID. He swatted weakly at Rebeka's hand. She ignored him, lifting his head to tuck her jacket under it.

"Stop jostling the stretcher." Kandi peered at her. She and Sorcha held opposite ends as they shifted it onto the lift; when she'd arrived from the *Lyra*, trailed by Grim, Kandi had found a room that looked like a medbay and ordered them to take Dustan there. For some unfathomable reason, Visi's sister was being helpful again.

Rebeka pursed her lips but did as she was told. She straightened and walked beside him, clutching his hand in hers. It was cold and sticky with blood.

Once in the cargo bay, he squeezed her hand. "Here."

"No, we need to get you to the medbay."

He struggled to sit up, almost tipping the stretcher. "Here," he said louder, then started coughing. Blood speckled his chin.

"Stop. You're going to make it worse."

He laughed, hoarse and deep. "It can't get worse." He shifted again, rocking the stretcher.

"Okay, fine." Kandi lowered her end of the stretcher and Sorcha had no choice but to follow suit. "Here."

"Kandi!" Rebeka stared at her part-time medic, who grimaced. Kandi turned to glare daggers at Sorcha, who Rebeka realized wasn't that much bigger than her part-time security officer. She just looked a lot scarier.

Sorcha rolled her eyes and lifted her hands. "You're welcome." She spun around and headed towards the ramp.

Kandi watched her go before turning back to Rebeka, laying her hand on her arm. "He's dying."

"Yes, that's why we need to get him to the medbay."

"It's not the wound that's killing him." She flicked her gaze to Dustan then back to Rebeka. "I should get back to the *Lyra*. Right now, Cass is in charge." With a last sad look at Rebeka, she turned and made her way towards the ramp.

Rebeka turned back to Dustan. "What's she talking about?"

"The lungs. Too much time disturbing ancient microbes in the dirt, maybe." Dustan clutched at her fingers as he took a shuddering breath. "Here."

"Again with the 'here.'"

He shifted, and more crimson blood soaked his shirt.

"Stop moving."

He shook his head and pressed something into her hand. When she looked at it, she realized it was the orb. She frowned, wanting to fling the infernal thing across the cargo bay. Dustan curled her fingers around it.

"Give it to Juniper."

"I'd rather give her you."

Dustan stared at her hand, eyes glassy. "Even if there's nothing left to find, she should have it. It's really her research. Remind her I...." His eyes closed.

"Dustan." Rebeka put the orb on the decking beside her and checked his pulse. Thready and weak but it was still there. She put her hand to his cheek, and his eyelids fluttered. "Dustan," she whispered as Grim came up and sniffed the orb. He started batting it around, and Rebeka plucked it away and put it in her pocket. Grim's green eyes stared at her. A sound pulled her attention away: boots on metal.

Looking over her shoulder, she saw the young archaeologist, who didn't look so young now. "Fennick."

"Sorry, I can go." He waved over his shoulder, back outside. "Surprisingly, Visi isn't killing us." He turned his gaze to Dustan, and his eyes glistened. "Not all of us. Not yet."

"Come here, my boy."

Rebeka's gaze swivelled to Dustan, awake and alert again. Fennick's tentative steps echoed in the empty hold. He knelt on Dustan's other side.

Dustan grasped the man's hand. "Use the treasure wisely."

"There's no treasure." Fennick shifted his hand in Dustan's grip. "Not for us."

"Ha, you don't know treasure." He turned to Rebeka. "Go get the treasure before it's taken."

"I don't care about the treasure."

"I do." Another cough racked him, and more blood oozed into his shirt. "Even more, I care about screwing Visi over."

"Something we can agree on." Rebeka said the words quietly, but she still almost missed Dustan's last breath.

Fennick reached out and ran his hand down Dustan's face, ignoring the tears on his own. "What do we do now?" he said, almost to himself.

"We see if there is any treasure to screw Visi out of." Rebeka's jaw clenched. "But first we take Dustan to the *Lyra*."

45: TINK

As Tink trolled through the *Celeste*'s data banks, Ish sat at her side to translate. Every minute, she looked sidelong at Visi. Somehow, they'd sold him on the need to translate the AI — although the labels were in an ancient variant of Standard, the ship still spoke an archaic dialect of Erivan. Even Ish had trouble with it. She shifted her regard to her friend, only to find him staring daggers at Visi.

She gazed back at the man. He peered over the cargo hold, standing for all the world like the captain of an old sailing ship, hands clasped behind his back. She only hoped Alek was able to surreptitiously search the crates for signs of a massive biological weapon under Visi's hawk-like gaze.

"What's up?" she asked Ish, keeping her voice low, as she turned back to the computer. Her real intent was to make sure there weren't any traces of specs for a biological weapon hidden in the code. The first thing she'd done when she sat down at the Tac station was insert a worm to seek and destroy.

He blinked and turned to her. "Nothing." His hair fell in front of his face as he shook his head.

"That wasn't a 'nothing' look."

"I...." He glanced at Visi again, who squinted at them, no longer appearing captainly. Ish said some words in what Tink was coming to recognize as Erivan. For their ruse to work, he did actually have to translate some of the AI. His shoulders shrugged. "I just don't trust him." He rattled off a few more words.

Visi appeared appeased and turned back to watch the progress of whatever was going on in the hold.

Kandi stood beside him and seemed to have all her weapons at the ready. She held the stave in her hand unextended.

Somewhere below, she heard Sorcha, the gang leader's sister, arguing with Alek, though she couldn't tell what the fight was about.

"Are you almost done?" Ish whispered, then shot a furtive glance at Visi. Tink followed suit, seeing that the gangster had shifted away from Kandi and spoke into his wrist patch. Even gangsters had patches.

Her tablet beeped, and she blinked at it. "Yeah. Done." Her forehead furrowed. "There's nothing."

"That's good, right?"

"Yeah, but I can't see what the worm ate. Not without taking it back to the *Lyra* and dissecting it. What if there's more hidden and I don't recognize—"

"We've done what we can." Ish grabbed her wrists and held her gaze.

Nodding, she stood and arched her back, then tucked her tablet into the front pocket of her overalls.

"Well, we should be taking our share and heading out," she said loud enough for Visi to hear.

Visi smiled at her and swept his hand towards the rail-less elevator, indicating she should go first.

"I think I'll take the stairs." She squinted at him.

He shifted his gaze over her shoulder, and she was surprised when Ish diverged and went to join him.

With barely a breath of indecision, Kandi stepped onto the pad with the two of them. Tink shrugged and headed down the stairs.

She reached the bottom shortly after the others, sliding down the railings to aid her descent. At the bottom, she shifted close to Alek.

"Anything?" she asked, her voice little more than a breath. He glanced at her and barely shook his head.

Visi reached the bottom, stopping in the middle of the hold. Grim stood on top of a crate and sniffed it, a low growl rising in his belly.

"Pretty cat." Visi reached out to pet him, quickly pulling his hand back when Grim hissed, his back arched, and lashed out with a clawed paw. "Vicious cat."

"Smart cat." Tink crossed over to Grim and scritched his chin. "But you shouldn't be here." He peered at her for a second, then flicked his tail, jumped off the crate and headed for the ramp. "Stupid cat."

A shadow paused in the doorway. Sorcha's hand went to her weapon for a second before the shadow stepped inside and resolved into Rebeka. A blood-soaked Rebeka.

"Captain," Alek said, staring at the blood.

"I'm fine." She continued to stare at Visi. "Time to deliver."

Visi ambled to Rebeka, pulling his lanky frame taller. "I'm afraid there's a problem." He shifted his gaze to Rebeka's front. "My deal was with Dustan Key. Null and void on his death."

In a heartbeat, Rebeka had her blaster at Visi's forehead. Kandi's stave flashed in Tink's peripheral vision.

"I wouldn't shoot if I were you." He shifted his head without pulling it away from the gun.

Tink inhaled. She had barely a second to realize he looked at her before she felt the cold metal of a blaster at her temple. Out the corner of her eye, she caught a sliver of fuchsia: Sorcha.

"I think we can come to a new agreement though." He shifted away from Rebeka's gun. She didn't move to follow. "I let you all live and give you a token crate as a gesture of appreciation."

Tink snorted, a sound echoed by Rebeka.

"And why should I trust you not to kill us as soon as I lower my weapon."

"Because I don't think my new employee would be happy about that. And I do like to keep my employees happy." He turned to gaze at her again.

No, not me. She shifted her head to gaze at Ish, who'd stepped up beside her.

"Ish?" Her eyes stung.

He shrugged and stepped towards the gangster. "He made me an offer I couldn't refuse."

Visi wrapped his arm around Ish's shoulder and tugged him close.

"But...." Tink started.

Rebeka peered at Ish, and her gun lowered. Visi took advantage of her distraction and grabbed the weapon.

"Well, you really should be going." Visi waved the blaster. "You know what they say about guests." He stared at the captain. "Sorcha, get their crate for them." He jerked his chin towards his sister. "I'm sure she's picked out something special for you."

Tink felt the gun leave her temple, and she stepped over to join Rebeka in peering at Ish, who stared at the floor.

Sorcha shoved the crate at Alek, who took it without protest.

After that, no one moved, and time seemed to stretch in the silence. Until Visi broke it.

"Are we going to have a problem?"

"Ish...?" Rebeka said. He shook his head and stepped back.

The captain sighed and turned to go.

"Captain? Rebeka." Tink waved an arm at Ish. "We can't just leave him."

"He's not being forced to stay."

"Really? They're the ones with all the guns."

Visi spun Rebeka's blaster around, and handed it back, handle first. "Now we're even."

Rebeka pressed her lips together and shook her head. "No, we're not." She grabbed the blaster then plodded towards the door. Alek glanced at her then followed.

"Ish." Tink peered at her friend.

"I'm staying."

She half turned towards the door but paused to look at him one more time.

"Go."

She turned to do as he asked.

"But...." Ish started.

She spun around. Visi frowned at Ish.

"Tell my father I love him." He glanced at his hands. "And I know how proud he'd be to see me navigator on a ship like this."

"Wha—?"

"Now, go."

Kandi grabbed her arm and dragged her, half stumbling, off the *Celeste*.

Back on the *Lyra*, the engines were already firing up, though Alek was still in the cargo bay.

"He's gone." Tink slumped to the floor, next to the crate Alek had dropped there. At the other end of the bay, Grim started howling and pacing. "He left me."

"He didn't leave us." Kandi crouched beside Tink, holding her closed stave between both hands.

"You saw what I did." Tink waved at the now closed ramp.

"But you obviously didn't *hear* what I did." The stave spun in her hands. "The bit about his father. To tell him that he loves him."

She shifted her head to meet Kandi's gaze. "And that he knows he'd be proud. That's not Ish's father."

"No, *that's* a secret message."

Tink grimaced. "But what's he trying to say?"

"That he didn't exactly choose to go." Rebeka tapped her wrist. "Cass, locate Ish."

"Ishmael is not in sensor range."

Rebeka slumped down beside her. "He's ...? How?"

"He's on the *Celeste*." Alek's voice was quiet. "Who knows what it's capable of."

"Well, at least we know it's not capable of manufacturing this weapon." Rebeka ran her hands over her head.

"Um, not for sure." Tink watched Grim stalk in front of them. Peering at them, he yowled before crawling into her lap, where he began a rapid purr. "I need to analyze what I pulled out."

"So, what are we going to do?" Fennick asked, standing beside Alek.

"There's not a lot we can do." Tink stared at the floor. "In case you hadn't noticed, the *Lyra* is ancient, and not in the *Celeste* kind of way." Tears welled up as she stroked the grating. "Sorry, girl, but it's true." She looked at Fennick. "If we don't know where he is, we can't trace him. And if we did know where he was, we don't have our own jump drive to follow."

"Seriously?" Alek glared at them, arms akimbo. "You're just going to give up?"

"If we can't trace him, we don't even know where to start looking," Rebeka added.

Alek's palm came down hard on the crate. "We have a crate's worth of ancient treasure. That should be enough to buy the information." His arms crossed over his torso, and a muscle in his jaw ticked. "We know who took him, and it's not like Visi is low profile."

A twitter fluttered through Tink's chest, and she stood up. "We should probably open it up and figure out how much we have to work with."

Rebeka pursed her lips then stepped to the crate. She flicked one latch then the other. A soft hiss escaped. She lifted to lid.

For a moment, Tink thought the laughter that followed was an expression of joy. Then Rebeka slumped to the grating, and Tink noticed the expression on Alek's face as he looked at the contents.

"What? What is it?" She shifted Grim off her lap and went to peer in the crate. She lifted the first book, then the next. Then shoved her hand down the side as far as it would go. *Nothing*.

"Books." Alek frowned. "Books in bleeding Erivan."

Fennick came closer. "These are priceless."

"Yes, *priceless*," Rebeka said from her spot on the floor. Tink went to sit beside her. "They won't help us pay for information on Ish."

"Oh." Fennick crouched facing them. He dug into his pocket. "Maybe this will help." He drew out a gemstone of the purest sea blue. It took up his entire palm. "I found it in the cavern."

"Wow." Alek peered at the stone. "That's a big rock to take. Much bigger than this." From his pocket, he drew out a necklace of green stones and silver metal and dropped it to the floor. Fennick placed his stone with it.

"If we tally everything we took, we might have enough." Kandi crouched again and a cascade of small, vibrant pink stones joined the rest. She shrugged. "They weren't watching the crates in the cargo hold."

"I'm on a ship of thieves." Tink cast her gaze around at her crewmates. "Are the captain and I the only ones who didn't take anything from the *Celeste*?"

Rebeka coughed. She pulled a pouch from her jacket and decanted the contents onto the pile. A series of unusual metal coins joined the rest of the items. "As Kandi says, we might have enough." She glanced over her shoulder at Dustan's form, covered in a blanket. "But first I have work to do."

Tink stood and took her friend's hand, helping her up. "We have work to do."

46: ISH

ISH STRUGGLED AGAINST THE restraints the Dominion officer snapped onto his wrists. An electric shock rewarded his efforts. He tried to repress the yelp, but it turned into a grunt.

The Dominion captain glared at him, eyes narrowed, then shifted his disapproving stare to Visi. "What were you thinking? Kidnapping wasn't part of the brief. Neither was bringing the enemy onto a Dominion ship."

"Come now, Low. Ish isn't the enemy. You're not my enemy, are you?" Visi ran a finger down Ish's arm. Ish managed not to shudder, but a small jolt still zapped his wrists as he jerked his arm away. Visi graced him with a vicious smile. The man's mood was foul, though for all Ish knew, he was always like this. Visi jostled the restraints, sending a spark through Ish's nerves before he shifted his regard to the other man. "And it's not kidnapping if he came willingly." He glanced sharply at Ish when he snorted. "Besides, I thought this was Halcyon's ship."

The captain — Low — pressed his lips into a thin line and huffed out of his nose. "Regardless of the chain of command, this is still a Dominion vessel." His gaze flicked to Ish, and Ish filed away the name Halcyon to investigate later. "And he's a criminal." He stepped forward, poking a finger into Visi's shoulder. "As are you."

"Touch me again and I'll—"

"You'll what?" Captain Low lifted a finger but stopped short of jabbing the gangster. "You inflated what you'd deliver and you failed her," he said, and Ish realized the man knew there was something more than jewels and gold on the *Celeste*. Something Visi hadn't found. "You'll be lucky if you survive our debrief." A ping sounded and lights flashed on the bridge. "Speaking of which...."

As if on cue, the ship came out of the stream. Ish swayed with the motion. A smile played at the corner of his lips as he watched Visi stop himself from stumbling.

Low arched an eyebrow. "Don't have your space legs yet, eh?"

"*My* crew gives me more warning."

"You need a better navigator," Ish mumbled but the captain still glanced his way before returning to Visi.

"This is a battleship. Lots of things happen without warning."

"Captain?" A voice came over the comms. "We're being hailed."

"Patch it through."

There was a pause for a second, then the woman's voice returned. "They're telling us to fly into docking bay 2." The sentence raised at the end, as it she wasn't sure her statement was true.

The captain's eyebrows drew together as his gaze flicked from Visi to Ish and back. "Docking bay 2?" he muttered, then his eyes widened. He turned on his heels and strode onto the bridge.

Visi followed, his hand on Ish's arm. Ish had no choice but to go along if he wanted to avoid getting shocked again. When he stepped onto the bridge, Ish's jaw dropped.

A dreadnought filled the viewscreen. Well, part of a dreadnought. He swallowed against the lump in his throat. His brain tried to tell him it was a mirage. They weren't supposed to be real -- half myth, half legend, all nightmare.

"Head for docking bay 2." Low's voice was tight.

"I take it Halcyon has left her tower," Visi said.

Ish turned his head to Visi. The gangster's lips quirked into a smile. He appeared to be the only one amused by the situation. However, the tension still lingered around Visi's eyes. He hadn't been happy with what he'd found on the *Celeste*. Or hadn't found.

Low pointed at Visi. "You, come with me," he said. "And show some respect if you value your life." He then strode off the bridge at a brisk pace.

Visi snorted but followed the captain, dragging Ish along again. Ish grimaced as a tingle coursed through his wrists.

The captain walked in front of them, long strides carrying him quickly down the dimly lit corridors that all looked the same to Ish: black on black on slate grey.

"Stay." Visi held his palm out then pointed at the enormous hydraulic piston beside them, the last one on the gangway. "I don't want anyone to take my new navigator." Visi's hand patted his cheek, and Ish bristled at being treated like a pet, or recalcitrant child, but he also had no desire to meet whoever was in command of the dreadnought. Low's second — Liet, Low had called her — took up position beside the piston on the other side, feigning a casual stance that was clearly anything but. Her gaze flicked his way, then focused on her captain. She had no weapons that Ish could see, but judging by her scars, he guessed she could hold her own in hand-to-hand.

The docking bay buzzed with activity. Techs checked the ship for contaminants while probably looking for hidden ordinance. Soldiers dressed in combat armour flanked the ship. A hush fell over the large space, and Ish peeked out from behind the column, his curiosity getting the better of him. Officers in crisp aquamarine and gold uniforms marched from a doorway across the docking bay towards the ship. Their steps echoed in sharp precision.

But Ish's attention was drawn behind the phalanx, where a woman glided towards Low and Visi. Her silver hair gleamed under the lights of the docking bay. It appeared that platinum butterflies fluttered around her head, an illusion generated by the metallic insects attached to the sticks holding her hair in place. Piled into an updo, it made her tall form appear even taller. Statuesque, his mother would have said. Handsome, Ish thought. Although her steps were smooth under her shimmering dress, the stride spoke of power. Real power that didn't need to be displayed.

Low stood at attention, arms ramrod straight at his side, shoulders back. Visi struck his usual inscrutable pose —

hands clasped in front of him — though Ish thought there was a little more stiffness that usual to his stance.

The woman came to a stop in front of Low, and the captain gave a sharp bow from his waist, staying bent. Visi's shoulders tensed; even from his position behind the piston, Ish could see the shift. Given her glance at the gangster, she could too. Ish almost smiled.

Her eyes flicked over the captain. "You're not in dress uniform, Captain Low." Even though her tone was even, the statement dripped with judgment.

"I had not hoped for an audience so soon, Lady Koning," Low said from his bow.

Koning. Ish mouthed the word, a tendril of fear snaking through his heart. The Archon Halcyon Koning.

"Stand." The Archon brought her long fingers to the man's chin. She almost seemed to lift him with her nails. "I want to look in your eyes when you speak."

"Yes, Archon." Low stood. After a second's pause at the top, he lifted his gaze.

"Twice you've failed me, Low."

"I—"

"I know you'll say it wasn't your fault, that you had to work with a wildcard." She waved her hand at Visi. "Yes, you had to work with the unknown." The butterflies flickered. "Did you ever consider this might have been a test? In politics, you have to work with all sorts."

Low gave a sharp nod, looking at the floor in front of him. "I am a lowly officer with much to learn."

"Mmm, yes. I can see that." She tipped her head sideways. "But I think you still have potential, so I won't kill you today."

"Thank you, Archon, for your grace."

"And you." She spun to Visi, who took an actual step back. Ish decided he could almost like this woman. Except for the fact that she scared the piss out of a Dominion officer and the leader of one of the most powerful gang cartels. "Where's my ship?"

Visi pulled his shoulders back. "I thought it was *our* ship."

Her hand lashed out, quick as a viper, nails raking across his cheek. Beside him, Ish heard Liet inhale, and the Archon's gaze drifted their way before settling back on Visi. She flicked her hand over her shoulder, and a cloth appeared from one of the soldiers in the phalanx. Visi's hand went to his cheek as she began cleaning his blood off her fingers. "The deal was you can have it *after* I'm done with it. And taking a person as booty was not part of our agreement." Her gaze flicked to Ish again, and he shrunk behind the piston. "Why a navigator, of all things? An AI can do the job." There was a pause. "Why not the pilot? Or the engineer?"

"I'm a gangster." Visi's tone had lost a little of its bravado, but not much. "A pirate. I see something I want, I take it." He peered over his shoulder, towards Ish and Liet for a second, as if some internal debate was going on. He turned back to the Archon and shrugged. "And I wanted him."

"I want my ship. And I will have it." She pulled herself up to her full height, but when she spoke it was a whisper. "Bring me the *Celeste*, undefiled. And the archaeologist's research."

"My sister may have already *defiled* the ship — she's talented that way." His jaw clenched so hard Ish could see it from where he stood. "And the research is on the *Lyra*."

"I will flay you and blow that little ship to pieces if I don't get what I want." She stepped back, her voice hoarse and low when she continued. "What I need."

It was only the look of confusion on Visi's face that made Ish realize she'd spoken the last bit in Ancient Erivan. He pressed his lips tight, not wanting to draw her attention.

His eyebrows pulled together, and his nostrils flared. Few learned the language nowadays, and even fewer understood the dialect she'd spoken. Ish only hoped she didn't realize he was one of the few.

DID YOU ENJOY A LOST SHIP IN A DARK GRAVE?

IF YOU DID, I'D really appreciate it if you'd leave a review — it lets me know people enjoy what I'm putting out into the void and helps more people discover the book ... which supports my long-term ambitions of taking over the world.

If there are words from the book you'd like to see in the list of people, places and events ... and insects, let me know.

And if you want to keep up on the series, have early access to side stories, and get special peeks behind the scenes, sign up for my newsletter at reneastle.com. Forewarned is forearmed: it's a process. I make you jump through hoops, do some tricks, say a secret word. But the tale of how Kandi ended up on the *Lyra* is coming soon! Keep flipping past the glossary and you can check out a sample.

People, Places and Events ... and Insects

Aconitia: A planet at the very edge of civilization, suspended between the Dominion proper and the wilds controlled by the cartels. Also Corican V, fifth planet in the Corican system.

Agrippian hawk: Large raptor, known to carry off pets and unattended children on its home planet of Melchior.

Alassi Fire: Oil distilled from the secretions of the Alassi beetle, it burns very hot and clean.

Andoran asp: Venomous snake that sounds like a cat hissing when riled. Easily riled.

Ansibles: Communication stations that relay signals across the vast distances of the Dominion near instantaneously. Origins of ansible tech unknown.

Archon: Ruler of one of the imperial clans in the Emperor's name. Technically reports to Taxarchon.

Argent, The: A ship, Barracuda class, under the command of Harbin Low, a leader in the Tau division.

Badlands, The: Area of space at the edge of the Dominion, nestled between the core empire and the Desolation. Home to the desperate and the destitute.

Bakweevil: Large beetle endemic to cargo ships that haul provisions.

Barnacles: Mild swear word, similar in intensity to Jacks.

Bleeding Hades: Swear word, stronger than Barnacles.

Cartels: Organized crime conglomerates. Some of the most prominent are Mantas, Kraits, Haggishi and Bullheads.

Cassandra Event: Destruction of spaceship and station, put down to a fault in a CASS-ANDRA AI. Afterwards, most Cass AIs were decommissioned.

Chit: Slang for official digital currency common of the Dominion.

Clan Koning: Prominent imperial clan, currently ruled by Archon Halcyon Koning.

Clan Erregina: Prominent imperial clan, currently ruled by Archon Tyre Erregina.

Connect, The: Interstellar information network spanning the Dominion. Reliant on ansibles.

Corican: Planetary system at the end of Dominion-controlled space. Home to a sad military station and Aconitia, also known as Corican V.

Custard Bug: Insect. Larval stage is plump with creamy insides. Used to create scrambles as well as desserts.

Desolation, The: Area of space, location of an ancient cataclysm. Few dare to tread there, fearing ghosts or aliens...or both. Home to only those too far gone for even the Badlands and to the Sisters of Elazir. Separated from the Dominion by the Wall.

Dominion, The: The empire that controls most of the known universe, both a spatial and political entity. The power of the known universe, spanning all the way from the Desolation to the systems claimed by the cartels. Ruled by the Emperor, supported by the imperial clans. Peace and stability are maintained by the Legion and SIPS.

Emperor: Reclusive ruler of the Dominion. The Emperor's power is absolute.

Emperor Tan: One of the old Erivan emperors, she was instrumental in laying down the foundations of the Dominion. Named 'The Magnificent' or 'The Terrible', depending on which side of history you were on.

Excelsior: Dayside port town on Ten Selva, coated in red dust and grime.

Exodus, The: The mass migration from the Desolation.

Fifth Echelon: Elite divisions of the Legion, with extra-special training and skills: Ki, Omega, Phi, Tau, Epsilon.

Fire wasps: tiny wasps, the size of a mudpuppy egg, with stings that cause a burning sensation. Congregate in swarms.

Green Zone, The: Area of space between core Dominion and the regions claimed by the cartels. Despite nominal Legion patrols, lawlessness is the norm.

Guilds: Corporations that drive the economy. Some say they control it.

Hail Hecate: Invocation of thanks to the goddess of magic, doorways, crossroads and jump gates.

Hera Wept: Curse, an utterance of exasperation.

Hudsonite Brigade: Under the leadership of Marpo Gothe, the most powerful faction of the loose, fractious organization of rebel groups. Fighting for the abrogation of the Dominion and divestiture of the Emperor.

Jacks: Mild swear word, similar in intensity to Barnacles. Also, card game played with a deck used for cartomancy as well.

Jump gates: Shortcuts between two points in space built and run by the Dominion. Alternative to the slipstream — cheaper and don't require a navigator, human or AI. But the Dominion knows your business.

Keplan Bindweed: Carnivorous plant that wraps tendrils secreting a digestive enzyme around its victims. It takes a long time for it to consume a human.

Klicks: Measure of distance (also kiloklicks and megaklicks).

Laurentian Brigade: Another rebel faction. Often disagrees with Hudsonite Brigade.

Legion, The: Main imperial armed forces supposedly loyal to the Emperor, and tangentially the imperial family. But loyalty can be bought as well as earned. Organized into divisions named from Alpha to Omega, each with special skills and training.

Leishmann's lung borers: Small parasite worm that infects the lungs when the eggs are inhaled. Encountered by early colonies, symptoms include shortness of breath and coughing up blood, followed shortly by death.

Luxe Palladium: Fancy schmancy hotel in Metropolis, only the very rich or utterly infamous can get a room there.

Lyra, The: Jack-of-all cargo ship, trying to stay on the invisible side of the law. Failing of late.

Mantadae Gate: Jump gate and its station, where the *Lyra* picked up Grim — or Grim picked the *Lyra*, depending on your point of view.

Masquerade: One of the most infamous clubs in the Dominion.

Mudpuppy: A fresh-water crustacean similar to a prawn that spends much of its life buried in the mud. Hence the common name mudpuppy. Sometimes added to stew, though it's an acquired taste.

Nefti Station: Dominion gate and station, shopping mall to the rich and famous, den of pirates and swindlers.

Passalida: Hedonistic planet of villas and eternal sunshine.

PhiRhoZeta: Spatial coordinate system to indicate where something is in relation to another object; for example, where your attackers are in relation to your ship.

Pilgrim's phage: Infectious disease encountered by colonists that eats away at the flesh, leaving raw, open wounds. Invariably leads to death.

Port Osoyoos: Dominion spaceport and gate hub. Navigators swear there are more monsters in the depths of the slipstream in the area.

Poseidon's Pox: A curse, especially when someone pisses you off.

Secretariat of Interplanetary Peace and Stability (SIPS): Local constabulary, keeping order maintained on planet and station. Sometimes they're overzealous.

Sepidilus: Small, tentacled marine animal, consumed as a fried snack. Considered sentient by the Thalassians, and therefore verboten to consume.

Sisters of Elazir (The Sisters): Nominally charitable association that tends to the sick in hospitals across the Dominion. Secretive about their treatment methods, cures can appear magical. The Sisters have amassed wealth and power but are always on the lookout for more.

Slipstream: Method of subspace travel. Alternative to the Dominion-controlled jump gates. Requires a navigator or sophisticated AI; best to have both — there are monsters in the deep.

Tanopolis: Ancient capital on Aconitia. Built by Queen Tan and named after herself.

Taursa Epsilon hemorrhagic plague: Infectious disease encountered by early colonists on Taursa Epsilon. Causes bleeding from orifices, hallucinations and death.

Taxarchon: Archon of Archons. Second most powerful office in the Dominion, after the Emperor. Selected from the Archons of the great clans (currently clan Ayaba).

Ten Selva: Tidally locked planet in the Selva system in the Green Zone.

Teramaki, Istio: A theoretical astrophysicist, Istio Teramaki's hypotheses revolutionized the study of slipstream astrodynamics. Also a renowned Kora player.

Tiger Ants: Reddish striped ant with a painful sting that can leave limbs swollen and aching. Dried and crushed, can be used as a numbing, peppery seasoning...just don't add too much.

Tower of Solitude: Home base of the Sisters of Elazir, stationed across the Wall. Marvel of technology, it appears and disappears from regular space.

Venusian Tickleweed: Large carnivorous plant. Its many fern-like appendages bear droplets of digestive secretions that glisten like gems in the sun. Recorded consumptions of humans have occurred.

Wall, The: Ancient mesh spread across the space to protect the Dominion from the Desolation. When active, it can slice ships into pieces, but it's assumed to be non-functional.

Zeus' Bollocks: A swear word, stronger than Jacks.

Exceprt: Part 1 of Kandi's Tale

Or How to Crew a Cargo Ship — Kandi, Part 1
"Kandira Sakherani, step forward."

Kandi tried to suppress her grin as she lifted her head to meet the eyes of her mentor, Surprefect Pilhadi Makterani. Unsure if she'd succeeded, her gaze flicked sideways to the Matriarch. The woman's indulgent expression did little to ease Kandi's nerves. The few times she'd been this close to the leader of the Antaran Commonwealth, the woman had appeared just the same — beneficent under the robes of office and the headdress that must have weighed 50 kilos. But then the Matriarch was always chosen from the ranks of the military so she had some experience carrying weight.

Taking a deep breath, Kandi slowly stepped up the two stairs that led to the dais, careful not to trip, to join the Surprefect and the Matriarch. Behind her, a rustle arose in her cohort. Some would be happy for her, and some upset. All of them would be jealous.

Kandi knelt in front of the Matriarch as the woman stood. The astringent scent of cat's paw cream tickled her nose, reaching her through the heavy robes. She knew the smell — her own mother had started using the cream on her old warrior's knees before she'd gone to serve as an ambassador. A heavy hand came to rest on Kandi's head, the fingernails digging in slightly. A welcome breeze disturbed the heavy heat, rustling the hairs at the back of her neck.

The Matriarch's gravelly voice spoke words in Middle Erivan, the precursor to Old Antaran, and still the language of deep ritual. Even though she was a haphazard student of the ancient language, the words of commendation were burned into the heart of every pledge to the Antaran Brigade. Kandi's cheeks flushed, and it wasn't the heat. She struggled to keep the smile from her face.

This was her second commendation in as many years. The first was for her acts of bravery, valour and self-sacrifice in the engagement with the Dominion army to suppress the Rezerian uprising. And now, for acts preserving the security of all Antarans at home by helping quell the latest Nouminen riots.

"Sarissan Kandira Sakherani, rise." Kandi glanced up, and her mouth opened slightly before she caught herself. Makterani half smiled as she looked down at her and held out the multi-functional dagger of a Sarissan, the insignia of her new rank embossed on the pommel. Anyone in her cohort who might have been happy for her probably wasn't now.

In a swift movement, she stood. Her head spun and she put it down to the heat and the speed of rising. Some soldiers served for years without a commendation, let alone a promotion. Being named Sarissan put her a big step closer to following in her mentor's footsteps. She reached out her hands to take the weapon. A smile tugged at the one side of her mouth as she thought of trying it out.

"Don't be irreverent," Pilhadi mouthed so no one else could hear.

Giving a sharp nod to the Surprefect, she turned to the Matriarch. As she bowed deeply, she spared a glance for the man at the woman's side. The Dominion Governor General. From what her mother told her, the position of Governor was usually a stepping stone to positions high up in the Dominion administration. However, Governor Quail had been the Antaran governor since she was a child. He seemed competent and nice enough to her. Yet he was still here.

A sussuration in the crowd caused her to come out of her bow sooner that was proper, but the Matriarch wasn't watching at her. The Matriarch's Own leaned over the old woman's shoulder and whispered in her ear.

"Now?" The Matriarch had switched from Old Antaran to the common dialect, and spoke loud enough for Kandi to hear. A frown marred her serene expression, and her fingers played at the Stave of Benevolence, which hung from her vestments — according to all reports, the weapon was *not* merely ceremonial.

"You did say you wanted him back." Governor Quail peered at Kandi as he spoke. Kandi shifted under his inspection. Other than an arched eyebrow, his face betrayed nothing of his thoughts.

The Matriarch's lips pulled down, and Surprefect Makterani shifted away from the woman and the weapon she now clutched. Kandi inched closer to her mentor, teacher, and now lover.

"What's going on?" she whispered. Makterani's head spun around, and she shook it, her lips pressed together.

The breeze had grown stronger, and lifted a curled lock of her short hair. A thrumming filled the air, causing her to turn.

A ship. And it wasn't landing at the main commercial port or the military base. It was coming down at the House Mount's pad, the Matriarch's private landing area.

"I didn't say right now." The words were a growl as the older woman stood, swiftly and stock straight despite the weight of her robes. She waved her hand, and Surprefect Makterani snapped a salute. Then she turned sharply on her heel to face the cohort.

"Attention!" Makterani's eyes flicked to her face before looking over her shoulder. Kandi's training kicked in, and she snapped to attention despite her confusion. "Honour guard formation. Hie."

In unison, boots squeaked on the marble paving stones, and Kandi jumped down the two steps to take her position at the head of the cohort. As a Sarissan. Makterani stepped into formation beside her. As one, they started marching, leading the Matriarch towards the landing pad.

When they passed through the colonnade that led to the House of the Mothers, the throbbing hum stopped. The ship had touched down. Kandi squinted against the midday sun to try make out its markings. But at this distance, in the heat, they shimmered, and the ship melded with the greenery of the House gardens. With the thrum of the ship gone, she noticed the buzz of the fire bugs — a storm was coming if the bugs, were to be believed. With sweat she couldn't wipe away dripping into her eyes, she glanced skyward: no sign of it yet.

The cohort kept up their march across the Lawn of the Martyrs before stopping sharply and separating into two even lines, forming an aisleway for the Matriarch. Surprefect Makterani stepped into the space to meet the Matriarch. Out of the corner of her eyes, Kandi saw that Governor Quail had joined them. Once the Matriarch passed through their aisle, the members of the cohort turned on their heel to face the ship. Standing at the front of her line, Kandi could finally make out the ship's markings: an eight-pointed star hugged by a crescent.

"The Sisters of Elazir." Kandi straightened and clamped her mouth shut when she realized she'd spoken her thoughts out loud. Regaining her composure, she examined the backs of the Matriarch, Makterani, and Governor Quail. The Sisters of Elazir hadn't had a real presence on Antaran soil since the Plague of Vesperas. For some reason, they were no longer welcome, though they maintained a hospice on Miina Station, the Dominion gate port parked at the edge of the solar system. Kandi felt the impulse to rub the phantom ache in her arm at the memory of her furtive visit to the Sisters, but she ignored it.

A ramp opened at the side of the ship, where no lines had been visible a few seconds before. As soon as the near end touched the ground, a figure clad in the cassock of a medical Sister appeared in the dark opening. He started down the ramp as two more Sisters took position on either side of the doorway. Kandi squinted trying to make out what was happening behind them, but all she got was a sense of movement. Finally, the man stepped onto the grass and approached the Matriarch, who tipped her head at him in the scantest bow.

From her position at the front of the line, Kandi made out a few words, her Standard being marginally better than her Old Antaran. Weren't expecting you ... main port ... Basherin.

Kandi's eyes went wide at that, and her gaze flicked back to the dark opening. Another figure emerged.

"Bash." Her mouth moved but the words was barely more than a breath. Still, the Sister's eyes slid her way and narrowed. She felt her cheeks redden. They'd take away her commendation if these slips continued. She forced her eyes forward, refusing to look at the ramp, but she still sensed the figure descending. It seemed to take an eternity.

"Kandira Sakherani, at ease." Makterani's voice broke her trance, and she forced herself to meet her mentor's gaze as she relaxed her posture slightly. "Stand easy." Kandi relaxed further, and her head drifted back to the Matriarch, who peered at her.

"Sarissan Sakherani, take charge of your brother." The old woman's expression was neutral.

Kandi nodded sharply and stepped towards Bash, a smile lifting the corners of her mouth despite herself. Her stepped faltered as she got her first good look at him. His appearance was markedly different from when he'd left three years ago. He'd always been athletic, ruddy. If he'd been a woman, he'd have been a shoe-in for the Brigade. Now, his skin had an unhealthy grey pallor and tugged at his gaunt form. She continued towards him as Makterani guided him in her direction. His gaze drifted towards her but it was almost as if he didn't see her. When she reached him, she snaked her arm around his waist, making her embrace look like she was supporting him. He tensed in her arms, and his head twisted as if to look around.

"Bash." She brought her hand to his face, realizing he might not recognize her. Screens were different from in person. "It's Kandi."

His eyes snapped to meet hers. "Don't let them tell you I'm crazy." His voice was hushed, the words rushed. "I've seen them. I know their secret."

She shook her head. "I—"

"The aliens."

Kandi sighed. Her brother had been fascinated by the idea of aliens since he was little, despite hundreds of years of searching by the best scientific minds in the Dominion had found nothing. Whatever was out there — if anything — had disappeared into stardust. "Bash...."

His hand came up to grasp hers, tightening to the point of discomfort. "It's real." His voice rose. "I studied them." His free hand waved towards the sky. "*They're* studying them, dissecting, injecting."

As his voice kept getting louder, Kandi pulled away, and glanced at her mentor, Makterani, and the Matriarch. Neither of them paid her any attention. Some members of her cohort, however, peered intently at them, even though they were supposed to still be at attention. She tugged her hand of her brother's grasp. "Bash, you're tired."

A shadow loomed to their right, and Kandi turned to see its source. The Sister stood beside them, his gaze on Kandi. Her eyes fell to the man's hand and the medpen it held. "It will help relax him." He peered at her, as if requesting permission. She gave a sharp nod. The medication seemed to take effect immediately, as Basherin became silent.

"What's wrong with him?" Kandi asked the Sister.

The man's eyes narrowed. "I'm his transport medic. I wasn't there when he fell ill."

"But—"

The man shrugged. "They say he broke under the stress of an imperial education. It happens."

Kandi snorted. "Not to Bash, it doesn't." Her brother was the smartest person she knew. The first man allowed to study off-world in...Hera knows how long.

"Kandira." Makterani stepped close. "Call Citizens' Hospital 1. Have them send a team to take your brother into treatment."

Kandi's eyebrows pulled together, confused as to why no one had mentioned her brother was sick, and why he was being taken to the citizens' hospital rather than the House hospital. Still she tapped her wrist patch to start the call.

"That won't be necessary," a voice said, the words cascading down from the darkness at the top of the ramp. "I called ahead. They're on their way."

Kandi's stomach fluttered. Her wide eyes latched onto the opening in the side of the ship. Sure enough, Arta Sakherani stepped out of the ship and strode down the ramp, coming to a stop between her and the Matriarch. The General Sakherani bowed low to the Antaran ruler, then straightened and pinned Kandi with her gaze.

"Kandira." The woman's chin dipped to her chest.

"Mother." Kandi nodded sharply.

Want to read more? Sign up for my newsletter at reneastle.com.

About the Author

Rene Astle is the scifi pen name of C. Rene Astle ... I know, super clever, right?

She gained a love of fiction, fantasy in particular, and a voracious appetite for story literally at her mother's knee, being read The Hobbit and Chronicles of Narnia — because those are the types of stories her mom wanted to read.

From her father, she got an enduring curiosity about the universe, earned shivering in the dark beside a telescope on cold, Canadian winter nights waiting to witness some celestial event.

Now she fits in writing between her day job, gardening and getting out to enjoy supernatural British Columbia.

As C. Rene Astle, she's the author of the Bloodborne Pathogens dark fantasy series, as well as a number of short stories.